Riding Shotgun

BOREALIS
BOOKS

Women

Write

About

Their

Mothers

Riding
Shotgun

Edited by Kathryn Kysar

Borealis Books is an imprint of the Minnesota Historical Society Press.

www.borealisbooks.org

The Minnesota Historical Society Press is a member of the Association of American University Presses.

Manufactured in the United States of America

10 9 8 7 6 5 4 3 2 1

♾ The paper used in this publication meets the minimum requirements of the American National Standard for Information Sciences—Permanence for Printed Library Materials, ANSI Z39.48-1984.

International Standard Book Number
ISBN 13: 978-0-87351-614-3
ISBN 10: 0-87351-614-1

Library of Congress Cataloging-in-Publication Data
Riding shotgun : women write about their mothers / edited by Kathryn Kysar.
p. cm.
Twenty-one essays by women writers explore their relationships with their mothers.
ISBN-13: 978-0-87351-614-3 (cloth : alk. paper)
ISBN-10: 0-87351-614-1 (cloth : alk. paper)
1. American essays—Women authors. 2. Women authors, American—Family relationships. 3. Mothers and daughters—United States. I. Kysar, Kathryn, 1960–

PS683.W65R53 2008
814'.608035252—dc22

2007047611

Photographs have been provided courtesy of the authors.

For Ardys Adelle Seabold

Contents

Introduction

Kathryn Kysar

On a dark evening, a tired farmwife is driving down a rural highway, her daughter beside her struggling to stay awake and watch the road. In Morgan Grayce Willow's essay "Riding Shotgun for Stanley Home Products," the daughter takes on the role of helpmate, protector, and assistant to the mother who is always with her, a guiding presence though her life.

In this remarkable collection of essays, twenty-one celebrated and accomplished women writers examine their relationships with their mothers with disarming clarity and love. Rich with complexity, these stories of caring and admiration, control and rebellion, intimacy and individuality are amazingly varied, yet readers will find resonances in every essay, recognizing their own mothers or daughters—and themselves—in startling ways.

Who are the twentieth-century mothers in this book? They were certainly not women of leisure. They worked hard: keeping an impeccably clean house in Kansas, struggling to raise a family of six on one paycheck in Chicago, cooking hearty midwestern meals in a California kitchen, operating a construction company in Minnesota, or managing a farmhouse with no running water in Iowa. Many strained against the restrictions placed on them by their small towns, their churches, and their communities: they were not supposed to work outside the home, be educated, have their own money, or, heaven forbid, be single. Some of the mothers triumph and blossom; all do the best they can as they push the limits and boundaries set for them. These essays offer tribute to and understanding of their joys and trials, their endurance and personal growth.

And who are their daughters? Smart women, writers who struggle to understand their lives. Their stories, sometimes uplifting and

x   humorous, sometimes dark and haunting, always insightful, raise many questions: How does my mother communicate with me? What was my mother's life like before me? Why was my mother absent in my life? Can "mother" be a web of extended family, adoptive and chosen mothers, or a generation of women? How can I live without her?

Mothers and daughters, connected with the deepest bonds of love, struggle when their inevitable flaws cause tensions and complications. Often by the time a daughter understands and accepts this, she is in the driver's seat, alone or with her own daughter beside her— fuming, giving directions, or staring out the window, riding shotgun. May you catch a glimpse of your own mother in the rearview mirror.

Kathryn Kysar

Riding Shotgun

Storm Warnings

Jonis Agee

The blizzard has coated the windows with snow and ice, filled the screens on the porch across the front of the house, weighted the branches of the huge old pine until they droop across the fence and lay on the ground, trapped by the heavy wet snow drifting the driveway shut, fixing the gate closed for the next thirty-six hours. I could not leave if I wanted or even needed to.

Everywhere I look familiar shapes are disappearing, and something new and smooth and impenetrable sits in their place while the sound of howling wind, muffled into the harsh, unexpected breath of an encounter with a stranger in a dark room keeps me rooted to my chair, listening. Listening once again to that voice.

For eight months I have been waiting to write about my mother, and it's not until tonight that she finally makes her appearance. For years my sisters and I have reported our parents' reincarnation in the plumbing—anytime we have water problems. On the anniversary of their deaths, ten days apart, in the deepest end of winter, on mother's birthday in June, or as prelude, announcement of a pending crisis. They're angry, we say, she's upset with my husband, we announce, don't tell me the water pipe burst, we warn each other, I can't take another disaster. The water is the least of it, you see, we can absorb the losses from flooding basements, exploding hot water heaters, faucets that turn on and off by themselves, toilets that won't stop flushing on their anniversary. It's the worry that accompanies the warning—will I lose my job, have I been speaking ill of the dead again, who is going to die now? When the well pump breaks just before Christmas, and the cistern pump last week, I pay the bills promptly, more worried about the messages than the cost. What do you mean? I silently ask. What should I do?

It is in the nature of our family to be superstitious. From the earliest trips back to the Missouri Ozarks with my mother hurtling down two-lane blacktops and gravel roads, with equal abandon, we were on the lookout for white horses—a sighting of which would slow her down long enough to touch her thumb to her tongue, tap the thumb to the middle of her palm and punch it with the opposite fist. Good luck, she'd announce, with a little lift of her chin and gleam in her eye. She had work for that luck to do when it arrived.

Spilled salt, she'd throw a pinch over her left shoulder. Don't kill spiders in the house, she'd warn. Or did I read that someplace, a book on Ozarks witchcraft, magic and superstition, perhaps. Your mother has healing hands, Father said the last year of his life. We have the sight, my brother said before he died. You're all witches, more than one of my husbands has declared. We know things, my sisters assure me, we know the future. No, sometimes we know the future, I caution. My dead sister knew who was calling before she picked up the phone. I know when a person is moving toward me across time and place. I think of them and they come back into my life. What does all this mean, I ask my mother. What have you done to us?

My mother talked to people who weren't there. One of the scary pranks of our childhood, once we moved into Omaha, was eavesdropping on mother's conversations with herself. Often these discussions were held in the laundry room off the basement recreation room in our small brick house. Quietly opening the first-floor closet door and lifting the lid to the laundry chute, we would lean in, staring down at the basket of dirty sheets and towels, while our mother ironed, pressing her arguments, her voice rising furiously up to our waiting ears until we backed away, momentarily stunned . . . Father was leaving us to hunt lions in Africa. We would be orphaned now. Sent to live on grandfather's farm, never graduate from high school.

We always hoped for new information, secrets that were to be kept from our young ears, but when we did retrieve something startling from her, it almost always turned out to be false . . . Her father was still alive, remarried, living with a new family, he had written in a recent letter. She was mail-boxed now, she shouted.

Telling Father that we heard Mother say it never released us from

6   punishment. She always looked surprised, not guilty, that we would
       lie at such a level. Each of the six children had to learn that hard les-
       son—nothing mother said to herself in the vanity mirror, in the base-
       ment doing laundry and ironing, or in the bath when we pressed our
       ears against the door, was worth a damn to us . . . the neighbor had
       not told her that her oldest daughter was going to run away and get
       married to a boy she had dated once.

       When I was six, my mother had a baby and my father went to what
       was then French Morocco to work as an accountant for a U.S. firm
       building an airstrip there. I have never quite understood why he had to
       leave his job working with my grandfather at the business college they
       owned in Omaha. Mother once told me a complicated story about his
       signing a loan to build a new school for our rural district north of
       town, so we could move out of the old two-room schoolhouse next to
       Sorenson's pig pen a mile away. When the district failed to pay the
       loan, my father was liable and needed to raise a sum of money much
       greater than what he earned working for his father. That was the glori-
       fied version. The other version was that my father, an accountant with
       a special hatred for the I.R.S., got in trouble during an audit and had
       to come up with a large sum of money to pay the fine and extra tax. It
       didn't matter why when Mother gave up trying to live in the country
       alone with four children and a new baby.

       It was January when she loaded us into the new Oldsmobile 88 with
       two four- barrel carburetors, our clothes, and as much of the contents
       of the freezer as she could manage and began the drive to her family in
       Missouri. She made the trip at night so that we would sleep while she
       smoked and drove too fast, fiddling with the radio for music that
       wouldn't wake the baby. I was already taking care of the baby by then,
       rocking and cooing to her while my brothers pushed against me for
       more room. Sometime in the middle of the night, I fought back in my
       sleep, and a box of frozen peas broke over me, dribbling down the col-
       lar of my coat like hard icy tears as we pulled into Columbia, Missouri,
       where we would spend the rest of the school year with my father's
       mother.

       The years Father was in North Africa were too hard for her, I've
       come to realize. Without her friends and familiar places, she must

have grown as strange to herself as she grew to us. The baby became my responsibility—and my grandmother Hetty's. For years after that time, I stayed home from school to take care of the baby when she was sick, got up in the night to fix her bottle, change her diapers, feed her meals, play with her until she slept. Having my own child was no surprise after that. But more than the baby she stopped caring for, my mother changed. She began to beat my older sister. She chased my older brother around the house with a broomstick. My younger brother and I hid from her, and worse things began to happen. For a while she was so sick that her monthly bleeding wouldn't stop. There was talk of her needing an operation. She lay in bed, pale, skin and bones, bleeding until the day came when it had to stop or she would be taken away. Then, miraculously, it did. Why am I telling this? Because no matter what she did to us, we were more terrified of her leaving. Father was already gone, sending postcards of exotic scenes in Morocco, promising to bring me a horse when he returned, sending Mother letters in his fine spidery handwriting on airmail paper so light and thin you could see through it.

In the summers we went to stay with Grandmother Ethel, my mother's mother, in Versailles, Missouri. My father called her Mrs. Willson to the day she died because they never liked each other. Their families never liked each other either, for some reason. My mother grew more strange when we got there. Maybe because her own mother never seemed to like or approve of her and made my mother feel small and worthless because there were so many children and my mother smoked, and her children were wild and made messes. My aunt lived two doors down, and by comparison, seemed grander, with her two boys and a husband who lived with her. On the other side lived Aunt Ruth, the widow of the beloved son who had laid down or fallen asleep on the railroad tracks south of town and been run over. A drunk, my father said, no good. An accident, my mother and grandmother insisted. Howard fell asleep. For years I was haunted by the idea that you could drop dead asleep without realizing it, no matter where you were, even on railroad tracks. Later I realized my father was probably right. Or maybe Howard heard the same voices my mother did, maybe he had a long argument with time too.

That first summer my grandmother spent half her time storming back down the sidewalk from the downtown dress shop where she worked, banging through the front door, and calling for my mother, Lauranell, with that high twangy drawl that was like the first violent note of an out-of-tune fiddle. Our crimes were multitudinous: My mother was smoking in public, we children were on the front porch waving and hollering at a funeral procession for an uncle, my mother was sunbathing nude on the second-story back porch roof, we children were having a rotten tomato fight with my cousins next door, my mother's fight with my older sister was followed by an emergency trip to the doctor to stitch up her leg, my mother wasn't wearing underwear in public again.

But there were joyful times too. Mother alone was so much more fun than Mother and Father together, when they were so preoccupied with each other that we children were merely the audience to their theater. She took us to swim in Gravois Creek, beyond the shallow place where cars could ford it, and we often roasted hot dogs and marshmallows. She took us for walks into the deep Ozark woods, pointing out flowers and trees, pawpaws and woodpeckers, and taking us to the natural stone bridge where she'd played as a child, and to Jacob's Cave, which her father had owned briefly and which she and her sisters had explored as girls. She gave us nickels for the Dairy Creme that opened a block away, and she let us stay out after dark to catch fireflies in jars, never reminding us that they'd be dead by morning. She drove us around the countryside in that big new Olds 88, smiling at the young men who stopped to admire the car at gas stations and tourist shops that sold cedar gifts from the Ozarks. Sometimes we drove slowly while she talked about her family and her childhood with her father who died of a stroke after he lost the bank and their fortune in the Depression. We drove by cabins perched along the country roads, men and women both with corncob pipes, or maybe that's a memory from my father's grandmother. It was the late forties and early fifties when we spent those years in Missouri with my mother—both during that two-year span when my father was gone, and before and after when my mother just had to go back.

What I'm trying to say is that I never knew the heart of my mother. I knew facts about her. I glimpsed the world of her past. I read the love letters and telegrams she and my father exchanged in college, in code, because their families had forbidden them to see each other. They did, though. In fact, we wouldn't know until after my parents' deaths, but they were secretly married in high school and kept it from us their whole lives. I know that when my father was dying she promised him that she'd be with him as soon as she could. And she was, ten days later. They had met in third grade, fallen in love, and spent their lives together. Romeo and Juliet without the good ending. The six children the wide-eyed witness to all that crazy love business that didn't include them except as a by-blow of passion.

How to write about my mother. I can only tell stories because that's how she saw life. One year for Christmas she sent boxes of stale Campfire Girl candy to all the relatives she disliked. Later, over ten Christmases, she sent me whatever craft she had made in rehab therapy during her most recent hospitalization: a pair of clumsily sewn fake suede slippers, a pair of brown ceramic mushroom-shaped salt and pepper shakers, a lopsided candle in shades of muddy brown with sequins, knitted orange potholders that burned my fingers through the spaces. I grew embarrassed and ashamed wondering why I deserved these presents. Was it because I stopped coming home? Because I divorced and went to graduate school? Because I opposed the war in Vietnam? Or because she knew something about me that I didn't know yet?

Her arguments with the world, with strangers, with family, with her children, were all a series of tales, fabrications laced with truth or facts, take your pick. She had a complex imagination, an unwieldy and powerful intellect, and a touch of genuine madness. Does that do her justice? Who can say. In the last twenty-five years of her life, I told myself and my sisters that Mother was mentally ill, so we shouldn't expect anything. It didn't matter. When she called, her voice sent shivers across my skin. My mind went numb and I stopped being able to think. I spent a lifetime learning to seek still waters with Mother, places that were shallow and quiet, where we could find no disagreement to send her into a spiraling rage. My older sister was drawn to her like a mouse to poison bait. When my sister died, my mother blamed herself and my father. She stopped taking medication and locked my father outside in the hundred-degree heat. She was right, but it was much too late. Driving her to the hospital, I so sympathized with her analysis. Yes, the pills were causing organ damage, yes, society did medicate women who objected, yes, she was dressed in angry colors—but what could I do? I still ask myself that.

I could write forever about my mother, you see. I have as many stories as the hours of this year. I will never know her. I never knew her, even when I thought I did. I felt sorry for her, anger for her, disgust and fear for her. I wanted to defend her. I had to defend myself. I barely escaped her. She always escaped me. When my father died, we joked and buried him as well as we could, singing loudly the old-time gospel songs he liked. "Rock of Ages," "The Old Rugged Cross," "Amazing Grace," feeling slightly cynical about the Ozark religion he'd thrown back at us. We served food on good china plates after the service and said nice things to relatives who showed up, and thought, well, that was that.

When my mother died, ten days later, we could not stop crying. Not one of us could raise our voice in song at the service, and when the minister who had never even met her talked about her bit of cheating at the bridge table, I wanted to get up and sock him in the nose.

I don't know who exactly I miss. Maybe it's the space around her, that woman who was called my mother, that person who took up so much room that it was hard to breathe. She was like the blizzard taking the world apart, silencing and blanking it into stillness, we were all pressed against the walls by her, blown and flattened, until we could make our way out and away, where the world gradually melted into color again. What discoveries we made then—what joy to realize we were still alive.

But most of all, I think that we carry her with us, everything she could not be, could not do, we do now—whispering to her, as if she is listening: Is this right? What's next? Knowing she will answer, that she will never, ever leave us alone.

Enough

Elizabeth Jarrett Andrew

I could trace my inheritance to an earlier beginning, but 1938 will do: the year my great-grandmother Martha was widowed. Her husband gone, she told her two daughters that, at age fifty-four, she was too old to care for herself. Kate and Elsie would have to live at home, to "look after her." Both daughters had postponed weddings because of their father's illness. At her mother's pronouncement, Kate fled. Who can blame her? And Elsie bent to her mother's will. After a honeymoon in D.C., she brought her new husband home. The house was small. The four children Elsie eventually bore took turns sharing a bed with their grandmother. Martha helped out a bit; she watched the kids while Elsie worked in the munitions factory, she crocheted, she cleaned, but still. Elsie rarely knew the simple pleasure of time alone with her husband until Martha, growing senile, chose a nursing home.

At least that's how my family tells the story. And this is what I hear: my great-grandmother Martha, grieving her young husband and stripped, suddenly, of that protective layer between herself and a confusing world, didn't know how to drive, balance a checkbook, earn a nickel. She could have learned, of course; she had the buffer of life insurance and her husband's pension. How much easier it is to let brokenness close us in! Especially with a daughter so willing to take the sputtering torch and run with it.

Through her seventies, then a widow herself, my grandmother Elsie knit up to a hundred pairs of mittens a year. By Christmas, every child who attended the Utica Neighborhood Center had warm hands. These were poor kids, generations of recent immigrants and the residents of Utica's run-down, jobless neighborhoods, and Elsie greeted each by name as they passed the reception desk where she volunteered. After she died, the Center named a conference room in her honor.

Elsie never learned to drive, and eventually the other elderly volunteers who had given her rides turned in their licenses. Grandma refused to take the Meditaxi. Instead she stayed home solving the *New York Times* Sunday crossword in ballpoint, reading about the Israeli-Palestinian conflict, and knitting. When her tea kettle boiled dry and melted, and she could no longer descend the steep basement stairs to wash her laundry, her children and grandchildren showed up with cardboard boxes. We carried her African violets from a windowsill abundant with blooms first to the floor of a dim assisted-living apartment and eventually to the top of a nursing-home radiator, where they withered. To help me remember what we were losing, I snapped off a leaf or two from each plant and stuck them in my own dirt.

With each move, Grandma's knitting meandered. One side of a cardigan drooped six inches below the other; the cabling hook fell to the bottom of her knitting bag. Her mittens grew malformed and weird—miniscule, ill-fitted thumbs, unmatched sizes, unfortunate stripes of acrylic pink and orange. They filled a basket beside her nursing-home recliner and caused my mother and aunts to talk in low voices out in the hall. Once I sat beside her on the bed. The room stank of disinfectant. She'd been toying with her chin whiskers, and I'd offered to pluck them for her. "Nah," she said. "What would I have to entertain me then?"

"I love you, Grandma," I told her. "I love being with you."

"Oh," she said dismissively. "I'm just a lump on a log."

Recently my father sent me a photo: My mother at a podium, her head tilted in an unassuming manner. She's wearing a rainbow stole and a sign around her neck with my picture on it and the words, "My Child Is of Sacred Worth." Perhaps this seems an obvious sentiment, except that we're talking the United Methodist Church, 2006—a dangerous place for sexual minorities and their families. The church refuses to sanction her daughter's marriage, will not ordain her, might not baptize her children, and, in some circumstances, denies her communion, and my mother works to overturn these policies. In the photo, she is accepting a regional award for service.

"All I've done is set up the display table at Conference," she tells me, referring to the booth that distributes these bright strips of fabric for delegates to wear in solidarity with those who are marginalized. My mother hates making phone calls; she attends plenty of meetings but prefers not to say much. Others are more powerful, better able to make decisions, more effective at bringing about social change. What she's best at is sewing dozens, hundreds, of these rainbow stoles which United Methodists from around the country wear year after year at churchwide events, hang from their rearview mirrors, don to march in Pride parades or to preach to their congregations. The material is exuberant, playful. All the seams are even.

"I was so humiliated," she says over the phone, as though she'd tripped on stage or been heckled. "The room was packed with lifetime activists. I don't know why I got the award."

My partner Emily's thirtieth birthday is in two weeks, and, once again, I'm in a bind. Sure, I bought her an iron wall decoration when I was in Guatemala, climbing vines with candleholders; I imagine it hanging beside the table on our porch, casting candlelight across late dinners filled with cricket-song. These days Emily drapes herself in the porch hammock for entire afternoons as she recovers from chemotherapy treatments. I'm certain she'll delight in the iron vines twisting up the side of the house and my story of clumsily toting them through customs. With the exchange rate, I've spent all of twenty bucks on this gift; my investment (of thought, money, creativity) is minimal. And thirty is a significant year, made more so by Emily's daily struggle to live. What gift would be appropriate? A handknit sweater? A poem I'd given weeks of attention? The trouble is, I'm worn thin from interrupted nights in a hospital bed, stacks of crusty dishes, the burden of paying our bills, my fear of losing my spouse so soon. It's too late to knit anything. What endearing words come to me, I speak.

Besides, it's this way every Christmas, every anniversary, every birthday—my gifts are insufficient; I dread the moment Emily or anyone unwraps my paltry representations of love. Within each box, amid the tissue paper, lurks ancestral inadequacy. There's no box right for this sprawling candelabra, so I cover the iron leaves and candleholders with tissue and scraps of bright ribbon—a funky tree bearing poorly disguised fruit. It's not enough but I give it anyway because, hurting and broken, Emily is more dear to me than life itself. And the real gift, as I dig out my maternal inheritance, air the shame, and look closely at what I can offer my loved ones, is this. Brokenness lets in light. See all these women? We shine.

My Mother's Heart

Sandra Benítez

In an effort to bring order to the mess my studio has recently become, I have been going through things, purging old files, digging into boxes filled with items I long ago set aside. In one of them, this brimming with black-and-white photos, my eyes fall upon a snapshot taken of my mother. She stands in the middle of the frame, wrapped in a dark coat, her gloved hands set, one over the other, at her waist. She has wound a patterned scarf around her neck, placed a Tyrolean-style hat aslant upon her head. All that is uncovered is her earnest face, her lips set in a tenuous smile, her left leg extended elegantly past the hem of her three-quarter length coat, her foot disappearing into a shiny leather pump. I turn the photo over and find her handwriting on the back: "New York," it reads. "I must have been fifteen or sixteen." I study the photo's background: what seems to be a '34 Chevrolet coupe is parked at the curb across the street from where she stands. Beyond it rises the expanse of a tall-storied granite and brick building.

I am amazed at the photograph. I cannot remember seeing it before, though I clearly must have. Of one thing I am certain: it is the only image that exists of my mother when she was young. Now that she is gone, it is a bittersweet discovery. Deeply missing her anew, I place the photo over my heart, longing to connect with her heart, concealed under her coat, her dress, her flesh.

Our hearts. It is where our stories reside.

As stories do, mine commences when I'm small. So small, in fact, that I'm floating in the watery haven of my mother's womb. Susana floats with me, the two of us, turned toward each other, our tiny faces nose to nose. Had we opened eyes, we might have noted the waxy down covering us, our fists bunched against our throats. Had I intuited what

was to come, I would have clasped my sister so mightily, held her so
tightly, never let her go.

To keep her, I might have projected myself into the past and told
Susana a story. My first story, burbling from the slit of my mouth to
enter the minute shell of her ear.

I would have told her about our mother.

She was a little thing, barely five feet tall and not a hundred pounds,
when, in Washington D.C., on a June day in 1940, she married our
father. In the photo that hangs in my dressing room, they stand on a
square of oriental carpet, a plain wall their backdrop. She wears a satin
sheath overlaid with lace. Her black hair is wavy and shoulder length,
and she has pinned an orange blossom at each of her temples to pull it
back fetchingly. A gossamer veil spills from a headdress that spans her
head like an arch. I wonder who helped her secure it, who helped fluff
the tulle prettily around her shoulders? Her mother, Abuelita? Her sister, Aunt Susana? And what mood were they in, these two, one as
fiercely independent as the other, both vexed perhaps by the sudden
presence of Abuelito who, after a troublesome absence, had arrived
from Puerto Rico, to attend his youngest daughter's wedding.

In the photo, Mami has poked an arm through Daddy's, and he stands
there, so sober and sure, in white slacks and shoes, in a dark double-
breasted jacket with a budding carnation pinned to the lapel. He feels
the small weight of her against him. Perhaps he is just beginning to
know that she will be there at his side, leaning a bit into him, for
almost sixty years. Jimmy Ables and Martita Benítez facing the world
together.

I might have told my sister this, gone on to add that after they race
westward toward a honeymoon in Idaho, traveling in "Betsy," the Ford
sedan Daddy purchased for one hundred dollars down and twenty-five
a month, after travel over the Great Smoky Mountains, along Chicago's Lake Shore Drive, through South Dakota, to a Fourth of July
rodeo in Custer, Wyoming, after they roam Yellowstone Park and cozy
up in a log cabin renting for a dollar a day, after they arrive at the folks'
Idaho farm, the folks being Daddy's folks, after our mother's initia-
tion there into the austere realities of country living—without running

water, electricity, or telephones—the newlyweds head back east toward their future and their new life.

I might have said, Look, dear sister, here is when you and I begin.

August 1940 to March 1941. We are to have only this time together. For these eight months, Susana and I are buoyed in the safety of our mother's womb. Around us, in the room, the house, outside, in the state, the country, the world, momentous events unfold: Germany gears up its war machine. Infantile paralysis and influenza epidemics strike around the country. German planes bomb the London suburbs on both sides of the Thames. Japanese troops are plundering China. American men, ages twenty-one to thirty-five, begin to register for the first peacetime conscription in U.S. history. Thirty-two states celebrate Thanksgiving Day and give thanks "for our preservation" in accordance with FDR's proclamation. Germany, Italy, and Japan establish a military and economic commission to implement their alliance. Oslo announces that no Nobel Peace Prize will be awarded for the year.

At home, after learning his family is expanding, our father scrambles to make a better living. He has been working as a clerk/typist for a government agency, the Reconstruction Finance Agency. His pay is $120 a month. Our mother, on the other hand, works as a stenographer for a law firm, but because she is pregnant, her job will come to an end.

One day Daddy hears that the head of the RFC Telegraph office, a strict old curmudgeon who cannot tolerate a woman working for him, is looking for a male secretary. The old man is of the opinion that women do not possess the discipline and concentration needed to send and receive vital messages. Daddy learns the new job pays more and, better yet, that it entails using the very same skills he is presently using. He rushes to apply for the job. Luckily, he gets it. Plus a pay increase of thirty dollars a month.

Our mother is growing larger. She gets so big she has trouble sleeping; she can't seem to settle herself, she says. But sitting, splay-legged, on the floor is strangely comfortable. One evening she sends Daddy out to buy a set of jacks. When he returns, they both sit down to play. Thump the little ball goes, thump. And Susana and I can hear it.

We hear it over the serene swooshswoosh sounds of Mami's heart. We hear it even over the sound her swift hand makes sweeping jacks off the floor. And we hear a tune playing on the Philco: "Three little fishies in an itty bitty pool . . . and they swam and they swam all over the dam." Better still, we hear their merry laughter when she tries to stand and finds that she cannot. He almost topples over her as he starts to pull her up.

Jimmy and Martita. The two of us. All four happily intent with playing jacks in the night.

A Dr. Verges is in charge of Mami's care. Over the months, he has become alarmed at her size. He does not suspect that she is carrying twins. It is 1941. No X-ray diagnostics, no ultrasounds are available. Dr. Verges is simply an old-fashioned practitioner who has taptapped our mother's big belly, and though he's placed a stethoscope to her flesh, he does not catch the beat of two little hearts.

Eight months into the pregnancy, on March 25, he decides to induce birth. Our mother is to drink a purgative. Daddy is to drive her to Sibley Memorial Hospital after that.

She will not drink a drop of it. Mami sets her mouth and will not take the glass Daddy holds out to her. He implores. He cajoles. In the end, he is firm. Do it for the baby, he says. And it is this that wins her over.

We have been purged. This forced birth has wrested Susana and me apart. They have placed us in separate Isolettes, our only comfort the radiance from the twenty-watt bulbs positioned in our incubator tops. They have wrapped us so snugly in swaddling cloths (around and around our little bodies, up and over our tiny faces) that we look like white panatelas. We are so small, in fact, we could actually fit into cigar boxes. Our bird-bone breasts heave with the difficulty of our breathing. Our hearts are fairy bell clappers and they knock quickly in our chests so weighted down with longing: already we yearn for the beat of our mother's heart, for the echoing resonations we sent out to each other. Our waif-like mouths open and close, with hunger for nourishment, yes, but with the hunger, too, for what so suddenly we have lost: Susana and I. In five swift minutes, we have lost each other.

★ ★ ★

Blithely unaware, Dr. Verges has made one, perhaps two, possible death-causing errors. He has attended to our birth and somehow introduced bacteria into our mother's body. He has delivered the placenta and is done with it. What he has failed to do is to make sure that the whole of the placenta was expelled. On the next day, when our mother develops a fever, then chills, a headache, a rapid heart rate, he does not check for retention of placental fragments within the uterus, nor does he order the blood count that would reveal a high white blood cell count and thereby confirm the presence of infection. Instead, he turns a blind eye to the tiny woman lying in bed number four in obstetrics ward number two. He has a set of twins to occupy his attention. The girl babies are not doing well. They are having trouble breathing. When fed, they cannot retain their formula.

Our father sits by our mother's bed. It is noon, and he's on his lunch break from the telegraph office. Daddy holds our mother's limp hand, talks to her about the babies. They have identical little faces, he says to her. When you're stronger, they will bring them both in and you can see this for yourself. Our mother smiles wanly. Tears slide down her cheeks. Her belly aches. Her head throbs.

"They won't let me hold them," she says.

"When you're stronger, you'll get to hold them all you want."

Our mother nods. She mouths our names. The effort exhausts her, but she says, "I can't feed them, Jimmy."

"I know," he says, "but remember I found a place that sells mother's milk?" He tells her again about the place across the Potomac, the convent where the nuns run a small home for unwed mothers. "I got milk for them this morning," he tells her. He had risen at dawn. Raced to the convent and then back to the hospital before reporting for work. "The babies took to it, Martita. I'll get fresh milk every day."

"Okay," she says. She closes her eyes.

He holds her hand and watches her. For three days he has watched her decline. Chills, pain, wanness. Her face is flushed. She refuses to eat. Today, when he returns to work, he will start to recruit people to sign up for blood transfusions. He does not know where he has gotten this idea. He thinks perhaps an angel in a dream has told him to do it.

And he will. He will ask at the telegraph office, and then, after the hospital visit at night, when he arrives at his moonlighting job at Western Union, he will ask there too. He feels her hand tightening around his.

"Jimmy," she says.

"Yes, little mother," he says.

"Jimmy, pray with me for the babies."

Across the river, past the trees, a drive winds up a hill. It leads to a convent door through which lost girls disappear to bear in shame the proof of what the world has labeled wantonness. These girls give up so much. Their innocence. Their good name. Their babies.

Oh, young girls, ever grateful for your sacrifice, I remember you still. You offered up your essence, proof of kindness, proof of love. Your bluish milk helped me to thrive. It prolonged the scant time I had with my twin sister.

Daddy is at Mami's bedside again, on the eighth night since we were born. They have moved Mami from the obstetrics ward into a private room. Daddy cannot understand the meaning of this sudden transfer for which he has no funds to cover, but the nurses know why. Call it what you may, childbed fever, puerperal fever, septicemia, blood poisoning, it spells one and the same thing: it is only a matter of time.

Silent and somber, the nurses glide in, adjust the edge of the sheet, study the chart at the foot of the bed, place a hand on Mami's forehead, trying to quiet her plaintive moans. Daddy watches their shoulders' slump and sends out a question with his eyes: She's dying, isn't she? But they turn away, leave the question to hang in the air.

He buries his face in his hands. He is not yet twenty-three. His wife is dying. In only a week, she has lost so much weight, her bones jut beneath her flesh. His babies are dying, too. Though Sandra seems to be holding her own, she is not yet out of danger. Little Susana is another story. Like her mother, Susana is losing weight. He stifles a sob. Tries to pray as she has taught him: Holy Mary, Mother of God.

He lifts wet eyes to her cry. "Jimmy!" She has thrown back the sheet and is trying to raise herself on an elbow. "Jimmy, I don't know what's happening."

He jumps to his feet. "What?" he says. "What?"

She begins to pound her belly. One dull blow after another. "I feel something in there, Jimmy. I can feel it." She kneads her belly as if it were dough. With the little strength she has, she grasps her flesh and pounds and pokes herself. "Martita!" he cries, watching helplessly as she pommels and prods and pelts. Soon she collapses against the pillows. "I am bleeding now," she says.

He draws back in horror. A river of bright blood erupts from her. The mattress and sheets soak it up, yet there is more. He charges into the hall, yells for help, charges back in with a nurse. She is a large woman, broad-chested, with powerful-looking arms. She takes one look, grasps the foot of the bed and, in one swift move, lifts the end up off the floor. "Get more help," she commands, keeping the end of the bed aloft. He does as she orders.

Upon return, he stands frozen at the door, watching as nurses stuff gauze, cotton, anything serviceable, into her. The sight is unbearable. He turns away and rushes to the phone, to do the only thing he can think of doing. It is 8:00 PM. He dials the homes of the people who have volunteered to give blood.

In the end, the hemorrhage is so severe that the transfusions provide her with a complete change of blood, a procedure that, in effect, flushes the poisons from her. In causing the hemorrhage, she has saved her own life. Still, she will have to endure yet another procedure, a dilatation and curettage, an enlargement and scraping of the womb. This will be performed without anesthetic for she is too weak to tolerate the potentially heart-stopping medication.

Three weeks after our birth, she leaves the hospital. She weighs seventy-eight pounds. She has not been allowed to hold us, has not once laid eyes upon us.

Susana Ables Benítez died May 3, 1941. She was buried in the Washington National Cemetery, Prince Georges County, Suitland, Maryland. Section "N," Lot 364.

Daddy once said to me, "Not long after we moved into our little apartment on Fort Davis Street, a salesman rang the doorbell. He was selling cemetery lots. I can't fathom why, at that stage in my life, a mere newlywed and short of money, I allowed myself to be talked into buying a cemetery lot. Maybe I thought it was a bargain or a good investment. But I bought it and that's where we buried little Susana, next to a small dogwood tree in full bloom."

My story leaps decades ahead. I am in a Miami hospital, with Daddy and my sister, Anita. Carlos, her husband the doctor, is with us too. So is Mami's heart physician. We are in a room the size of a large closet, huddling around a monitor viewing the results of Mami's latest echocardiogram. The scene is surreal: the only light in the room emanates from the little screen. Upon it, the image of my mother's heart expands and contracts so vividly I feel my own heart attempting to match its rhythm. On the screen, Mami's arteries cascade in a per-plexing tangle, like the aftereffects of fireworks. The heart doctor touches a pointer to the hot spots. "This one is half-blocked. This one is a total."

The "total" is a white bulge, like a plugged up section of garden hose with the water built up under the pressure.

I am stunned into silence, my eyes fixed on the pulsing mass on the screen, on the milky tendrils showering around it. I think, This is my mother's heart I'm gazing at.

Her heart.

The loss of a mother is a partial loss of the self. It was for me. Mami's death, years later, in 1999, cast me adrift, for she took with her her memory, both spoken and untold. She took all she might have divulged about herself, about me, for from the moment she passed, from the moment I watched her face soften and ease as she took death's hand, as she grasped her Susanita's, a myriad of questions I might have asked descended on me like a sudden sleeve of rain. With her went all that possibility.

It's often said that life is a circle, but I see it as a spiral, that ancient symbol of unity and multiplicity, of wisdom and eternity. A spiral, con-centric swirls where all is a continuum. I think about how our own DNA is represented by a helix, that lovely ascending spiral. The circles upon circles of code it contains. The stored memories, the stories.

Stories captured by the orbit of our eyes. Stories reverberating in the volute shell of our ears. Stories imprinted in the whorls at our fingertips. When we speak, are we not surrendering stories by the pursed circle of our lips?

When Mami died, her stories went with her, and now, I long to have her back. For just one day. Twenty-four hours in which I might persuade her to lay aside the cloak of silence and sorrow that all her life she wound about herself.

Tell me, Mami, I would say. *Dígame.* And I would look deep into her dark eyes. Truly seeing. Truly listening.

When We Were in the Projects

Barrie Jean Borich

The first day of my visit with my mother in Florida, she comes home from Wal-Mart with a brand-new electric coffee percolator.

Why a percolator? Ever since the first Mr. Coffee came out in the 1970s, when I was in high school, Mom's had a drip coffeemaker. I've admired the one she's had for the last few years, sitting on the counter in her kitchen overlooking the golf course. It's the kind with a thermal pot, the type that keeps the coffee warm without burning it up.

But still, Mom's come home with a percolator, and now she's fiddling with it, complaining about all the things it won't do. It doesn't have a timer, she says. I can't set it up the night before. It doesn't have instructions. Can I use my regular coffee?

I ask her, why did you buy it? I'm the child who worries her by not trying hard enough to own all the right appliances. She'll buy me the televisions or electric can openers she's sure I need, whether or not I want them. But when it comes to her own home, she thinks before she spends. She's frugal to the point of haranguing my Dad if he buys a book. The percolator, though, was an impulse purchase. She just saw it and picked it up. She didn't even read the box. She used to have percolators all the time. She remembers the coffee was good.

For my mother, the kinds of appliances she has in her kitchen, the kind of house she lives in, the size of the television she watches, and the features of the car she drives are all responses to her childhood spent in the Projects. Her Projects were in South Deering, also called Irondale or Slag Valley, on the far south side of Chicago, a few blocks from the old Wisconsin Steel plant. Her Projects are to me like a 3-D slide of Graceland, or the bleak setting of an English novel, or the 1893 Chicago World's Fair—places I've never visited but feel as if I have, because I've heard so much about them.

My brothers and I grew up within my mother's mantras, the countless sentences that begin, When we were in the Projects. When Little Grandma Luschak finally moved out of the Projects, she relocated only a couple blocks away. My mother always pointed out the Projects when we drove past, on the way to or from her mother's apartment, but all I could see were yellow brick buildings laid out like train cars, just two stories high, with flat roofs and teensy lawns. The Trumbull Park Homes, built before the infamous towers farther north and closer to the lake, were the old style of Chicago projects, originally designed for steelworkers, mostly Yugoslavs, Poles, and Italians back then, row houses clustered around a bland courtyard. It wasn't just my mother who called them the Projects. Nobody in the neighborhood called them the Trumbull Park Homes. The Projects were their proper name, pronounced with a hard capital P. Your father used to pick me up for dates in the Projects, my mother always says. In the Projects I used to scrub the walls until my hands turned red.

In the 1950s, when my mother lived in the Projects, they were not quite the forgotten spaces of today's inner cities. Still, my mother talks about them the way veterans talk about battlefields, the way hurricane survivors talk about the big waves. The Projects were her disaster, her big war, her burning house. She still smells the scent of smoke on her skin.

Recently I spotted a red 1960s percolator with gold starbursts, set on a high shelf of an antique store. Right away I wanted it, even imagined it in my kitchen surrounded by white walls and red accents, perking away—dare I say perkily? It would match the red diner-style kitchen table my love Linnea bought at some poor slob's get-out-of-town-quick garage sale, across the alley from the duplex where we lived our first ten years together. But I didn't ask the sales clerk to pull the red perker down for me. Linnea and I already own both a French press and an espresso machine, not to mention the stovetop percolator Linnea takes out when a retro coffee mood strikes. I don't need a red percolator.

Linnea and I used to be attracted to older styles of design. On our very first date, dinner in my south Minneapolis studio apartment, one of us commented that the type of furniture we loved best was Art Deco and the other one of us, I no longer remember which, whispered, Me too. It was our first mutual turn-on. The next thing we knew, we were stretched out on my couch, kissing. The couch was a 1950s wagon-wheel foldout I picked up for a hundred dollars in a local used furniture store, the first big piece of furniture I'd ever bought, made of turquoise Naugahyde. It had a saddle imprinted into the back cushion, wheels built into the sides. It was the sort of couch you see in movies about women who went west to Reno in the 1940s and '50s to wait for a divorce. So Linnea and I fell in love in the 1980s on a Reno divorce couch, just before the mid-twentieth century qualified as antique. That's when it began, Linnea and my collections of items that could have been in our parents' apartments the year we were born.

I still lived with my mother the last time she used a percolator. That would have been in the old house at 14200 Emerald. This brings me to the smoke that I still smell on my skin—not actual smoke, but a smoky shadow, a sheath of the past that perhaps I could shed if I wanted to. For some reason I work to preserve it, keep it like a souvenir, a long-dead spider perpetually crouched in an amber haze, frozen but still visible, suspended and unable to sting.

Across the alley behind our house was Halsted Avenue, always busy, always rattling with semitrucks driving down from the south-side mills and warehouses of the city. Across the street was an open tract of land we called the Prairie. We called any empty lot in Chicago a prairie. It was one of those words nobody thought about, but everyone spoke. Now I see how poorly the word fits that weedy stretch, bordered by train tracks and semitruck routes and the brick bungalows of the working class suburbs and canopied by the giant steel frames of high-tension wires. That was no prairie. It was open ground, an undeveloped industrial patch too close to the wires to make room for homes or stores. Now I know what a prairie really is. The tall grass that stoops in the wind. The green sea of inland America, swallowed by the plow. That semi-open space across the street from 14200 Emerald was no prairie.

But then again, it was the prairie, or had been once. All of Illinois was once tallgrass prairie. The first outsider settlers, French priests trading with the Pottawatomie, had to part the grass with their arms and knees before shaking hands or smoking the pipe called the calumet with indigenous locals who would soon become history. That's what our industrial stink plain was named, long before I was born. Calumet. The prairie land that turned into a rail yard, a slag heap, and little brown brick houses with percolators pumping perkily on Formica countertops while the black-and-white televisions flickered with newscasters intoning through a cigarette mist or with the perky smiles and pointed training bras of the Disney Mouseketeers.

Across the street from the house on Emerald Avenue, in the center of our prairie, sat an abandoned grain mill. If I pressed my cheek against the glass and craned my neck I could see it out my bedroom window. The south side of Chicago in the early 1970s was full of forsaken factories and mills. We took school field trips to the Wonder Bread factory and the Museum of Science and Industry, but no one ever mentioned the plethora of dead warehouses and broken-down manufacturing plants, shells of the post-industrial age. Whatever wreckage we couldn't see from our yard, we drove past on the way to Little Grandma's apartment in the old neighborhood. Sometimes my mother scrunched up her nose.

The kids in the blocks around our house called that old grain mill the Rat Factory. It was russet-colored, the outer walls smeared with graffiti. The windows were punched out. If the square-shouldered Rat Factory had a face, it looked as if birds had pecked out its eyes. When we kids, walking home from school, got too close to Rat Factory—by this point Rat Factory had become a proper name—we hunched over to make ourselves smaller. We slowed our steps and shrunk our voices to a whisper. Our lunchboxes banged against each other's elbows. As we got closer to 142nd Street, Rat Factory stood up on its haunches. What would it do? Suck us in? Swallow us whole? Grind us into flour and feed us to the rats? We ran, cutting across the grass of the corner houses, screaming and barreling west toward Emerald Avenue, two blocks, one block more. Emerald Avenue beckoned like the lights of the Emerald City, as Rat Factory retreated into the background, settling back into its prairie bed.

★ ★ ★

The first pot of coffee my mother makes with her new Florida percolator is pale brown. Coffee that's too weak has a dirty taste. I can't drink it. My mother, on the other hand, is happy with supermarket coffee that comes in a vacuum-packed can. She's suspicious of the beans that cost ten bucks a bag and is leery of the grinders set up in the coffee aisle for the people who don't have grinders at home. So I'm surprised she's making such a fuss over this percolator. Mom, I ask her. Why don't you just use your old pot? You used that pot just fine for years now. No I didn't, she says. That pot's terrible. It's supposed to keep the coffee warm, but the coffee gets cold anyway. And I keep setting up the timer and forgetting to put the carafe in. What a mess, all over my counter.

That sounds like operator error, Mom, I tell her.

Even though I've always known that my mother's Projects really exist, I'm not sure I really believed it as a kid. No, *believe* is not the right word. I believed, but that belief wasn't physical, not the way our actual house with its brown bricks and prickly hedge and heavy basement door with the wood barricade instead of a lock was physical. The Projects were a faded movie, the kind that burns up when it gets too close to the projector bulb. I couldn't imagine actually walking through the Projects. The past was not a country my parents returned to. No guided tour. No packet of historical data. The past was a place you leave, a place to forget, a place to change away from, to pile up on the curb until the truck comes to take it away.

I imagine the walls of the Projects were bare, but clean, because my mother told me how often she scrubbed, until her elbows hurt and her knuckles were raw. I don't see how those walls could have been dirty enough to need all that scrubbing. It must have been a feeling my mother was trying to scrape away, the shadow of the mill smoke, so thick it could have been meringue, except it was too gray to be like meringue, and the eggs had gone bad, and there is no stink like eggs gone bad. She wanted to scrub all of it away, the coppery slag pilings, refuse from the mills that looked like pyres of collapsed bones, the sanitary district where her father worked, the whole stinking toilet-scape of the far Southeast Side. The memory of smell is almost all it takes to recreate that smell; she can't ever get rid of it completely, just like she can't scrub away the odor of cigarettes and whiskey that wafted out her father's pores, even though he's been dead since I was a freshman in college.

And too, I think my mother must have been scrubbing away at her certainty that there might never be enough, that it might all go down under her, that she'd sooner or later have nothing left, nowhere to sleep, nothing solid against her skin, nothing pretty or valuable to call her own. It's the pull to get up out of the urban underclass that motivated her every move, no looking back at the pile-up of people lining up behind, the ones looking forward to moving into the same space she wished so badly to abandon.

When I visit Florida we go to a restaurant near my parents' retirement house, the nice fish place down the road, the one where muscular gay men who work out at the same gym as my father have replaced the old-lady waitresses with high hair and cigarette-crossed voices. We don't eat the rolls, so my mother asks the waiter if he will wrap them up to go. They're just rolls. Just half rolls, some of them, the ones I'd picked at, pretending I wasn't eating the bread. Not worth saving. But Mom will not leave uneaten food on the table. One of us— her kids who try to fill her in on all the ways the world has progressed since she lived in the Projects—must have told her to ask the waiter for a bag; she used to just dump the rolls into her purse when the server's back was turned.

Mom, I'd say, why do you need those rolls? You've RETIRED in FLORIDA. This isn't the PROJECTS anymore. Outside the restaurant window, the dock water glistens. Boats rock against the docks, the swooshing barely audible through the glass. No, this is nothing like the Projects. Mom, you can afford to buy rolls, I'd say. Why should I pay for new rolls? she'd say. I'm already paying for these rolls. The waiter brings back our half-eaten rolls in a Styrofoam box. Mom wraps up the conversation the same way every time. You'll never get the Projects out of me, she says.

Every time Linnea and I clean out our cabinets for our annual South Minneapolis neighborhood yard sale, we realize we might have trouble letting go of the past. I make fun of the way my mother moved half of Chicago into her little wood A-frame in Florida, but I'm no better. I forget that it's not memory that collectors save, just objects that look like memory.

Such is my collection of mid-twentieth-century TV lamps. I have more than twenty of them now—pairs of poodles and birds of paradise, lilies and leaping gazelles, an abstract cluster of leaves that looks like a head of lettuce, and even a ceramic fireplace made with translucent clay, my collection incomplete until I find that ceramic light-up accordion. They are my favorite things, silly ceramic statuary, sold in the 1950s to set on top of the TV, a hood ornament for then-new TV consoles, modern and practical, and promising to reduce TV-tube eye strain. TV lamps, along with atomic curtain-fabric design and anything that pictured a poodle, were part of the twentieth-century, mid-industrial-era, American domesticity fetish. Finally, a nice house. In a clean neighborhood with lawns and freestanding houses. Finally, we are out of the Projects.

Linnea broke one of my lamps recently, while moving the furniture to plug in the digital TV connection. Honey, I said. Be careful of my TV lamps. Yeah yeah, she said, and a few moments later I heard a crash. When I saw the broken ceramic birds, no longer poised for flight above a porcelain planter, I cried, as if I'd lost something that mattered, something crucial and imprecise as memory itself.

Linnea glued the birds back together. I can't see the cracks unless I look closely. Still, I don't know what I'm doing, gathering up these objects, more things to dust. It may be enough to just say I like them, that they are silly and useless and make me laugh, but I suspect they are more. I tell myself I want to know about the past but it could be I prefer a kitschy history, the kind I can control.

My mother is frustrated with her new percolator. She can't control it. The coffee doesn't taste like she remembers percolated coffee tasting. She asks me, am I doing this wrong? She asks me, doesn't Linnea have a percolator? What does she do to make her coffee so good? Linnea does have a percolator, the type that sits on the stove and shoots coffee up into its glass-knobbed lid. And Linnea makes good coffee. But she has the kitchen thumb. It's not fair to compare. When my parents come to visit, she makes them coffee in that percolator, because it looks more like a coffee pot to them than the press pot or espresso machine we'd otherwise use.

So I call Linnea and tell her, Mom wants your advice on using her new percolator. Well, Linnea says, first be sure the coffee cooks long enough. It takes longer than the Mr. Coffee. Oh, my mother says, and frowns. This is not good news. She doesn't want it to take longer. She just wants it to taste better. And stay warmer. She wants to make it at 6:00 AM when she gets up, and she wants it to stay warm until 11:00 AM, when she pours another cup. She wants a lot, I almost point out, but then don't bother. I might not be able to help her with this percolator problem.

Then tell her, Linnea continues, that my grandmother used to toss in eggshells. Eggshells, I ask her, What does that do? I don't know, Linnea says. It's some old Italian thing. So tell I her, Mom, Linnea says her grandmother throws in eggshells. Eggshells, my mother asks, Do I have to wash them off first? No, no, I tell her, just save the shells and put them in with the coffee grounds. Well, I'm not going to waste an egg just for the coffee, Mom says.

Before my parents moved to Florida I absconded with two collections—my Dad's battered old jazz albums and the dusty reels of home movies that no one had looked at for years, ever since my Dad's old projector finally broke down. A year or so later I pulled that box of film out of the closet under my stairs and decided I wanted to see what I had. So I rented a projector. The film flickered against the white paper I taped against the wall in my dining room, the film images harder and crisper than they'd look later, once I had them transferred to videotape. I watched scenes from the day my mother brought me home from the hospital, swaddled in her arms, and scenes of one of my birthday parties, a swarm of children playing London Bridge on the front lawn, and then the scenes that really surprised me, footage of the Projects. My mother's middle brother, the one who used to look like

Elvis, sat in an upstairs window and waved. My other uncle, a skinny teenager who would later work on his Edsel collection in our garage, opened the front door and beckoned us in.

When I saw that footage I shivered. It was as if a story had transmogrified into a hologram, as if language had suddenly become a body. The buildings were not remarkable. Plain brick, windows square and open. My Elvis uncle was younger and more relaxed than he seemed to me later, when I actually knew him, living in a messy back room of his mother's apartment. No, the difference was this: My mother's mantra became a body of space, the province of her constant and repetitious storytelling, the place her whole life has been dedicated to leaving, but also a geography that exists without her, in real time, in history, in the annals of my family's old Super 8 film reels. I couldn't tell if this made the Projects less of a story, or more.

When is a prairie a plot of industrial detritus, and when is it a sea of wild grass? When is a percolator an item of nostalgia in an antique shop specializing in overflow from middle-twentieth-century-American kitchens, and when is it the best way to make coffee? The percolator is a cliché for bubbling over, for fresh, fast, and new ways of thinking, but the coffee my mother makes in her new Wal-Mart percolator just doesn't taste that good.

Linnea says maybe my mother bought that percolator so she could make coffee for me. She comes to our house, Linnea says, and our coffee is different from hers, not regular coffee. Maybe to her the percolator seems fancier. Maybe she's just trying to make coffee that you'll drink. At first I say no no, that's not it. She told me she didn't know why she bought it; she just saw it and placed it in her shopping cart without thinking. But the minute I say it I take it back. My mother has always told me she doesn't believe in psychological reasons for things, so if I asked her she would pooh-pooh the idea. But the more I think of it, the more I can see it.

Back in the 1960s, when Mom replaced her old percolator with a Mr. Coffee, she had stepped into an ever-cleaner world. Fill the paper basket with coffee. Pour the water in at the back. Push the button, and the coffee streams out into a clear glass carafe as if out of a kitchen faucet, and the dirty grounds never stick in the basket holes, never touch her hands.

Nostalgia is the past with the messy grounds removed, nothing but the surface remaining. Those 1950s ads of well-groomed housewives with starry smiles serving dinner in crisp yellow dresses and comfortable heels are funny to us now, but back then they were a promise. So my mother is wheeling her way through Wal-Mart the day her only daughter is coming to visit, the kid who turned out so different, who likes that fancy strong coffee, and she sees the image of a gleaming percolator on the box and remembers when the perky fountain of coffee sitting on her kitchen counter was the picture of her escape. The percolator was fancy; that's what she remembers.

If that's true, then she must be disappointed when I set on her counter the Italian Roast that I'd carried all the way from Minneapolis and proceed to make coffee in my new toy, a silver mug with a press pot plunger built right in. I show the French press cup to Mom, demonstrate how it works. That's pretty fancy, my mother says.

People I've told in my adulthood about Rat Factory have imagined a pinched-face, stoop-shouldered gangster called Ratty, ugly enough, but too small. I don't always remember to mention that our Rat Factory was tall as a ten-story office building, and wide as well, the width of four or five of our houses.

Truman Capote once described midwestern grain elevators as Greek temples, but he was writing about Kansas, towers rising out of wide swaths of open farmland. Rat Factory, more pyramid than temple, had brick neighborhoods and train tracks and electrical lines huddled around it from all sides. Most of the time, we sensed it more than saw it, the way we were aware of tornados and presidential assassins, real enough on the nightly news, but not the kind of thing you want to look in the face.

According to neighborhood stories, there were really rats inside Rat Factory, although I never saw them. All grain mills had rats, because in a grain mill there is plenty for rats to eat. In the 1960s, before we lived there, Rat Factory caught fire, causing the rats to run for their lives. An army of rats fled the mill, filing into the prairie, crossing 142nd Street, burrowing into the basements of the homes in the streets surrounding.

Rats or no rats, Emerald Avenue, while fancier than the Projects, was not nearly fancy enough from my mother's point of view. Yet today when I type that old address, 14200 Emerald, into an internet street atlas, what comes up on my computer screen is simply a pale yellow map, not Rat Factory, not even a palette of my mother's fears, those invisible perpetrators she named "unsavory characters," hiding like rats in the broken prairie brush. A red star marks where our old house stands, at the corner of a tight grid of streets that cup the bottom of the city. Emerald Avenue was a block of boxy houses, evenly spaced. The lawns were square and the chain link fences hemmed us all in neatly. I might remember the name of the avenue, not as I knew it but as it sounds, green and cradling an inner flicker, or I might remember it as it was, not a gem, just a residential street a few blocks beyond the mill smoke, or I might remember all of it at once. The abandoned prospects of the post-steel American metropolis. The fear of rats that may not have been actual rats but only my mother's unspoken shadows, not just her father's poverty but also his fumbling whiskey hands. I might remember the actual avenue and also the promise of some fancier city, awaiting both her and my escape.

My mother had a dishwasher in the Emerald Avenue house, not the built-in kind she has now, but the kind with wheels. My dad, a member of the camera club, built a darkroom in the basement. The weeping willow in the yard fingered its way into the foundation, the flowering bushes in the yard popped into bloom each spring and shook showers of pink petals across the grass, and in the garage my uncle sanded and painted and re-sanded and re-painted another old car. Once I squeezed into the dome-like front seat of his latest Edsel with one of my brothers, and my uncle drove us along the perimeter of the prairie, safe inside the tank steel skin of the car, while the prairie weeds billowed and Rat Factory glowered but couldn't get near us. Back home my mother set a cup of percolated coffee on the yellow speckled counter and forgot about it until it was too cold to drink.

A prairie is a fancy plain of grass, diverse and spectacular, billowing like the sea. A prairie is an industrial dump with wire-laced skies and rat-faced factories. The Projects were supposed to be planned communities, orchestrated fanciness, a shelter, a nice clean place to live for people who worked hard for their money, but they turned out to be, for my mother at least, her purgatory. The memories we collect are the smiley faces and un-cracked hearts, pressed like pretty leaves between the pages of the dictionary. The memories that stick without our efforts have dirty walls and rat-infested basements. When we were in the Projects, my mother begins, and she means not just then but also now.

I will never ask my mother if she finally does what she's been threatening the whole week of my visit, which is to clean up that percolator, put it back in the box, return it to Wal-Mart. I won't get involved in her arguments with Dad about whether it's too late, now that she's used it. Dad and I both know if she wants to take it back, she will.

But if what Mom really wants is to make me a cup of coffee fancier than the Projects, then we are at an impasse. She reaches for the percolator at Wal-Mart because the fancy picture on the box reminds her less of coffee than of her old longing to leave. I long for the percolator at the antique store because I love the funniness of the lie, the snazzy starburst design and the swanky spout, the promise of a perkier-than-possible future. My mother's and my ideas of fancy meet, then part again.

Before I leave Florida, I try to brew a pot of my dark Italian Roast in Mom's percolator. I'd like to say that this is the winning equation; the daughter's content plus the mother's technology equal a fancy cup of coffee we can both enjoy. But my coffee is ground too coarsely, meant for the press pot. It clogs the works of my mother's percolator. Neither of us can drink it. We leave the cups of grainy black brew on her counter until the golfers outside her kitchen window, retirees from the northern mill cities or midwestern suburbs or the southern Air Force bases, drive their carts back to their half-life arcadias, the course turning blue under the setting sun, the coffee cold.

Grown Folks' Business

Taiyon Coleman

On Saturdays, Momma sat alone in our yellow kitchen, smoking cigarettes and drinking Coca-Cola from its contoured glass bottle. Momma usually sat between the kitchen window and the table. Her long slender legs crossed each other, and cheap, blue flip-flops dangled from her feet. She shook one foot back and forth to the steady rhythm of the music. I sat with my sisters and brother on the couch in our sparsely decorated living room. Our house was shaped like one big rectangle, and from the living room, we watched Momma flopping her foot, smoking her cigarettes and drinking her pop. The couch faced a big broken television set, and on top of it sat the smaller black-and-white television that worked. The room could have been improved a bit by more and newer furniture and by moving the smaller television to the bar and the broken one downstairs, but Momma wouldn't let us move the TV. It was a gift from her dead brother, Wayne.

Wayne and Momma were very close. He was the only one we saw regularly, and he brought the TV on one of his visits. He'd even shuttle us the three hundred miles from Chicago to Sparta, Illinois, and back when we couldn't afford to buy six Greyhound bus tickets. When Wayne died in a coal mining accident, it was the first and the only time I ever saw my mother cry. She hurt so much; I wondered if she ever realized how much we were hurting, too. We tried to convince Momma that we could carry the TV downstairs by ourselves without damaging it any further, but our suggestions, like our questions about our parents' divorce, were always met with a swift and solid "no."

"I am grown," was Momma's response to me and my four siblings whenever we asked her about Daddy and their divorce. Usually, the question came in rare moments of play and intimacy when Momma seemed happy and at ease. That usually meant on Saturday afternoons, when the house was clean, and everybody was tired and a little loopy from a morning of sweeping, scrubbing, and vacuuming. On the good Saturdays, there was even enough food for the weekend. Momma didn't worry about what bills not to pay in order to pay the bills she needed to pay. Momma called it robbing Peter to pay Paul.

Next to the television was the bar with the record player. From black vinyl stacked on top of black vinyl, waiting its turn to drop, the smooth '70s R&B sounds of Luther Vandross, Peabo Bryson, and Phyllis Hyman streamed out of the record player speakers into our small, one-story, two-bedroom house on Chicago's south side. Like most offspring of Motown parents, my siblings and I could sing all the lyrics to Momma's favorite songs. It didn't matter that we didn't understand the words, their joy and their pain. We just liked how happy the music seemed to make Momma feel. When we watched and heard Momma sing those songs, she was no longer a single mother of five kids abandoned by her husband. Momma was the lead singer, and we were her snazzy backup singers with synchronized moves, dancing nice and looking mighty fine in the height of the '70s disco era.

When Phyllis Hyman sang "Somewhere in My Lifetime," I was too young to have kissed somebody's lips in that "special" way that Phyllis was crooning about, but I somehow already knew in my heart and soul what Phyllis's longing was about. I missed Daddy, and I missed the part of Momma that Daddy took with him when he left us. I knew that Momma missed Daddy too, and listening to music and singing together was the only time she could afford to feel it. It was during those carefree times that I, like many children of divorce, asked my desperate questions. It seemed as if one day Daddy was at home, and the next day, Daddy was gone.

"Momma . . . what happened between you and Daddy? Momma . . . why isn't Daddy coming home?"

When Phyllis Hyman was playing in the background, I just knew that Momma would answer. At age ten, it was easy to be courageous. My ignorance and childhood forgetfulness made it easy to come back to the same questions over and over again. I was analytical and inquisitive, unlike my siblings. I was already a critical thinker, which in my family translated into a reputation for talking too much, asking too many questions, and having a smart-ass mouth. I was reading Stephen King and Danielle Steel novels, and I had watched too many episodes of "The Young and the Restless" and "General Hospital." My parents even took me to see *Cooley High* when I was six, although I feel asleep before the sex and violence part of the movie. I thought I knew everything and that I could handle anything.

"Momma. What happened? Why is Daddy not here?" I asked again, thinking that maybe she didn't hear me.

"I'm grown," she responded for the second time.

Momma took a drag off her cigarette. Phyllis was singing "You Know How to Love Me," but right then, I could no longer hear Phyllis's words or the music.

Momma stood up and placed her hands on her size-ten hips. She hung her head and turned it to the side to face the kitchen window, allowing her long, straight black hair to fall over her face. Her cigarette was gone, and she calmly reached down over the kitchen table to free another Winston from its squished red and white package. The sound of the match striking and lighting sucked in the room's silence.

I looked back into the living room to see my oldest sister, Cheron, sitting on the couch. She was giving me a look that said, *Shut up and sit down because you are really gonna get it if you don't stop.*

I rolled my eyes at her the way good little sisters can, and I turned back to face Momma.

An exhaled white fog circled my pig-tailed head like a ghost, and Momma turned from the kitchen window to face me. Her five-foot-eleven-inch frame towered over me, and through the smoke, her eyes widened into my own, which were exactly like hers.

"Momma. Please tell me what happened, so I can understand?" I asked again. My desire to know was making me very brave.

"Please," I begged. For some reason, her eye contact made me hopeful.

Momma's full, pink lips closed to pull in more smoke from her cigarette, and with this physical movement, I knew my questions had gone too far. Our conversation was over.

I about-faced and walked back to the living room, a soldier shamed and defeated in battle. Cheron gave me a smug "I told you so" look. A little of my pride was intact because I knew Cheron had the same questions, but she didn't have the guts to ask. Cherisse, Jacqueline, and Ronnie were too young to care. For most of their lives, Daddy had hardly been at home. It seemed that I was the only person who couldn't let go.

In Momma's world, children did not ask adults questions. Adults were grown; therefore, adults were absolved of all self-explanation, especially to their own kids.

"It's not fair, Momma! It affects us too!" I yelled at her from living room into the kitchen, knowing that I was cutting it really close. It was a safe distance, but even from the living room, I stepped back a little in case her hand somehow sprung out of the kitchen to slap me in the face. Momma did have magical powers.

"If you ain't paying the bills, then sit your ass down and shut up!" Momma yelled back. It was her only response, and it was Momma's motto. I believed that it came from *The Black Momma Handbook, Volume II*, which included popular Momma phrases like "I'm not your friend, I'm your Momma," "I brought you into this world, and I'll take you out," and "Have you lost your mind?" The first volume is subtitled, *None of Your Business Because I'm Grown*. They were phrases that stung harder than any open hand slap in the face, and they cut me to the bone.

Momma's smoky silence left me in the pre-adolescent haze of my longing, but she clearly conveyed what my ten-year-old brain and heart could not understand: she and Daddy were through, and he was never coming back home. Although it affected me in every fiber of my being, to my mother, it was absolutely none of my business.

Before the divorce, I remember school mornings filled with hugs and kisses. When we left for school, Momma always licked her thumb to wipe dried breakfast cereal from the creased edges of our mouths. Late in the afternoon, we ran to the bus stop at the end of the block to greet Momma and walk her home. But when Daddy left, we, like most single-parent families, were instantly thrown into poverty; we lived one paycheck away from starvation. Momma's communications became, primarily, fierce directions for survival: "Take care of your brother and sisters, keep the house clean, leave me alone because you always want something, and I can't never have nothing because of you!" I learned early on not to want anything or at least not to show I wanted anything, but I could never stop wanting to know why my parents divorced.

According to my paternal grandmother, who prided herself on being lighter than a paper bag, Momma was having too may kids. It didn't matter that Grandmother had five kids of her own. Grandmother could do that because she was middle-class, and her husband hadn't left her.

"She just kept popping them out," Grandmother said as she rubbed her chest underneath her weekend robe. It was an involuntary moment and something that seemed to soothe her. She often was relaxed and in her best moods when she was wearing her weekend robes and rubbing her breasts.

It was Sunday morning, and sometimes we stayed Saturday nights and all day Sundays with Grandmother. She read the paper and watched the White Sox on WGN if she wasn't torturing us with straightening our hair with chemicals.

As a hard head makes for a soft behind, one of our favorite topics of discussion was how sorry she was over Momma and Daddy's divorce. We were lucky to see my father once or twice a year after the divorce.

"I know it hurts, but at least you have a father," was always her response to my eternal questions of why.

"Your grandmother never knew her daddy," she said, as she rubbed one breast, then the other. The rubbing seemed like a form of meditation, and I wished, at age ten, that I had breasts to rub, too. Maybe it would make me feel better.

My grandmother migrated from Arkansas to Chicago as a young girl. Her father's name was Red, and Red made a living playing piano in juke joints across the South. Grandmother's mother, Beulah, babysat Red's and his wife's children when Red traveled and when his wife worked. Red came home a lot when his wife wasn't there. At the age of fourteen, Beulah gave birth to Red's fifth daughter, my grandmother, and Beulah's family quietly shipped Grandmother to Chicago to stay with relatives.

Grandmother never saw her father much. When she was a toddler and still living in rural Arkansas, Red took her to the home, the back-door to be specific, of his Irish father. Apparently, Red hadn't grown up with his father either, but he wanted the opportunity to show off his beautiful, light-skinned daughter with her red hair to his white father for approval. Grandmother's family never talked about Beulah's rape, Red's pedophilia, and Grandmother's abandonment.

It seemed that fatherlessness, secrets, and abandonment were a family tradition, and Grandmother really believed that that kind of hurt was normal.

"Pain is a part of life, child," she slipped into black vernacular to finish her point. We weren't ever allowed to use non-standard English around my grandparents, or we would be slapped in the mouth.

"Why?" I asked.

"It just is, baby. Be grateful for what you have because it could be worse," she said, and her attention went back to the White Sox and to rubbing her breasts. Grandmother was so sincere. What was being a child of divorce compared to never knowing your father and your mother?

To Grandmother, I was lucky and spoiled, and she was doing me a huge favor by encouraging me to learn to live with my parents' divorce and my father's absence. Hadn't she done a good job learning to live with her hurt, and her parents weren't even married, let alone court-ing? What right did I, a little black girl from Chicago with black nappy hair, have to expect a normal family life with my father?

"After your mother had the second baby, Grandmother asked your daddy if they were using something," she said, coming back to what she thought was the most important point of our conversation.

Grandmother regularly referred to herself in the third person.

"What do you mean?" I asked, really understanding but wanting her to explain.

"They just kept having children, one right after another, and Grand-mother wondered if your mother had ever had the talk about birth control," she said.

The White Sox hit a home run, and her attention left me and her breasts. She jumped up and ran to the television, screaming, "Yes! Yes! Yes!"

I thought that maybe my parents just really loved each other. Isn't that why they had all those children?

Is it possible that my parents' love was really about lust dangerously paired with my mother's fifth-generation Roman Catholicism? Grandmother said that she wanted somebody to talk to Momma, and I have always wondered why didn't she just talk to Momma herself. Who would talk to my mother? If these people couldn't even tell me why my parents divorced, how could they talk about sex, birth control, and babies? Everyone that Momma ever knew was over three hundred miles away in her small, rural hometown. All of Momma's married family and friends disappeared the day she left my father. Who could Momma trust enough to tell her to stop having children and that the man she loved did not really love her? Who loved Momma enough and knew enough to tell her?

If they did tell Momma, what did they say to her? "Your man loves you, Cheryl, but he is no good for you, girl," or "Cheryl, you better get a hold onto yourself tight so that you won't end up in a jam with all these children."

Maybe that was the mistake: thinking that children, like spoiled leftovers, were the problem when love and a marriage ended.

No one said anything. They kept silent, and I kept asking questions. By the time they said anything, it was too late. My siblings and I were here, and saying something about it became gossip, judgment, and talking behind my mother's back. They said nothing, and another woman, another black woman, another poor woman, another single mother, another Catholic woman, and another inner-city woman almost choked herself to death upon her own love.

I have a sort of bald spot in the back of my head. It is short and smooth, like freshly trimmed grass, right at the place where my head hits the pillow when I sleep on my back. It is my habit to periodically touch it and think about it involuntarily. It is not caused by male pattern baldness or hair breakage. I was born with a full-size afro, which was appropriate to the 1970s. It was only when women other than my momma started putting their hands in my hair that I was made aware of the bald patch.

It was Cheron's job to braid hair in our house because Momma didn't have time to do our hair. Plus, Momma didn't have a nappy piece of hair on her body, so she really didn't know how to comb the coarse hair of her own children. One day while Cheron was french-braiding cornrows into my hair, she crudely informed me of the spot.

"I can't braid your head here in this spot," she said as she yanked on the small patch.

"Ouch," I said. I pulled away.

"Be still, or I won't braid it," she said, and the thought of looking ugly for the next week made me put up with the pain.

On other grooming occasions, it was my next-door neighbor and sometimes babysitter, Doll. I cringed when Doll pressed my nappy, black hair in that spot with her hot comb and Blue Magic grease, because the short hairs couldn't protect my tender scalp from the fiery heat of Doll's metal comb.

"What are you doing in the back of your head, girl?" Doll said out of one side of her mouth while her cigarette hung out the other.

I stayed silent. Doll had sugar (black vernacular for diabetes), her husband died right after he bought her their first and only house, and it was rumored that her daughter ran away from home after she beat her with an extension cord. She watched neighborhood kids to make money on the side. Doll was seriously old school. Doll asked children questions that were not meant to be answered. The question itself was the statement.

The patch on the back of my head needed different treatment when my grandmother first straightened my hair with lye. After she worked me over with chemicals in her basement, wannabe beauty salon, I placed my head under her hair dryer. When Momma came to pick me up, Grandmother boasted proudly that her work, the destruction of my coarse hair for straighter, whiter-looking hair, was a masterpiece of orange, plastic rollers, except for the smaller green ones. Grandmother motioned me to get from under the dryer, and she pushed my head down with her hand for Momma's inspection.

"It's beautiful, Cheryl, except for this spot in the back of her head. What happened?" Genuinely puzzled, they stared at the back of my head for a moment, and I stared at my big feet and the floor. While

Momma and Grandmother tried to imagine why I had such a marking, the green magnetic rollers, my newly processed hair, and I hung on for life.

"I think I can cover it up," Grandmother broke the silence and the staring, and it meant I could go home believing I looked beautiful, at least for that day.

After my mother's death, my aunt Linda told me that my father was cheating on my mother with a woman who lived in the neighborhood. My mother convinced my uncle Harold (my father's brother and Aunt Linda's ex-husband) to take her to the house. It was a hot August day in 1969. My mother found my father with another woman at that house. I was born a few weeks later.

My father was not only having an affair with the woman, but he furnished the woman's bedroom when he and my mother were living in a house with no furniture at all. I cannot imagine how devastating that was for Momma: to have one child not even a year old, one child about to be born, to have left your family and your education for a man, and to find he was cheating on you, your child, and your unborn child with another woman.

I imagine that after I was born I lay in the crib crying a lot. I imagine that I was never picked up. I imagine Momma not having the physical and emotional energy to do anything beyond nursing me. Because I now consider myself an emotional eater, I imagine that breast-feeding time was the only opportunity I had for love, comfort, and attention. It is in the months of crying in the crib, neglected because I could not walk like my sister, that I developed the bald patch on the back of my head.

"I should have known," Momma said.

Two plastic cups full of pop and ice sweated out a late June day on our concrete steps. Aunt Linda was visiting us on her way home from work.

Aunt Linda and Momma were very close. They had a great deal in common. They were both married and divorced from Coleman brothers. Their conversation was free flowing, and because I had finally gained a little "grown folks" status, I was not asked to leave the porch to let grown folks talk their business.

I was no longer an adolescent in the kitchen singing Momma's favorite songs. The '70s were over, I was in college, and it was a Friday. It was one of those good days. There was no music playing. There were Pepsi and cigarettes, two of my mother's favorite things in the world, and there were fewer mouths to feed in the house. Three of her children were away in college, and that left only two kids at home. Plus, the Cook County courts had decided in Momma's favor, so Daddy was still paying child support, back child support, and health insurance for us all.

Now, let's be clear. There was no way I was ever going to be grown enough to smoke cigarettes or grown enough to try to drink Momma's Pepsi out of her cup, but I could stay on the porch and listen to her talk if I played my cards right. I had to be cool, and from the way I liked to ask questions, you all know that cool was a very hard thing for me to do.

Aunt Linda and Momma were talking about Momma's first meeting with Daddy. They were riding a bus in Carbondale. Daddy said that Momma had the prettiest legs he had ever seen, and Momma said that Daddy was a little young but smart and handsome. She said, when Daddy smiled, it was like the slow opening of dark house to morning sunlight.

"I should have known," she said again and took a long drag off her Winston Light 100s.

"Should have known what?" I asked. I was trying to be really cool.

"This is grown folks' business, Taiyon," Aunt Linda said. She stood up from the concrete porch and faced Momma from the bottom of the steps. They both laughed.

I was losing my cool.

"I should have known then," Momma said. It was becoming a mantra, but finally, the story came, and I got the business.

Momma had a serious collection of Motown forty-fives when she met Daddy, and their relationship started with them just getting together to listen to her music. Once they were a hot and heavy item, Momma said they were planning to attend a big campus dance together, but Daddy said that he was sick and didn't feel like going. Momma initially decided to stay home with her girlfriends, but later, she and her girlfriends went to the party anyway. Momma said she found my father at the dance, hanging out with another girl. She said she tried to confront Daddy, but he just ran away.

"It was like that the entire time we were married. He was with me and everybody else, too, but this time, I didn't have anywhere to run. I just should have known," she said for the last time, and it sounded like the words meant something different to her because they meant something new and different to me. It was as if I heard the words and their meanings for the first time.

"I told you it was grown folks' business," Aunt Linda said, and she laughed, knowing Momma's story had not satisfied me, as she watched me look at Momma. Aunt Linda shrugged her shoulders, took a drag off of her cigarette and drank the remaining Pepsi from her cup.

I suddenly felt shy and looked away from Momma's face. I should have known, too. I should have trusted Momma to have a really good reason. I should have trusted Momma to be grown.

Unlike me, Momma was cool.

Momma said the important things just once, and if you didn't listen, the consequences were all on you. This was her way. She never pushed me into anything I didn't want to do. She would always make a suggestion, and she would leave the decisions up to me, even when she saw me heading for an obvious wreck. I guess she knew that wrecks cannot be stopped, at least not by people standing on the sidelines.

"How old is he?" is the only question she asked me. We were talking on the phone about the trouble in my marriage. My first husband could sell sand in the desert, and it did not help that he believed that he was God's sexual gift to every willing woman who crossed his path.

"He is thirty-two years old," I replied. There was silence on the line, and then, Momma spoke.

"He is not going to change. He is going to be that way forever, Taiyon," she said it calmly without any hint of persuasion. It was a fact offered to me without any judgment or chastisement. It was a fact given to be left or taken.

"It's going to hurt," I said, trying not to cry. I didn't want to show myself as weak to Momma. I was embarrassed and shamed enough that I had married a complete idiot, someone even worse than my father. But I was lucky. I had finished college, we had no children, and we owned absolutely nothing together. It would be a divorce free of legal problems, and most importantly, the scars would only be internal. My price for failure would be permanent but manageable unto myself. My price would not be as high as Momma's.

"It's going to hurt," I said again, pretending that Momma didn't hear me the first time. I wanted her to give me a way out, but this time, she came back with a quick response.

"Yes, Taiyon. It will hurt, but you'll live," she added the words like forgotten items on a grocery store list. Oh, I almost forgot. I need the tomatoes to make the stew, and the pain and the hurt are integral ingredients of life, especially when mistakes, change, and the hope for something better are involved.

Momma was giving me the best advice she could give. I knew that it was as persuasive as she would get. She knew love was blind, and she would never try to convince me to do something that I was not ready to do. It was advice she had learned the hard way. I would be a fool not to listen.

By this time, I still knew only a little of why Momma divorced my father and why it took her so long to leave him, but the small details were no longer important. The big things—commitment, responsibility, love, trust, and self-respect—were.

At twenty-six, I could finally start to see my mother as not just my mother, but as a brave woman who risked everything. She swallowed her fear, her pain, and the abandonment and judgment of others because she knew there must be a better way to live a life than allowing herself to be continually hurt and humiliated by another person, even when that person was her husband and the father of her five children. In that moment of talking about my divorce with my mother, I became grown. I was thankful Momma left Daddy. Who might I have become had she not?

★ ★ ★

"I just got the papers today. The divorce is final," I said over the phone. It was around nine in the evening, and it had been six months since I filed. I had just arrived home from a seminar in my first year of graduate school to find my final documents. Without thinking, I immediately called Momma to give her the news. I wanted her to be proud of me.

"Good. It is done," she said, and it was a short conversation. We exchanged our "I love you," to each other, and I said I would call her the coming weekend. It was our last conversation. Before the week was done, my mother went into cardiac arrest and never regained consciousness. It happened at home in the kitchen. For the first time in twenty-six years, Momma was alone in the house. My brother, the last born, had left for college earlier that year. There was no one there to call the police, to unlock the bolted doors and to revive Momma's heart. As she had wanted, we removed Momma from life support and let her go.

Momma went to the grave at age forty-nine, never telling me the entire story of how and why she and Daddy divorced. I guess for so long Momma was forced to focus on survival that she didn't talk or share about how she felt. Her job was just to make sure that the five of us had food, shelter, clothing, and a decent education. The basic necessities of life didn't include the privilege of emotional well-being or putting all your business in the street. Momma worked full time, and fulfilling her parental responsibilities sucked away everything else, including her ability to share the pain that all of us were going through. For a long time, I even thought that she didn't love Daddy and that she didn't really love us. For a long time, I thought that she didn't love me. But she did love me. She was only a woman, with five kids, trying to be grown.

Indian Princess, Girl Guide, Plains Mother

Heid E. Erdrich

In a room of blondes, my mom stood out. Easy to spot in a town full of Norwegians and Swedes, her dark head held up a bit above the rest, a beacon to kids lost in a crowd. Mom had seven children and one or another of them was always about to be lost, lagging behind, scanning the crowd for her. Good thing she was easy to find.

Mom's difference always made me proud. She was tall for her day, though only average height for my generation, at five-foot-six. Her glossy black hair has held off most of the grey until this day. She has good hair, as lots of Chippewa women do. At least we have that, I've heard it said, good hair and strong knees. And a good laugh.

Mom's hair was her crown. Did you ever wear your hair long? I asked Mom. Never, she said. But it was so thick and rich, why not wear it long? This was the 1970s, era of the straight fall, the hippie head. There were other looks, of course. Did she want to seem mod and sporty? For me it was all about the hair.

The deepness of Mom's hair gave her beauty-queen appeal, especially when she wore red lipstick, that instant glamour several generations' worth of American mothers never failed to apply just before they headed out the door. That and those sheer scarves to hold the hairdo gave our mothers the look of movie stars fleeing paparazzi—all they needed were the dark sunglasses. And some of them had those as well.

As for those icons of fashion, Mom's beauty seemed public in our small town. Her good looks were often remarked on by my friends' mothers and fathers: Oh, you are one of Rita's daughters? Your mother is so beautiful, they would say. You would think a girl would be flattered, but I knew what would come next and I dreaded it. Inevitably the claim would be pronounced: She's an Indian Princess!

My grandfather was chairman of our tribe, the Turtle Mountain

Band of Ojibway, but that did not make my mother a royal. I knew this because Mom made it clear to me: There are no Indian Princesses, she'd insist. And as an offer of response for me to use, she'd say, Tell them our tribe didn't have royalty. Interestingly, she left it open as to whether other tribes might have had such designations and thereby taught me a lesson: Not all Native peoples are the same. Or two lessons, because I also learned that not all Indian things are Indian.

In fact, there are Indian Princesses, just as there are Homecoming Queens and Rodeo Royalty and Little Miss Hometown titles. It's honorary, that's all, not cultural in the fuller sense. It is an American thing, not an American Indian thing.

Yet, many times in my childhood, I insisted my mother was not an Indian Princess. Thank you, but my mother is not an Indian Princess. Our tribe didn't have royalty. I took it as a challenge, really, an early unconscious lesson in revisiting stereotype. Mom was beautiful, yes, but she was not to be crowned by anyone.

Maybe my mom inadvertently resisted stereotype in her eventual choice of coif. Sometime in the early '70s she had her straight black hair done in a perm of short tight curls. Yes, Mom got a 'fro. Not just once, but for some years, it was her chosen style. And as the perm grew out each month, her hair got Angela Davis wild. Once, a little girl who was staying with her grandparents asked me, in her southern accent, What kind of colored is your Mama? and I had no idea how to reply.

When I told my mom, she laughed. The hair was just the style of the day, and lots of blonde moms were wearing it that way. But the memory of how Mom's hair choice could be read so differently by others really stuck with me. Again my mother had been noticed as different. Had I been a little older, I would have used the chance to say she was not an Indian Princess, but an African Queen.

We think of our mothers as changeless in our childhood. They are then as they always were. Then we grow enough to see our mothers as other females, even women who once were girls. Still, imagine my shock when in my teen years I asked my mother to share her school yearbook and discovered that she had a college annual as well. I had no idea that my mother had been to college in our hometown the year before she married Dad. And yet paging through the black-and-white pages for 1953, I found she was active in clubs and won honors. She was also clearly the apple of the photographer's eye, appearing in many shots, always neatly coifed.

There she was under the title, "Enter at Your Own Risk Geniuses at Work," in striped shirt, neat wool skirt, and jaunty scarf tied at the neck. She looked positively French. Next, page 39 finds her head-to-heels in leather—her chemistry apron described as regulation in the caption that suggests the danger she and her lab partner apprehend there with all the tubes, flasks, and Bunsen burners. They just might blow up!

Mom appears in several club shots, a standout in each, Home Economics (across from Students' Wives) and something called Sacajawea Club, noted as responsible for the Big-Little Sister Tea, basketball games, and a formal Mom claims she did not attend.

Imagine my surprise when, in one photo near the center of the book, my own mother appears as, of all things, an Indian Princess. Her hair in thick braids flipped forward to lie along her chest, her beaded headband and modest pose in leather-like dress, propped against a convertible's open top, ready for that wand-like wave of the royal hand! My mother *was* an Indian Princess.

Once. Only once, she said. This is what came of her membership in the Sacajawea Club and of her coaxed willingness as one of the few Indian girls at college that year. But what about her hair? I could not comprehend the length, the sheer luxury of the braids' foot-long fall, and their gloss and gorgeousness. The braids, she explained, were attached to the beaded headband. Her "brave" beside her was someone I nearly recognized, which alarmed me since he was certainly not my Dad. Just one of the guys, she said, to reassure me that the coupling was purely political, not by preference. Yet how odd to see Mom done up in tribal drag, draped on the arm of some charming fellow imitating the Sioux.

Discovering those photos explained a great many things. I knew then how that North Dakota off-reservation town had come to claim my mother as royal. People saw her once in the role they expected and her one-parade's designation became permanent to some: Mom was an Indian Princess.

Still, she resisted the title and all it implied, and for that I was grateful. Especially when I went East to study and learned a whole world out there knew nothing more about American Indian women than the princess myth. Unless, of course, they also carried in their collective cultural imagination the concept of that savage drudge: the squaw. And somewhere in between these two imagined figures falls the truth, or multiple and diverse truths, the reality of Native American women.

Of course I had no such thoughts as a young woman when I saw those pictures of my mother. Gazing at the mother through the lens of the past, we see another version of the familiar, but as through water: she's magnified or made small and strange. My mother had another life before her children and husband. Once my mother was a girl away at school, far from her own mother. That story always drew me, the one about the girl alone in the world. I went away myself, to New England, before I turned fifteen.

In the East, I learned that the myth-making American Indian Princess, Pocahontas, stands as female cultural ancestor. Her story is one of the first. In the West, Sacajawea works that role. The Girl Guide to the Lewis and Clark expedition appeared on posters and roadside signs in my youth. She was portrayed in North Dakota pageants and she, along with dancer Maria Tallchief, became the subject of numerous well-meaningly assigned book reports for a generation of girls seeking American Indian role models. It was either The Girl Guide, the ballerina, or Cher, when I was a kid.

When I was a girl in North Dakota, the "real Sacajawea," was presented to me by my mother's dear friend, Esther Brunett Horne, or Grandma Essie, as she asked to be called. Mom met her when she was a young woman in college, in her days with the Sacajawea Club. I first knew Sacajawea as the woman this kind elder claimed as her great-great-grandmother, a strong young woman who led some lost white guys through hostile territory, all the while with a baby on her back.

Sacajawea did this, Essie gave it to be understood, in order that she might once again see the land she loved. After the expedition, she went on her own way, traveling eventually by rails (using her medals as passage) and dying as a respected elder.

I liked this version of Sacajawea, but I had tucked it away into my thinking. When I was young, Sacajawea had stood as an example of how an Indian woman could do hard and important things. But then I learned the phrase "race traitor," used for those who gave up their own people for members of the dominant culture. Of course, that was before I understood the complexities of marriage in other centuries, how women might have seen their roles as wives more politically, more professionally even. Somehow I had let my vision of this strong role model, this motivated Sacajawea, get turned into one of shame. In fact, when I heard she was going to be on a dollar coin, my first thought was *why her?*

It wasn't until years later that I looked at the coin and thought, All right, an Indian woman *and* a mother. I became interested in reclamation of Sacajawea as a female figure, an ancestor of sorts who is both character and author, whose stories and actions told the expedition's tale. Without her there not only would not have been success for the expedition, but the very journals that chronicle the exploits of Lewis and Clark likely would not have survived. Yes, she saved their bacon and their goods more than one time.

In the first pages of her biography/autobiography, *Essie's Story: The Life and Legacy of a Shoshone Teacher*, co-authored by Sally McBeth, Esther Horne explains her relation to the woman known as Sacajawea, whom she calls her great-great-grandmother:

Bazil, Sacajawea's sister's son whom she adopted, was very solicitous of his mother and her comfort throughout her later life. Tradition has it that after many years of travel, at about the age of eighty, Sacajawea returned home to her people in what later (1890) became the state of Wyoming. Maggie Bazil, my maternal grandmother, was Bazil's daughter. We had connections to Sacajawea from both sides of our family. We were related through our mother's side, but my father's side of the family also had a long-standing relationship with her.

The way I remember Grandma Essie telling it, Sacajawea was not an Indian scout for the enemy, but an ambassador and a translator. She did not betray the people; she kept the peace. It was delightful to read *Essie's Story* and find in its pages confirmation of the image given to me as a child: "Sacajawea's presence, as a woman with a child, and her knowledge of sign language clarified the peaceful intentions of the explorers." What's more, *Essie's Story* suggests that Sacajawea's role with the expedition prepared her for a career of sorts:

Sacajawea spoke English and some French, as well as Shoshone and Hidatsa. She was also fluent in sign language and so was able to help the Shoshone make their wants known to government employees as well as the military. Oral tradition also suggests that she was instrumental in keeping peace between Shoshones and other tribes. So, that was her great service there.

Certainly Essie Horne's vision of this historical figure speaks against the many stereotypes of indigenous women as despised slaves or elevated princesses. This Sacajawea is a woman with her own intentions, a woman who might have survived walking to the west with her child on her back not as a service to men, kind as the captains could be or cruel as her husband, but as a way to once again see Shoshone territory, to speak her language and embrace her family.

What strikes me in Essie's portrait is that her Sacajawea (kidnapped and married off, to be sure) is not simply compelled by her servitude, but motivated by it. Essie paints the older Sacajawea as an adventurer, a woman in unhappy circumstances who makes the best of her situation: "Charbonneau had taken another wife and was abusive to Sacajawea. So she left him in St. Louis and began her migration back homeward to her Shoshone people."

This Sacajawea gains freedom and the independence to live out a ripe old age as an inspiration to others.

My relationship to Sacajawea is by no means the most important of my life, but I will admit that my connections to this well-known heroine have brought me a great deal of attention in my eighty-plus years. From the time I was a small child in Idaho, to the time spent around the Wind River reservation, to my days as a student and teacher in the Bureau of Indian Affairs boarding schools, the oral traditions of this woman have inspired me to hold on to my traditions.

Essie Horne made her Sacajawea a heroine to emulate, someone we might shape our lives around as Indian women. Maybe, beginning with my mother's service to the Sacajawea Club, that is what we women in my family did as well.

A nest of clear bowls, a stack of dolls, orbs within orbs. Such images always come to me what I think of the central amazement of biology: we were each an egg within our mother when she was within her mother. Once we were all three in one place, in part if not in whole. Then birth and we separate again and again as girl, woman, mother, grandmother. We follow each other, but never truly reunite.

My own maternal grandmother lived hundreds of miles from where I grew up. Her circumstances of age, income, and the care of foster children made it difficult for her to travel often. She was, as many have said, a saint. But my grandmother was not the person I most often called Grandma. Far from our home reservation, but bound in relation to other American Indian people, my family called two women Grandma who were not related to us by blood.

Other American Indian families did this too and do so still today. In our case, the women we "adopted" were not even from our tribe. Grandma Farmen was Dakota. My mother had been best of friends with her daughter Nettie, who died when they were both young mothers. Afterwards, my Mom took on something of a daughter role to her dear friend's mother. We visited Grandma Farmen often. She touched my face with hands so tender I can feel them still. My mother would light the stove, and then Grandma Farmen baked her truly perfect pies. I never understood she was blind until one day my mother told me. It's Grandma Farmen's recipes I had by heart by the time I was a teen. By then she was gone.

For a long time we had our Grandma Essie, proud descendant of The Girl Guide. She lived to an old age, suffering the loss of her husband and a daughter, and dying with my mother and sister comforting her in her last days. She had come to our weddings, celebrated our graduations, and even my nephews and nieces got her special attention, her careful cards, signed and sent until the very end. Who else does that but a grandmother?

Mom remembers Grandma Essie telling her, "Don't look at your feet" when she walked—an admonition I am sure that I heard, too. She meant that my mother should be proud. In those days that also meant be proud you are Indian. Pride meant everything to Essie and was the message of her many talks on Sacajawea. Pride is probably why she urged my mother to take part in that long-ago parade.

When I asked again about that event, I learned another amazing fact. The wig Mom wore when she dolled up as Indian Princess was woven of braids from Grandma Essie's own daughter. My mother says she remembers it being quite an honor—not being Princess, but the fact that Essie trusted her with something so precious, those braids that had come from her own daughter's hair.

When I asked my mother if Grandma Essie was like a mother to her, Mom was thoughtful, then said that Essie encouraged her in all her interests, especially her painting and art. She sounds just like my own mother.

Both women we called Grandma were, it seems, mothers to my mother. Through them my mother found grandmothers for her children, women who were bound by love as well as American Indian kinship, who guided us as wonderful elders, who taught us what it meant to be related in what we called the Indian way.

M(other)

Diane Glancy

My mother was the other in the house. She was something of which I was not part. I was left alone with her in the house until my father came home and my brother was born. A child is an island. A child is a moth. A child is a spot on the distant sea. My mother was in the house as I was. A dimmer light. An unwanted smot. I made up words for the land I inhabited. I found it moved like a floating island bumping against a continent that didn't want it bumping. I rowed my island back to the sea. Bypassing as it bypassed. What was it that was the connective? I was where I had to be when there was nowhere as yet to go. Going and ungoing. My dreams always were of travel. To speak of a mother is to speak of my father's grandfather who ran because he had to run to cover his tracks. Even his gravestone says he was born in Arkansas, but it was Indian Territory. He lied and ran, as my mother wanted the same cut and run, but I was the moth that kept her in the house. I was the cement block that tried to drown her. She swept with a broom that was her tongue. Her insistence on the mothership of which I was the dingy with cords that could be cut. I was the object to which she objected. I take this language of words though language at first is soundless. It is a longing for a connective, but it is separation that first rows across the sea. I am here. You are there. It is the first realization of (m)otherness. A filament of sound called language that could never breach the break. That took me to the shipwreck of my own motherness where my own children found the same sea. Mother of dry grass. Mother of flatlands. Mother of sharp boulders by the sea. Mother of vast loneliness and disappointment who thought she was escaping a farm, but ended up nonetheless stranded in a field. Forgive me for my attitude. I was a worse mother than she. My language was a suitcase. Forgive me, mother, for the ungraciousness of this written text. I am speaking to you as if I stood at your grave, which I have done. I know your sacrifice. I was what you didn't want to do, but did nonetheless. You yourself were shipwrecked. Marooned. Stranded on an island you only wanted him to reach. What did you think when you married him? Idea and the actuality that surrounded that idea were different. The disappointment you received as your paycheck. Recipient of undefined sadness that was the crop on the Kansas farm where you were raised. It sent you away on a vessel. Good-bye. I look back to your formidable shore that I would never reach, but took the broken boards and made a wooden shore that almost looked like land.

Motherfood

Jan Zita Grover

I didn't understand my mother's cooking until I moved to Minnesota after her death. I didn't realize it had been torn from its native soil—south-central Minnesota German-American farm life—and dropped into the alien setting of suburban postwar California. Working her way west by teaching during the Depression, my mother brought her tastes and kitchen techniques into a culture in which they were superfluous, even foreign.

Like many couples with young children during the critical housing shortage after World War II, my parents bought the first house they could afford. We ended up in the White Cliffs of Dolger at the furthest reaches of San Francisco's foggy Sunset district, three blocks from the ocean, surrounded by fellow immigrants from downtown apartments and flats. Most of our neighbors were new not only to the sand dunes west of Twin Peaks but to America: first- and second-generation immigrants from Ireland, Germany, Italy, Eastern Europe.

Everyone's cooking seemed breathtakingly exotic to me, my mother's included, for by the time I was seven, I recognized that lunchroom food and meals downtown at Manning's Cafeteria or at Ott's Drive-In in North Beach were the true American food. Only the Irish in our neighborhood cooked like that.

Food was one of the primary lenses through which I viewed the world as a child. I recognized the Muni's bus and streetcar routes by the food I saw along them: kosher poultry shops and bakeries along the 15 McAllister's route, specialty greengrocers and bakeries and candy stores that still dotted Market Street along the 72 Sunset and N Judah lines. I tormented my sister, Jean, with chicken feet I gathered free from the poultry store on the 48 line, just two blocks from our house.

The only notable exception I knew to immigrant fare in the Sunset and eat-out white-bread food elsewhere was Nanty's. Nanty was a family friend from my mother's home state of Minnesota, the daughter of a prosperous family from Rochester. She was my mentor, succorer, and honorary mother, offering me the warmth and interest that my unhappy mother could not.

Nanty was an inspired cook. She introduced me to the marginal but critical distinctions between produce from the carriage-trade Grant Street Market and that from inferior grocery stores; she explained why it was worth our time to take the 19 bus all the way to the expensive specialty butcher shop, Stonestown Meats, for two-inch-thick lamb chops rather than buy them at the neighborhood butcher near her house on the L Taraval streetcar line. She taught me how to order pullets cut into four pieces, wings tipped, please. Thirty-three years since I last ate it, Nanty's cooking remains a loving, intuitive adaptation of midwestern cooking to local ingredients—what has since been celebrated (and inflated) as California or West Coast cuisine.

Many of Nanty's ingredients were the same ones I saw my mother pull wearily from the icebox each evening: chickens, roasts, chops, green-yellow-orange vegetables. The difference lay in their respective quality and what happened to them as they passed from the raw to the cooked. Nanty sought out individual fruits and vegetables at the Grant Street Market, where they were displayed in pyramids and whorls in which each piece stood out like an individual artwork. My mother bought hers in bulk from the neighborhood supermarket except at the height of summer, when truck farmers from down the Peninsula drove into the neighborhood in their stake trucks, scales swinging, and sold melons and tomatoes from the back.

Like most of our thrifty Sunset neighbors, my mother clung to her wartime habit of cooking with grease or margarine, that marmoreal lipid that came from the store white as Crisco. One of my childhood tasks was to squeeze yolk-colored pigment into a bowl, mashing and combining it with the margarine until it became yellow as butter. Coloring margarine was my introduction to politics: I remember being astonished, at eight or nine, when a *San Francisco Chronicle* story reported that the California dairy industry had again defeated a legislative bill that would have allowed margarine manufacturers to sell their product precolored, like butter.

Butter was Nanty's universal culinary solvent. She rolled it into balls with deft short strokes of two pale ash paddles to put on her butter plates, and she lavished it on raw ingredients. Even her unctuous lamb chops received dollops of it when they rolled sputtering from the broiler. She served those two-inch-thick chops—meltingly tender, pink within—with corn custard and tiny new peas. Nanty's scrambled eggs, cloudlike suspensions of eggs, cream, and butter with the giddy instability of thunderheads, trembled on the cusp of collapse, riven by molten channels of butter.

At Nanty's, I ate these confections on a child-pleasing variety of china plates. Nanty hadn't settled for a single china pattern in an era when women chose a china pattern; instead, she bought single place-settings of every pattern that pleased her. When I stayed with her, which was as often as possible, I loved to open the china cupboard, smell its fresh enamel, and pick out a different plate for each meal: birds, dragons, grapes, shepherds and shepherdesses, flowers, sailing ships, patterns eighteenth-century, Regency, Victorian . . . and a plain, restful Lenox the color of sweet butter for dull-day use. Since I wasn't present when she acquired any of this fairytale assortment, I invested Nanty's dishes with the timelessness of tale or fable: like Boston women's hats, they seemed irreducibly hers, possessed rather than purchased. Later in life I was shocked to spot her china in Gump's and realize it could be bought.

At home in the foggy western avenues, my mother produced a succession of gray roasts and heavy homemade breads with dark, bitter crusts. Later, as she grew sicker, she served us hamburger mixed with undiluted Campbell's soup over split Kilpatrick's hot-dog buns. I chewed my way determinedly through my mother's Spartan meals toward Nanty, longing for her butter balls, lamb chops, and the steam that arose from her cooking, sealing us into intimacy as it condensed on her kitchen windows and African violets, shutting out the world. Winter mornings on my family's ocean-side front porch, my robe whipped by the salt breeze, I bit off the cream plugs that rose frozen from the tops of the milk bottles and waited for the cold-hot freeze in my mouth to subside to a heavy warmth reminiscent of Nanty's sauces. Mmmmmm: I could invoke her even when she was absent. Yet I ate my mother's food happily enough, the watery stews, entropic vegetables, corned beef hash, occasional chaste pies (rhubarb with only a trace of sugar). In the discontinuous universe of my childhood, I occupied a satisfying culinary niche, gluttonously consuming two worlds.

When my sister and I were still small, we trick-or-treated at one of the few remaining earthquake cottages still standing on the Sunset's dunes—those improvised homes built after the 1906 earthquake and still standing fifty years later, thanks to San Francisco's mild climate. This particular earthquake cottage was a tiny, whimsical, brown-shingled house tucked deep at the back of a standard city lot, fronted by a garden a-tangle with Martha Washington pelargoniums, agapan-thus, fuchsias, nasturtiums, serpentine aloes and jade trees, and a monkey-puzzle tree.

The other children on our block believed that the old woman who lived in the cottage was a witch. Her house and garden were odd and irregular compared to our parents' pastel row houses and postage-stamp lawns, and what other evidence did they need? Their suspicions of her peculiarity were compounded each Halloween, when the old woman greeted the few trick-or-treaters who groped their way down the narrow path through her dark garden not with the miniature Toot-sie Rolls and Charleston Chews we received everywhere else, but with rosettes.

Almost sixty years later, I remain haunted by the beauty of her gift and the misunderstanding with which it was generally greeted. Rosettes are a northern European pastry: a crisp, fragile latticework formed around the armature of an open-work iron that has been plunged into hot fat. Once the crêpe-y flour batter has fried, a sharp shake frees the rosette from the iron. After it has cooled, the rosette is dusted with powdered sugar. In shape, it resembles a snowflake or flower.

My mother, indifferent cook that she was, nonetheless made rosettes for my sister and me occasionally, perhaps an evocation of her

Minnesota Germanness, and I knew how time-consuming and exact-ing they were to produce. Their symmetry and sweetness proceeded out of nothing, like those of a poem. They shattered at even the most timid bite, like shards of sugared glass.

So when the old woman in the brown-shingled cottage came to her door each Halloween with a plate of perfect rosettes, I was excited and impressed by her offering. My sister and I each accepted one and immediately guided it into our mouths.

Our mates turned away from the old woman's door in disgust. "What're these?" they grumbled, and hurled the rosettes into their sacks of candy, where I knew they would quickly perish. Soon, soon, they would be nothing but sugar crumbs in the bottom of the ignora-muses' bags.

My sister and I didn't try to tell our friends about the exquisite treats they casually spurned. In dismissing the rosettes, I feared that my playmates mocked my own family: my mother's inarticulate northern-liness, her loyalty to bitter-crusted breads in the face of the ubiquitous Kilpatrick's and Wonder Bread, some root difference that kept our family at a remove from everyone else's dream of jolly sameness. I loved the old woman's cottage, garden, and delicate Halloween ges-ture, but I was embarrassed by that love. Some part of me hung back, ashamed at my own avidity for the rosettes, abashed at what it said about the foreignness in me.

When I was eight, my mother left us, driven away to the sanitarium in Marin County by my father while my sister and I stood at the window, watching. She disappeared for over a year, hospitalized for what I later learned was acute depression. At first her absence seemed fun. The air in our house lifted and cleared, emptied of her mournful presence. Now I could read as long and hard as I wanted to, even at the dinner table. Being motherless was a distinction; my mother became invested with a glamour she wholly lacked while present, poor wraithlike chain smoker, listless crier. When Nanty asked me to send notes to my mother in the hospital, I wrote telling her to stay there.

Assisted by Carrie, a day housekeeper, my father tried to keep Jean and me at home. Standing at the stove at dinnertime with a metal spoon, he tried to cook for us. The aluminum pan burned dry as he stirred, and peas caromed around its bottom like BBs. These he spooned onto our plates, brown and scorched, his anger rising at our disappointment. I knew then that this was never going to work: my father was no cook, and he raged at doing anything less than well, made even more furious by our involuntary witness. To him, cooking was woman's work and beneath him, yet he could not do it competently. I stirred the burnt pellets around my plate and knew that even bigger changes awaited us.

We were sent to stay with family friends in Salt Lake City, then in Reno. No Nanty, no San Francisco: my ninth summer is the only period in my life unmarked by memories of the food I ate, from which I conclude that my pain was so comprehensive that even that most trustworthy anodyne could not relieve it. Our months of wandering ended when my father reappeared in Reno in August to announce that my mother was coming home and that we were, all of us, moving to Sacramento.

I returned to San Francisco mutinously, resentfully; I wanted to stay in Reno with my cousins. It didn't occur to me to wonder about my mother's feelings: I was too deeply mired in my own misery at leaving Reno, San Francisco, Nanty, my friends, our neighborhood.

My mother's misery, as I sensed then and know now, was not merely personal; it was pervasive—what used to be called an organic depression. She was a person displaced from herself and the culture that had formed her, unable to adapt to the place she came to. What I have come to understand since moving to Minnesota is that she was uneasy with what she found in California and estranged from what she had left behind.

She was adrift.

We moved to Arden Park, one of Sacramento's first postwar suburbs, a place embodying what a friend later described as the *Sunset Magazine* ethos—"A barbecue, a patio: the antechambers to heaven." My friends' families ate the peculiar foods of suburbia: balloon bread, Lipton's onion soup mix and sour cream with potato chips, canned spaghetti, and other bizarrely named convenience foods. In

Sacramento, iceberg lettuce salads were accorded the status of main dishes, and entire families seemed to live on chilled Kraft macaroni and cheese, six-packs of Pepsi and Coke, and Dayglo-colored Popsicles. In Sacramento, my mother's cooking was odd enough that even my friends noticed it.

She started cooking again. We ate ponderous stews on shadeless summer nights in the '90s, two-crust tuna pies every Friday, regardless of the weather. There was no discernible connection between the Sacramento Valley temperatures and what my mother cooked; she fed us, I've since believed, for northern springs that didn't begin until late May, for northern winters that wore people down unless they stoked themselves like boilers, for snow and ice that hung around six months of the year. She fed us in the seven-month heat of the Central Valley as if we were going to head out after breakfast to plow the back forty.

Each fall, she added hasenpfeffer to our alien diet. At Christmas, she baked spritz and rosettes. My friends eyed them suspiciously, then ate.

"What're those?"

"Spritz."

"What're spritz?"

"Butter cookies. You press them through a cookie press."

"Why?"

"Because they're German." As far as I knew, German was just another way of saying Minnesotan, just as my mother's antiphonal Ja, sures were simply Minnesotan for the Yes, mmm-hmmm, I see I heard my friends' mothers murmur on the phone. I did not understand my mother's unassimilated holiday cookies, her unseasonably heavy meals. If they sprang from her heritage and showed up on our table to keep her connected to it, I did not know it.

Only once a year did my mother's internal clock coincide with that of the Central Valley. Each June, she planted three summer crops in our half-acre backyard: sweet corn, tomatoes, and ground cherries (Physalis virginiana), strange little low-lying annual fruits encased in parchmentlike husks, which she made into pies and jams that the rest of us wouldn't eat.

She was adamant about the corn: it could not be eaten unless it was fewer than several minutes away from the cornstalk. First you put on a full pot of cold water and get it to a good rolling boil. Then you go out and pick your ears, ones whose silk has already turned brown. Pull back the husks first to make sure the corn's ready—if you pop a kernel with your fingernail, it should shoot white sugar juice at you. Pick the ear—and this is very important—and run as fast as you can to get the ears into the water, shucking as you go.

Don't wait a second. You've got to get that corn into the boiling water right away, or the sugar will turn to starch and the corn will be tough. No right-thinking person would want to eat such corn. Get it into the pot in under a minute, and that corn will be as sweet as sweet can be.

She was not a spirited gardener of anything but these crops. Our yards weren't planted with the flowers and shrubs that softened the foundations of other families' houses. They weren't shaded by the Modesto ashes and sycamores that other families quickly planted to shield themselves from the hot Valley sun. Our neighbors' dichondra lawns and olive trees, their juicy Meyer lemons in front-porch pots, the camellias that dropped their fat flowers all winter long in nearby flower beds didn't interest her. When we moved to an old house in 1962, my mother was unimpressed by its elaborate, established gardens. She quickly found new homes for the old rhododendrons, roses, camellias, and irises, many of them rare, that grew there and had them dug out. Eventually she had the splendid, spreading Royal Anne and Black Tartarian cherry trees chopped down too. "Too messy," she said. It was as if she could be comfortable only once our yard resembled the remembered fields of Sibley County, Minnesota, clean and spare and plain.

Then she could begin planting her crops.

I don't miss my mother. I wish I did; I feel regretful, humiliated, by my lack of sorrow over her death. She was an unhappy person, and through a combination of character and historical circumstance, she was unable to transcend her depression. The drugs weren't there then, and she did not seek out talking therapy. Her illness pooled, then spilled over into the lives of her daughters and husband. I dreaded coming home from school or play; I dreaded our meals together; they resembled her embodied sadness. My mother's cooking mirrored her depression, and like it, fueled in me a longing to be somewhere— anywhere—else.

When I think about her life now, I remember chiefly the sudden avidity with which she awakened to eating during her last two years. It was as if something erupted, and it took the form of an appetite for food, and she could not be sated.

I realize this may sound self-justifying, since I was the chief source of what she ate in those years. And perhaps she was simply playing to my own interest in food. Perhaps my interest kindled her own. I'll never know.

What I do know is that she became a zealot: a seeker of fresh spinach and broccoli, a fan of local poultry growers' barnyard chickens, the first poultry in California that reminded her of the chickens she'd eaten in childhood on her parents' farm, a regular for Mandarin takeout each Saturday evening. She wanted me to bake her pan after pan of blackstrap gingerbread. Although she seldom left the house, she seemed to enjoy my accounts of the X-Y-Z farmers' market, held beneath a flyover of the I-80 freeway a mile north of her house.

"Food is the only pleasure I have left," she said flatly when I asked her once why she, a ninety-pound woman, ate so heartily.

I don't miss my mother, but I do miss cooking for her. She was an easy eater to please, once she discovered her appetite: there wasn't anything she wouldn't try, and she ate it all. Having another person to feed is sometimes critical to spirited cooking, and these days, living alone, I miss my mother as an appetite to be fed. I would never choose to welcome her sorrow, which pervaded my childhood and adolescence, but her willing mouth, her relentless appetite, were blessings to fill.

She swung her head to the side and looked up at Jean. My sister and I had just broken in through a window and discovered our mother lying on the bathroom floor, brought there by too many diuretics and not enough fluids. Delusional. "Isn't it funny how Janny can walk up the walls?" she said.

After that incident, which ended with her being admitted to the ICU, pumped full of saline, she reluctantly gave me a key to her house. It wasn't by any means a key to her heart—only two apparently held that: depression and her new-found appetite. Depression itself didn't need a key; it had become an in-dweller long since, the host who answered the door when I came to visit, deftly ensuring that whatever I did wouldn't work. The most it permitted my mother was a tight-lipped grimace or several seconds of attention to news of the world before she broke in with "Should we have turkey loaf or Rocky the Range Bird for dinner tonight?"

Depression is determined not to be amused. You can take it and its companion human out for a drive in the country, read it a story, and it won't respond—its awareness is always somewhere else. You're merely an irritant, a distraction. Depression doesn't want to do: it wants to withdraw, to pull down the shades, to swing closed the rusty gates, to suspend.

My mother shuffled around her dark house, shades drawn, in the iron rounds of depression, little familiar tasks that marked off each day's long hours.

7:00 AM:

 Start the water in the poached egg pan.

 Take the juice out of the refrigerator, the eggs.

 Get the bread out of the package. Put the slices in the toaster.

 Pour water into the tea kettle. Set it to boiling.

 Turn on the radio to the news station in the breakfast room.

7:30 AM:

 Crack the eggs into the poaching cups. Cover and simmer them.

 Push down the lever on the toaster.

 Get out a plate. Get out the margarine. Get out a cup and saucer.

 Pour the juice.

 Put tea in the tea ball. Set it in the cup.

 Scoop the eggs out of their cups and onto the toast.

7:45 AM:

 Eat.

This invariant sequence began my mother's day as far back as I can remember. It began her last conscious day, August 15, 1989. She got as far as *Take the toast out of the toaster* before a thrombus hurtled into her heart or brain, and she fell into final darkness.

When I arrived at the house that afternoon from the hospital, the state of her breakfast told me she had fallen about 7:35—toast margarined and cut, tea darkening in its cup, no eggs yet.

I fell to battling the house officer at the hospital, who had put her on a respirator after her housekeeper found her on the kitchen floor that morning and called 911. My mother had a do-not-resuscitate order in her chart and no discernible brain activity, so after talking the situation over with Jean, I told the hospital to obtain my mother's records and take her off life support. In the rush of getting my sister and her daughters to Sacramento, I forgot about the state of my mother's unfinished breakfast.

Two weeks later, in a heavy ground fog, I drove Jean to the airport and saw her off. A great weariness descended on me as I left the airport, a physical tiredness so complete that my neck buckled under the burden of it. If it hadn't been so foggy, I would have pulled to the side of the road halfway back to town to take a nap. But I drove on, reached the house, and crept into it, intent on sleep.

I came in through the back door. As I crossed the kitchen, I noticed for the first time since my mother's death her stainless steel egg poacher, still standing on the back burner of the stove, haloed by the light glowing from the back panel. How had we missed seeing it while we worked from room to room, deciding what would go to Jean, what to me, what to St. Vincent de Paul's?

I was fully awake now. I walked across the big room to the stove and took off the lid. Inside sat two poached eggs, ambered, two weeks old, seemingly preserved.

In late June, sitting mild and content among new acquaintances on my screened porch in Minneapolis, I listened to their soft, flat Minnesotan voices talk about growing corn and tomatoes each summer. Their words sounded primal and urgent, almost like a chant to allay pain.

They homed in on the proper way to cook corn like heat-seeking missiles. As if in a dream, I already knew what I was going to hear.

Beneath the dappled shadow of the front-yard maple, in a dozy reverie, a green shade, I heard their faith in Minnesota's soil to bring forth tomatoes and corn, a faith already planted in me decades ago by my wandering mother, Minnesota vegetable gardener, farm-born, since lost.

My Mother Is a Garden

Denise Low

American Robin

Cold sun brings this mourning season to an end—
one year since my mother's death. Last winter thaw
my brother shoveled clay-dirt, she called it gumbo,
over what the crematorium sent back. Not her,

but fine powdery substance, lightened, all else
rendered into invisible elements. That handful
of a pouch, un-boxed, was tucked into plotted soil,
the churchyard columbarium, a brass plaque the only

permanence, and the brick retaining wall. So finally
my mother is a garden, day lilies and chrysanthemums
feeding from that slight, dampened, decomposing ash.
Her voice stilled. One ruddy robin in the grass, dipping.

After Mother's Episcopalian funeral, my husband conducted a
Native American Church memorial in our backyard. We gathered
around a fire pit and spoke about her life. Then my husband burned
her master's degree hood, which she had left folded in a closet. The
smoke rose straight into the winter clouds, toward the heavens of
both traditions.

I had almost forgotten about my mother's college years, after we
four children left our home in Emporia, Kansas. I was the youngest,
and in the 1970s, I launched full-speed into rebellions at the state university. I was caught up in my hippie identity—and glad to be away

from her supervision. It never occurred to me she might be glad to be rid of my sulky presence as she finally attended college after a lifetime of deferred ambitions.

These disconnections were the curse and blessing of our tie. We were not at peace with each other in this world, but now, when I look over the funeral pictures—church flowers; the altar of cedar, eagle feathers, and Bible; the firewood brought by a friend; the circle of friends and family—I feel a warm affection. I think of her often as I handle kitchenware she used and as her iris bloom in my garden. One of the greatest surprises for me was how our relationship would continue to evolve after her death.

Recently I felt her ghost, or some similar presence, protect me: I was chopping onions with a cleaver, and it slipped. In an eerie moment, I felt another person take the blade and put it in my other hand. I heard her voice: "Don't hurt yourself," as I must have heard it a thousand times when I was a baby.

From the first, though, we were not a natural mother-child pair. She wanted me to be a blonde, curly-haired, bubbly, and male, like my father's German-British family, but I was born with straight black hair and brown eyes, like her mysterious Bruner relatives. After six weeks, perhaps in an effort to please her, my hair turned wavy and ash-blonde. But I always knew it was not blonde enough, like my one sister's. My other sister had the straight, dark hair of the Bruners; later she told me how she suffered burning permanents all her childhood as our mother tried to make her resemble Shirley Temple. With natural curls, I was spared that fate. My mother was a strong-willed person. But so was I. My eyes remained brown, I seldom smiled, and although I was a tomboy, I was undoubtedly a girl.

From the start I was a somber, reticent little being with my father's brooding quality, which did not endear me to my mother, an explosive extrovert. She often became enraged at me and my siblings. Early on I felt the whack of her yardstick and heard "Spare the rod and spoil the child." Years later she would tell me how her own father, of Native heritage, never laid a hand on her; how he would instead take her roller skates and put them up high as punishment; how he explained everything very patiently. She never acknowledged the contrast between her upbringing and the way she punished her own children. For me, her temper was a fundamental fact of life.

I did not have an awful childhood, and perhaps my memory selects a sepia-colored picture of the past. My parents were present; I had food and shelter; I was clothed. Perhaps most childhoods abound with conflicts, and no doubt I am sensitive by nature. But I did not feel my mother loved me. And I found some advantages to this cold relationship.

I understood early in my life that I was on my own. When my mother erupted in anger over tangles in my hair or spilled sugar, I learned to pull within and keep going. I had a high threshold for emotional pain. She had a Jekyll-and-Hyde temperament, an animated personality for public life and a very different one for her family. Even when she seemed calm, I knew it would not last. In my forties I read Sally Carrighar's autobiography, Home to the Wilderness, in which she writes about how her mother had a double identity and treated her daughter differently—hatefully—in private. She had a particular kind of unnamed insanity, Carrighar thought. Once again the secondhand magic of books comforted, as I learned that someone else's mother was like mine but much more extreme.

My mother later remembered keeping house in those early years as an enormous, endless task. Our family of six lived in a three-story house and generated endless dust for the vacuum and endless piles of laundry for the hand-cranked washing machine. Money was tight, and the six-member family had no car and no labor-saving household devices. She was from the generation that expected fresh, ironed sheets once a week, and her temper flared often as she strove to meet impossible housekeeping standards.

As a child, though, I understood only my own point of view, and that was survival. Seldom did I give my mother the satisfaction of a response to her tirades; instead, I remained stoic. I learned I would never please my mother, and I should look elsewhere for warmth.

Most immediately, I found succor in relationships with my three older siblings. We had resisted our mother's rule in an unspoken conspiracy. My older sister read books to me, sang, played games, and called me her little monkey. Every Saturday she listened to opera on the radio and baked while I "helped." She was the mother-sister I adored. My only brother tolerated me among his plastic cowboys, "Indians," soldiers, and Crusaders. He taught me wrestling moves and rules for football. Somehow he persuaded us to clean his room so our mother would not unleash her anger. Once she struck him with a hairbrush, and I ran at her with my fists flailing. I could not stand to see my big brother hurt. This one time, because I was so tiny, she thought I was cute and laughed. I felt that child's sense of justice. This was one of the best days of my life.

And my other sister, just three years older, stayed with me, morning to night, as we avoided our mother. We played dolls and house and jacks and jumped rope. When we were old enough to read, we acted out further adventures of the Little Women or Anna of Siam. We talked about when we would be famous writers and make up stories like the Brontë sisters.

I found refuge in my father's shelves full of books: bestsellers, Asian philosophy (*Tibetan Book of the Dead* and yoga), fantasy (Conan, Tarzan), Nancy Drew, science fiction, history (C. W. Ceram, Will Durant), nature (Rachel Carson and Thor Heyerdahl), and every other imaginable genre. I discovered very young that ecstatic trance induced by good writers: one night I read Twain's *A Connecticut Yankee in King Arthur's Court* for hours before my mother caught me. However she upbraided me, she could not take away my profound escapist pleasure of those hours, nor the stirring of my imagination. Reading and then writing were assertions of my identity separate from my mother's expectations of me, especially as a girl. Like Tarzan, who navigated a violent jungle and survived surly gorilla pack leaders, I maneuvered the hazards of my household.

My mother herself must have had very mixed feelings about gender roles, since her family had taught her to be an active, assertive woman. She had done very well in school—ancient history was her passion—and she started college during the Depression. Her family could not afford tuition, so she learned shorthand and began a career as a medical stenographer. She loved it, she said, but when she married at twenty, into a well-to-do family, her father-in-law insisted she quit.

Her employment would compromise his social standing. So unful-filled career plans colored her treatment of her daughters, and she pushed us all to succeed, sometimes mercilessly. She had our IQs tested early by local college officials. If I brought home an A-minus, she wanted to know why.

After my mother completed her own bachelor's and then master's degrees, when I was twenty-two, she relaxed. As a "nontraditional" student in the 1960s, years before that term was coined, she majored in one of the accepted fields for women: Home Economics. Her mas-ter's thesis, a history of costume design, deepened her love of history, which was considered a masculine pursuit.

At the same time, my mother pushed feminine arts as well as aca-demics. She herself was a skilled seamstress and expected her daugh-ters to follow her lead. She taunted us with how our pretty girl cousins could sew beautifully. But in this area, I had a reprieve. When I was about eight, she gave my sister and me a formal lesson in sewing. I hated it. I had poor fine-motor skills and little patience. Finally, she released me to go outside and play with the neighborhood kids. The rest of my childhood I was not forced to cook or sew.

As long as I behaved, did chores, and did not draw attention, I could play outdoors with the small gang of neighborhood boys and girls, and we had great times. We kids did everything together, from base-ball to dolls to playing with trucks. Just about everything was shared between genders. Boys could not join certain girls' activities, like jump-rope, nor could they wear shorts. But they did play "house" and take the male leads. In the winter we built elaborate snow forts and threw snowballs at each other. One year we buried rocks in the snow-balls, and I broke a sixth-grader's nose; I did not feel as bad as I should have, and I wondered at that.

I was fortunate to live across the street from a truly kind boy with a boston terrier and a country-bred mother who benignly oversaw our play. From her I experienced another style of parenting. Other neigh-bors like her opened their homes to me. One family taught me to shoot pool and enjoy ukulele music. Another friend's father took me to Boy Scout shooting lessons. I went horse riding in the country with girlfriends. I reveled in the refuge of these households, as I learned give-and-take with peers of both genders and their parents. My frequent day-long absences also eased the tension between my mother and me.

We were not farmers or ranchers, but the influence of the countryside was part of the town culture, including gender roles. In the Flint Hills of Kansas, many women herded cattle, fixed cars, and farmed as needed—although they deferred to male willfulness. Many widows in shirtwaist dresses continued to farm their family land. One neighbor told me that she had herded cattle on horseback with needlework in her saddlebag. In school we read stories of Annie Oakley and Calamity Jane, so we knew we were not helpless.

My mother also felt herself the equal of any man. For example, when my father refused to help her build a stone patio, she did the heavy landscaping work herself, with a bandana twisted around her forehead. She went to the country and transported heavy stones. Then she dug out the entire patio area, laid a bed of sand, and fitted the stones together. In her seventies, she still painted the fence and house. I took this for granted, that women could be physical. She could sew and cook, but also she ordered the household, often overruling my father's wishes.

Men, in those days, never cooked or cleaned, although my father did so on occasion. He lamented that although we were supposed to be German, he did not get the obedience he saw in local German families, which were truly patriarchal, he thought. My mother and he argued throughout their marriage, until in their sixties they learned to co-exist and occasionally laugh.

Unwittingly, I followed my mother's example and developed independence. When I could drive legally at age fourteen, I cruised country roads and learned to enjoy the open expanses. I often biked to the Neosho River dam, about two miles away, and spent happy hours sifting through crinoid fossils and gravel on the small beach. I learned basic laws of physics as well as life. History worked its way to the surface of the ground every time it rained or thawed, so I became curious about geology. Nodules of flint lay scattered in the alleys, and we kids struck them for sparks. Horsetail ferns grew in a damp, shady spot next to a neighbor's garage, and then we found fossils of pressed ferns. On a nearby empty lot, unplowed grasses grew to six feet and provided another playground. Throughout the seasons, about two hundred different kinds of wildflowers bloomed. Bird families teemed in our backyard, as well as rabbits and garter snakes. My knowledge of interconnections and relationships came from the flora and fauna around me and their cycles.

This world was beautiful. I watched watercress grow in lime-green fans around the front porch drainpipe. Sunsets smeared the sky with cerise or tangerine or orchid. Winter skies were delicate lemons and grays. In this Willa Cather grassland, I learned awe. Navajo people have a saying, "The Earth is a mother," and like them I believe this is a literal truth, not a metaphor. The surroundings provided me physical and spiritual sustenance. I cannot imagine my life without those years of healing interaction with wildflowers, sky, and free space. I went outdoors every day, and that was the time when I felt loved by something larger than any human mother.

There were dangers within this idyllic setting. Two of my playmates drowned in a boating accident. Once when I was walking home from school, a man exposed himself to me. But I knew almost every family on the block, and I ran to the front porch of a neighbor. The police arrested that man, and the process of justice taught me another layer of security. Mostly, my mother could let me out of her sight and not worry. And what my mother did for me, despite our disconnection, was to maintain a safe environment for me to explore on my own. I thrived under her regime of benign neglect, and she was seldom cross with me.

And as I grew older, we found a common ground—her love of gardening. From spring to late fall she immersed herself in grapevines, strawberries, asparagus, dogwood, iris, Memorial Day daisies, roses, hollyhocks, lemon balm, sweet rocket, shasta daisies, and chrysanthemums.

She told me the small plot outside my bedroom window was my own garden, and there she planted hens-and-chickens. The small, round shoots grew from a center rosette, broke off, and became new plants. This was her model of mother and child, I thought. She loved images of the Madonna and child, which I could not understand, but the plant world was visible before my eyes. And she took me with her to visit other gardeners in the town. I loved the exotica—tropical banks of daffodils, day lilies, coreopsis, and tiger lilies. She introduced me to a living tradition as old as any on earth, which I cherish. I overheard discussions of soil, hybridization, and weather. Some of the women were quite elderly, from the covered-wagon days, so I also learned local history, another dimension of the land.

Near my eighteenth birthday, my mother and I had a horrible quarrel that ended our friendly overtures. I seldom spoke, and some days I took my dinner to my room to eat alone. I was not allowed to be openly impudent, but I had a good set of nonconfrontational defenses in place. Soon after, I left for college in the northeast part of the state, and while my dorm roommates suffered homesickness, I only felt freedom. I already had years of survival on my own.

The first bridging of our estrangement came when I bore children, in my early twenties. These were the first of my mother's grandchildren to grow up near her, and she cautiously offered help. She recalled her own difficult new-mother situation, when four grandparents came to her home every day at dinner time and interrupted her new baby's meals. They sabotaged her discipline, she said, and so she made up her mind to do better. As I struggled with my transition to adulthood, she offered much-needed encouragement. This was the first time I remember hearing praise from her. And I was surprised how she stepped aside so I could find my own way through natural childbirth, La Leche League, babysitting co-ops, and vegetarian cooking.

When she held my son for the first time, she tried to explain how she felt such satisfaction with her youngest child now producing a baby. Despite our differences, she demonstrated for me a biological connection among the generations that transcends compatibility and Hallmark greeting-card slogans. Underneath all her frustrations, she never denied her own identity as an earthly creature. Perhaps on the starboard side of the Flint Hills, where nature's gales explode in epic proportions and ripples of green waves reach to the horizon, this sense of connection is more vivid.

During these years I gained insights into my mother's own mothering values. When my first son played with Legos for an afternoon, she praised him for having a "good attention span." I had not thought of that quality as anything worth nurturing, but now I realize how she had allowed me to stay with my toys uninterrupted. I sometimes see Native parents encourage this same quality, and this may have been a holdover from that family heritage. I came to understand how she molded my inner sense of direction more than mothers of other girls in the neighborhood. This was a quality that allowed me to withstand the difficult aspects of my growing up years and thrive. It sustains me to this day.

My mother used a vocabulary with my babies I had never heard before, as she called my baby "cunning," in an Elizabethan usage. She played baby games. She taught me how to pace the babies' days and have patience with their needs for exercise and willfulness. She gave me perspective on the stages of a baby's growth; implicitly, she suggested stages for her adult daughter as well, and for her as an elderly woman. And she told me that she wished she had spent more time enjoying her children, rather than struggling with housework.

I was the only child who remained in the area, and I returned to visit her every holiday and birthday, as long as she lived. Despite my new insights, though, most often I saw her dutifully and still dreaded the shift in her personality that occurred after several hours. I kept visits short, and she used her company-manners charm with me as long as she could. I visited her for a few brief hours, exchanged news, and drove her to view neighbors' gardens. I had the satisfaction of those good visits later, as I grieved her death.

After the charred ring of the memorial fire pit faded into new grass, I recovered from her death. Images from her dying moments stayed in my mind for days—with her last breath, she exhaled bright red blood, which was awful. I felt the helplessness of not saving her. I had learned to get along without her years before, so after she died, I did not miss the relationship as much as some daughters might. Although I did not feel a loving attachment to her, for which I felt guilty, I had a guarded respect.

As the first year of mourning ended, the guilt left, and I remember the moment. It was in the garden as I tended violets. I wrenched crab grass from between their rhizomes, and I saw my hand become her hand. Then I began to have memories of her laughter. I began doing the *New York Times* crossword, as she and my father had done together, and this somewhat compulsive activity staved off depression. Now I can accept the hard fact that as I age, I resemble her more and more.

And after her death, I began to piece together an occluded family history, as I sorted forgotten photographs of the blond Millers and the dark-skinned Bruner family. She cut off from her family when she married and for years hardly saw any of them, including her parents and grandmothers. So I found cousins and traded family stories and found, despite our involuntary distancing, that we had similar tales. We speculated about how the claustrophobic small-town life puts pressure on people. Our parents worried about their Sunday hats, about the men's income, about ironed sheets—so much that it stifled everyone. We discussed how part of the midwestern ethos is based on fitting into community life, at some cost to the individual. We speculated about the American Indian heritage in some of our family—and indeed found some census records—how it was suppressed, and what that denial cost us. Through the years I have learned that many other Flint Hills families have mixed heritages, although it is seldom explored. I discovered the "German" grandfather Miller was actually Irish and his parents lived just twenty miles south of my present home. Somehow that "bumpkin" background also was erased from the family lore.

As I discover these disparate pieces of my mother's hidden life, I feel more at peace. I understand her chronic anger had myriad causes. I learn a few of them, and others I will never know. My mother's insistence on attending college, over my father's wishes and before feminism, was heroic. Now I see my mother as a strong woman born in a time when she did not have tools to sculpt her life. She did the best she could, and in her way she loved me, as well as she could. And her somber fourth child, who would become a poet and literature professor, must not have been an easy connection for her.

I wish I had been able to understand her achievements at the time. Perhaps, in writing this, I can reframe those times and find some healing; perhaps, in the world of spirits, she can be touched by this effort. Even after her death, my mother resides in my memory, where I revise our relationship as I grow older.

I can celebrate the good, heal from the sad times, and finally turn back to the gardens and countryside she left behind and never really left. In our funeral fire pit, we symbolically released her to the grassland winds and the earth. Over two seasons the burnt scar remained, and then green growth reclaimed it. Because of her, I know land is the true mother who never abandons us.

Shall I Jump Now?

Alison McGhee

At twenty-five I dreamed a dream that has haunted me ever since: My mother faces me on the sloping deck of a gunmetal-gray ocean liner. Perhaps it is an aircraft carrier; it has that same forbidding, ominous look. A narrow rail runs along the edge of the deck. No deck chairs, nothing to hold a body to the surface of the ship—and that slope, that slope is strange. Should you slip on that sloping deck, you would careen right over the edge.

I peer over the side. Huge waves boil and heave, flinging angry spray dozens of feet in the air and still not even close to where I stand clutching the rail. If I fell overboard, I would drown within seconds. No one would hear my cries. No one would even know I was gone.

Something, a sixth sense, makes me turn around. Gabrielle stands yards away from me on the sloping deck, her arms held out for balance in the strong wind. She is smiling. She's wearing her blue velveteen bathrobe, the one that zips from ankle to neck. She's wearing her blue slippers, too. She looks the way she looks first thing in the morning, when she moves about the kitchen making coffee.

She smiles at me. Her arms are held straight out to either side. She looks light and joyful.

"Shall I jump now?" she says.

Years later, I tell only one friend about my dream. I describe the blue bathrobe, the happiness in my mother's eyes.

"The blue bathrobe," says my friend. "Hmm. What does the blue bathrobe represent to you? Security? Warmth? Comfort?"

I suppose the blue bathrobe represents all those things to me, but that is not what I focus on. What I see are those arms, lifting as if to catch the wind.

★ ★ ★

When I unravel time, the furthest back I can go is this: my mother was ahead of me, climbing up brown stairs that had little bits of gray on them. I know this because I am crawling up the stairs, looking down at them inches from my nose. My mother carries a bucket. I am wearing diapers; I can feel the plastic heaviness rubbing on my legs and back. I look out through the railing on the stairs and I see the world going by and time passing, and my mother is climbing, climbing up beyond me and even though I cannot think in words yet I tell myself: Remember this.

My young mother is lovely, slim and straight, with beautiful long legs. Unruly chestnut hair frames her dark-brown eyes. She wears red lipstick. She shepherds her three small girls (our brother is not yet born) out to the bus for school, so that she can get in the car and drive to the high school where she teaches algebra and geometry. She drives to graduate school for her second master's degree. She places an X and a Q on a Scrabble triple word space; has she won again? She has won again. She weeds the garden, plants flowers, hangs the laundered clothes out on the line. She sautés zucchini in her electric skillet. She does the *New York Times* crossword puzzle. Castanets in hand, she dances the flamenco.

I remember her sitting at the kitchen table before her worn sewing machine, feeding lengths of flowered cotton through the presser foot and needle. She senses my presence and looks up and smiles.

"Look," she says, and holds up a sleeveless shift trimmed with cotton lace at the neck and hem. Flowers against a background of green. Red for my sister Laurel and yellow for my sister Holly. In the photo taken on Easter morning a few days later, our mother stands on the steps surrounded by her little girls, all three bathed, ribbons in their hair, wearing flowered dresses.

Years later, standing on the faded blue concrete of the porch, my mother wears her blue velveteen bathrobe and her navy velveteen slippers. She is waving good-bye to me. One arm rises and falls in a slow circular motion. She will wave until the car that is bearing me away is out of sight, rounding the curve of Route 274.

Where am I going?

Maybe I'm sixteen and heading to Lisbon, Portugal, as an exchange student.

Maybe I'm eighteen and off to college in Vermont.

Maybe I'm twenty and on my way to Taipei, Taiwan, for a semester.

Maybe I'm twenty-two and moving to Boston.

Maybe I'm tweny-five and driving west, to Minneapolis.

Wherever I'm going, it's away.

My mother stands on the porch, waving and smiling until I'm all the way gone. See her now. She cups her hands around her mouth. Good-bye, she calls. Good-bye, darling girl.

"The dream," my friend says. "Why the ship? Why the ocean? What sort of journey does this represent?"

Who the hell knows, I want to say. Who the hell cares? Can't you see my mother, dammit, standing there, asking me if she should jump now?

My mother's slender hands are always in motion, her fingers long and expressive.

"I talk with my hands, don't I?" she said in astonishment, the first time she saw herself on video.

Sometimes. Sometimes you do, Gabrielle. Sometimes you don't talk at all, but go still and silent, as you did when I was seven and your mother took the train up from the city to visit us.

Something was wrong and Grandma knew it. She had a sixth sense. A shift in the universe, molecules rearranging themselves six hours downstate in the New York City apartment she shared with my grandfather. Grandma picked up the telephone and called. My mother watched her. Grandma called again. And again. She paced back and forth, the telephone cord dangling as she walked. Finally Grandma called the building superintendent, and the superintendent opened the apartment door with his master key to find my grandfather dead by his own hand.

I remember driving to the city with my mother and father. I remember going up and down in an elevator, back and forth from their apartment to the street below. I remember the elevator full of boxes and bags on the way down, and empty on the way up except for me and my parents. I remember my mother's weary eyes. She was thirty-one, an age so young to me now and unfathomably adult to me then, when I was seven.

And I remember the years following, eleven years of daily 4:30 PM telephone calls from my mother—home with her four children, home from teaching all day—to my grandmother. My mother, steadfast companion, she who does what needs to be done.

At twenty-two I graduated from a prestigious college with a highly marketable degree in Chinese and Asian studies, student loans, and a single-minded desire to write fiction. I did not even try to find a real job. Instead, I lived in a tiny room in Boston and freelance typed to pay the bills, while rising at dawn to write my stories.

Gabrielle said nothing. She let me be, as she always has. She did not try to steer me in any particular direction, despite the fact that she longed for me to be financially secure, the way she never was as a child.

She used to visit me in Boston, in that scraping-by former life of mine that I loved so much. We roamed the streets and drank coffee and ate muffins from DeLuca's Market, sitting on the floor of my tiny chairless room. We wandered through the Public Garden and along the Esplanade by the Charles River. At night I unrolled a camping mattress onto the floor (no room for a bed) and she slept next to me. She read the short stories I typed out on my rented IBM Selectric II.

Gabrielle stands on the sloping deck of the gray ship. Her arms are out to her sides. My heart seizes. I try to move toward her, take her winged arms in mine and lower them, but nothing happens. Dream paralysis.

"Do you suppose the dream means that she's just tired?" my friend says. "Sick of responsibility, maybe?"

My mother was a math teacher at a middle school in downstate New York when she found out she was pregnant for the first time, with the baby who would become me. She was twenty-three years old. She ran down the hall to the gym, where a pep rally was taking place, so happy that she couldn't resist telling a fellow teacher: I'm going to have a baby! I'm going to have a baby!

"Maybe," I said, "but my mother would not leave me unless she had no choice."

When I was twenty-four, the man I had abandoned my heart to died. Suicide. A friend drove me from Boston to my parents' house. It was a six-hour drive in a rattletrap car and my friend chattered to fill the silence and sometimes I bent over in the seat and pushed my forehead into the musty vinyl of the dashboard.

I remember my mother waiting with outstretched arms on the porch. I remember the ticking of the kitchen clock that marked off each fifteen-minute block of time. I remember the plate of pork chops and applesauce and bread and butter she set before me, none of which I could eat.

In a photo from that time, I sit in a bikini on a beach by my mother's favorite mountain, up in the Adirondacks. Every rib shoves itself out from my skin; I am knobs and bones and angles shivered in pain. Exhaustion in my eyes. My mother is invisible behind the camera, silent witness to her child's grief. My mother, patient companion.

My sister Laurel and I are at Laurel's house in New Hampshire, lazily flipping through one of our old high school yearbooks, cackling at what dorks we were. We come to the teachers' section and see our mother's photo in the math department.

We stop laughing.

"It was the year Grandma died," Laurel says after a while.

My mother was my age when her mother lay in a coma in a room at St. Luke's hospital in Utica, New York. The nurses told my mother that Grandma's blood pressure was dropping, and my mother sat vigil in the quiet room. At some point in the night, my mother went out to the nurse's station to lie down on their couch and try to sleep. She startled out of sleep to hear her mother calling, in a young, happy voice, "Gabrielle, Gabrielle." Thinking it was a dream, my mother went back to sleep. Half an hour later the nurse came to waken her and said that Grandma had died.

"I have always felt that this was her way of telling me that she was fine," my mother tells me.

Who else did my mother have to see her through her grief? No sister, no brother, father long dead. All my mother had in the way of a patient companion, a witness to her sorrow, was that fleeting call from her dying mother, that young and happy voice.

Our mother in black-and-white smiles out from the old book, weariness in her eyes. Oh Gabrielle, how thin you are, too thin. How young you look. The present me looks like the past you. If only I could reach into that book, into the room where you sit alone at your desk, and put my arms around you. Comfort you. Make you a plate of pork chops and applesauce. Tell you, as you have told me in the dark hours, that all will be well, all will be well, and all manner of things will be well.

"So Gabrielle is off to Guatemala," Laurel tells me. "Some house project for Habitat for Humanity. Can you imagine her, pouring concrete?"

She laughs. So do I. It is entirely possible for our mother to be pouring concrete and we both know it. There is not much that is impossible to imagine our mother doing. Close your eyes and pick a day, any day, in the life of Gabrielle. Here she is driving north to the mountain lakes, her yellow kayak in the back of her van. Playing Scrabble with a housebound elder. Teaching English as a second language to Bosnian refugees. Working at the local food bank, putting together a charity mailing, begging for pledges for her latest ski-a-thon, walk-a-thon, canoe-a-thon, take your pick of any and all worthy causes.

I rise in a summer dawn and steal glimpses of my children, asleep in their rooms. My youngest has taken off her pajama shirt in the night and lies on her side, hands tucked together under her chin as if in prayer.

Behold her smooth brown back, her spine a tender curve of buttons, her ribs a pair of cupped hands that hold her heart. The moment I had a baby was the moment I understood terror, my heart blown sideways with adoration and fear. How dazzling and how awful to love someone this much.

★ ★ ★

Not long ago Gabrielle and I sat in her kitchen, talking of children, mine and hers. Dogs, mine and hers. Teaching, mine and hers. Fiction writing: mine. Projects that make the world a better place: hers.

"I could tell you anything, my darling girl," she says at one point. "You have been through the fire."

Fire, meaning the kind of loss and grief that cracks your heart. Fire, meaning joy so deep that it, too, opens your heart. Fire, meaning life, the way it stretches and hurts and raptures you, if you let it all in.

There is one fire I have not yet been through, though.

I see my mother standing on the porch in her blue velveteen bathrobe, smiling and waving, waving until I am out of sight.

And I see her standing on the sloping deck, waves hurling them-selves at the smooth sides. Her arms rise up, wings in blue velveteen. Why does she sound so light of heart? No. But I am frozen in my dream and cannot scream.

"Maybe you're interpreting it wrong," my friend says. "Maybe what the dream is really asking you is this: are you ready to let her go?"

Soon I will wake. My throat will ache for the rest of the day. Twenty years later, my throat still aches when the nightmare imagery conjures itself. The only real lesson the years in between have taught me about my dream is this: that when the time does come for my mother to jump, to call my name in a young and happy voice, then the enormous work of staying behind and waving, waving until she is out of sight, will be mine.

Your Mother

Sheila O'Connor

How old was I before I realized you were nothing like the other mothers? Not gentle-eyed June Lockhart calling Timmy home, or high-heeled Donna Reed putting pancakes on the table, not the small-town mothers on our street—mothers in hair curlers and housecoats, their packs of happy kids eating peanut butter picnics in the yard. By four or five years old, I understood you were a person beyond *Mother*, a busy mystery who had a full life someplace else.

You worked. Young, a single parent by 1963, you left your tiny daughters in other mothers' homes. Cozy foreign countries with strange rituals like sewing, knitting, canning, crafts, dolls constructed out of Styrofoam and plastic Hi-Lex bottles. Bleached sheets flapping on the line. Women with leafy backyard gardens, fresh roses and tomatoes, rhubarb coffee cake cooling in the window. *As the World Turns* playing on TV. By early evening, pork chops and potatoes frying on the stove. Their homes a yellow glow of waxy kitchen floors and oiled woodwork; yours, a cramped basement apartment with canned spaghetti and a litter of kids' toys.

House life with all its mother glories left you cold.

Always, you believed you belonged at work beside the men. Gender equality, not dream or theory, but in your case simply practice. You believed it so you claimed it. From the start, you were the ultimate un-mother: a spoiled boarding school princess, a brainy beauty who became the head and heart of a road construction firm. The one home you ruled until you finally retired. Well-loved and feared by burly men—you were a controller who controlled, a taskmaster, a tight-fisted shrewd accountant who understood the bottom line. I used to marvel when the tattooed backhoe drivers cowered at your desk, shamed small by your quick tongue.

Your mother, the road crew often said to me that summer you sent me to flag construction. *Your mother.* Two small words and the road crew shook their heads. Laughed in disbelief. Those were the same two words my father often said, years beyond your short-lived marriage. *Your mother.* A phrase meant to convey wonder, delight, immeasurable respect.

Your mother. How differently it sounded in the mouths of parish mothers, teachers, nuns, Monsignor, the proper neighbors who watched your wild daughters run barefoot on the streets. In second grade, Sister Leonette led me out of lunch to say: *Your mother must be saved. It's up to you.*

Me?

Back in the cafeteria, my normal classmates with two Catholic married parents got to eat their turkey gravy and canned peas.

You were never Catholic. At home, you dismissed my fanatical devotion to the church, the martyrs, my sacred Children's Bible, my book on Holy Saints, my obsessions with sacraments and sin. You didn't go to church on Sundays, didn't genuflect or pray. In the days before your marriage to a Catholic, you agreed to see a priest for " premarital instruction," an exercise you called *a good-natured theological debate.* Father Truman lost, left the church, got married. Another noncompliance triumph you liked to share with us at supper.

I was never going to have the strength to save your soul.

Here's one thing I came to understand too late. All those parish mothers—Mrs. Hardman, Mrs. Beckwell, Mrs. Moore, Mrs. O'Keane, Mrs. Shannon—those good mothers who wouldn't allow their daughters to play over at our house because you worked, because you were divorced (and later, worse than that, *remarried*), because you weren't a Catholic, because you shunned the PTA and parish pancake breakfasts, because you dropped your girls at church—all those mothers were sinking in dark domestic waters. Mrs. Shannon spent her days in bed; Mrs. Beckwell went away for *rests*; Mrs. Moore's dentist husband left muddy bruises on her cheek. Proper matriarchs of perfect Catholic families who lost their children early to drugs, insanity, suicide, or booze. Dark secrets in those parish households, and still because of you we were cast as the pariahs. You, who may have been the only sane one in the group.

Sane because you failed to surrender?

Busy, brand new to Minneapolis, barely scraping by, somehow you signed me up for lessons at the Minneapolis Institute of Art. You trusted me, a nine-year-old, to take the bus, find my own way through the city, left me to spend my restless summer mornings drawing portraits in the gallery or painting cityscapes among the drunks at Fair Oaks Park. The beginning of my love affair with art, my early recognition there was sacred in the silence, in marble, in sky and field, in other artists' dreams. A soul shift that left me different from the other fourth graders I had to join in school that fall.

A gift that made me see.

I hold two rare days in memory—rare because I spent them both alone with you.

The first: A doctor's appointment that ends with a soda-fountain lunch at Butler Drug, the two of us on stools at the counter. You order California burgers for us both, even though I don't eat lettuce or tomato, then you order me a phosphate, cherry, a dreadful fizzy drink you say you always loved. It's bitter, bubbly, unbearable; but, thirsty for your past, I force myself to drink it. Afterward, another mother-daughter oddity, you announce you're going to take me shopping. Extraordinary, because you hate to shop, especially for me, your scruffy middle daughter who dresses like a boy. Besides, we don't have the cash to hobby shop.

This amazing day, you choose for me a knee-length formal coat, inky blue, fake plush fur. It's hideous; I hate it, and still I let you buy it, let you dress me because I know this is an *ordinary mother* thing, to buy an ugly coat the daughter hates, it happens often to my classmates, and I know for me it won't happen again.

The second: On a day I stay home sick from school, we drive to downtown Minneapolis through the snow, a strange day trip you don't bother to explain. Instead we take a number, stand silently in line.

You're tense, nervous—two traits I rarely see; usually you're happy, confident, full of easy conversation. Worry, you leave that to your anxious kids. But when you finally have your chance with the woman at the window, there's trouble. Your birth certificate isn't quite the way it should be. This piece of paper that they gave you has been altered. It's incorrect. *This isn't it*, you argue. *The date. The place. The names.* The indifferent clerk calls for the next number. *I'm sorry ma'am*, she snaps. *You have to leave.* Finally you surrender, one of the first fights I've watched you lose. On the elevator down, you're too preoccupied to answer any of my questions.

Don't you ever tell anyone what we did today. I mean it. You need to promise me.

What we did? I'm not sure of that myself. Still I'm thrilled we have our first and only mother-daughter secret. *Sure*, I say. It seems an easy promise. And for eight long years I don't.

What about that day? You're thirty-four years old when you discover you're adopted, born in Sauk Centre at a home for wayward girls. Your birth mother isn't the doting mother you adore, the good woman who's given you the moon. The patient saint who kept you in cashmere, a new gown for every boarding school ball, who let you go to college at sixteen, the mother who admires your mind, your pluck, your strength, the beloved mother who owns your only-child heart. That strange day you learn you didn't begin this lifetime in her body. And your father, the man of deep integrity, the dad who never told you no, who put his family first, who earned every shining penny for your pleasure, whose hands were always there to help, that man—he's not your father after all.

What does it mean, the high cost of that secret?
Nothing. It means nothing.
Or if it does, you're busy, you can't be bothered with that now.

Can you be bothered with this, Mom?
I'm a high school senior; Mrs. Stern, my shorthand teacher (you insist that I take shorthand so I'm never unemployed) is alarmed by the condition of my uniform, the ugly brown plaid skirt you bought

me in ninth grade. It's stained dishwater gray; I've stapled up the hem, replaced the missing waist button with a silver paper clip.

Daily, with that familiar blend of pity and disgust, Mrs. Stern stops beside my desk to see that I have three sharpened pencils lined up for dictation, my legs crossed at the ankles. Always she bends low, whispers her social worker question in my ear: *Your mother? Does she realize the condition of this skirt?*

My mother, Mrs. Stern?

My mother sends her kids across the alley, five-dollar bill in hand, when something must be sewn. A First Communion dress. A Girl Scout badge. My older sister's formal gowns. My too-long pairs of jeans. Her famous phrase: *Go ask Mrs. Mertz to do it.* My mother? She works. I'm eighteen. This plaid skirt isn't on her radar.

Finally, Mrs. Stern takes me out into the hallway, and in that instant all my classmates know I'll never be a secretary, never own a proper skirt. A flashback to Sister Leonette and the host of other baffled teachers who can't understand my mom.

Your mother. Mrs. Stern scrunches her nose. *That skirt.* She shakes her head, squints her beady ferret eyes at me. *I'm calling her today. I mean it, Sheila.*

Oh yes, I say. *Please do.*

A Partial List of Things You Can't Be Bothered With

My clothes, my grades (*just so you do your best*), the books I read, the company I keep, TV, nosy neighbors, the endless stream of boys stopping by the house, clean bedrooms, bedtime, curfew, piano practice, Brownies, our stereos or music, homework, fashion, taste, our weight, our hair, what anybody else thinks, our maudlin girl dramatics, angst of any kind, how much money someone makes, the state of anybody's house, recipes, Christmas cookies, gossip, guilt, organized religion, parents, teachers, priests, plants, baking birthday cakes, diets, who did and didn't do what, women's magazines, the future or the past, breast cancer (*what can I do about it, dear?*), mistakes (*everybody makes them*), double standards (*how utterly ridiculous*), hypocrisy, shame, the men I date, formal weddings, formal anything, death (*sweetheart, it can't be helped*), old age, retirement, rest, the house I buy, the furnishings, the dust, the papers piled up, the work I do, the way I raise my own kids.

Mom, you never worried about me?
  I guess I always knew you'd be okay.
  Uncommon Mother Wisdom: Faith.

More Uncommon Mother Wisdom:
Refrain from Judgment. Let Everybody In.
Everyone was welcome in your house: Our boyfriends, old and new, the elderly, the lonely, your good friends Steve and Earl, a devoted male couple in the years before anyone said *gay*. An open door we always took for granted. For years, our house on Elliot was filled with ragged teen girl strays. Bookworms, hippies in hoop earrings and small halters, smokers, runaways afraid of what they faced at home. Always that leggy nest of adolescent girls sleeping on our floors. On weekend mornings, bleary-eyed, we'd stumble to the kitchen to find our friends already at the table, smoking, eating Captain Crunch, laughing, telling you their sordid stories. *Your mom,* they'd sigh, a mix of longing, envy, awe. This meant, of course, you were nothing like the one they had at home.

Me? I never found another mother that I wanted.

This week, you call me at 6:30 in the morning, brokenhearted, to say your best friend is dead. Gone, the girl you've loved since both of you were babies. Another brutal cancer death; you knew that it was coming. You've done the bedside vigil, reminisced, clocked the hours at the hospital, said your last good-bye, hoped for an end to pain, and now it's come. All of that and yet . . . your voice cracks, a sound I've hardly heard. In our long life, I've rarely seen you cry.
  Oh Mom, what will you do? I say.
  Do? You repeat; you don't understand the question. *Well, today I have my bridge.*
  Your bridge, of course. At seventy years old, you're the Senior Doubles whiz kid; you don't like to miss a day.

And besides, to survive means not to dwell.

I dwell. All your daughters do.

I wish you could have stayed, say, sixty-three forever. No doubt you would choose younger, but I'm the selfish daughter, I want to freeze-frame you retired, home at last, my children in the picture. Sixty-three, a perfect age, you're full of life, free to spend your days playing with my kids.

And my children—they adore you. Your maverick spirit, the way you dress in wild costumes, play make believe, a floppy Minnie Pearl hat on your head. You sing off-key, dance, finger snap, watch endless cartoon movies I can't bear. You take them to the pool, dive for pennies, teach them to play poker; bridge will have to wait.

In their young eyes, you are already a legend. In their young hearts, you've left your fierce nonconformist mark.

Your mother, they will both grow up to say. Two words that mean they think you are a marvel.

In fact, they already say it now.

This is my un-mother story. No doubt my sisters have their own. Maybe I was the ultimate un-daughter, the middle child happy to roam free without rules or restrictions, blessed with an older sister who made sure that I stayed safe, in love with life, certain I'd find the future for myself, content to know I could call you if I ever needed anything. You'd be at work, but still you'd take the call.

And I do; I call you every day, mornings now before you're off to bridge or lunch dates. You're busy; if I want you, I have to catch you early. Most days we talk about the books you're reading, you plow through two a week, trade family updates, obituaries, you always want to hear the news about my kids. You're the only one who listens to my endless list of mother worries; apparently, you can be bothered with those now.

And, as always, I'm happy that you're home.

Articles from Your Mother

Shannon Olson

Approaching forty this year, I've decided it's time for a big purge, something significant to indicate to the universe that I'm ready for the next part of my life. I've been cleaning and organizing closets, taking bags and boxes to the trash and to Goodwill: a gigantic sweater, for instance, that I suddenly realized I'd had since I was nineteen; a pan I found at some garage sale when I got my first apartment; worn, pointy boots from the 1980s (which I think are back in style now); a broken blender that my ex-boyfriend left behind; a Wisconsin sweatshirt, purchased on a visit to Madison in 1987, with holes in it. Room by room, closet by closet, I envision a life less burdened by the past, something more portable, so that when I make my next move, whatever it is, only the essentials will come with me.

I leave office clutter for last, six big boxes—the kind you can buy at Cub Foods, with reinforced handles for especially heavy groceries. The boxes are overflowing with yellowed tax returns, old checks, journals, cards, graduate school papers, outdated auto and health insurance information, and the countless articles my mother has been clipping and mailing to me since I left home. Those articles are all marked in the top left-hand corner with her shorthand for me: S, which I mostly interpreted in my twenties and early thirties to mean, "Shannon, here's another article about what's wrong with you. Love, Mom." And so, since the '80s, they've gone unread, tossed into a pile or a box. I couldn't bring myself to read them, but neither, for some reason, could I bring myself to toss them away.

My mother has never been much of a book reader, but any newspaper, magazine, or newsletter that comes into the house receives her full attention. The newspapers struggling to stay afloat in an electronic age, trying hard to skew to a younger, Web-fed audience, have forgotten my seventy-one-year-old mother, who sits down with her Folgers and reads every page, every day, of the Minneapolis *StarTribune*, beginning with the obituaries, "to see," as she says, "if I'm dead yet." She calls me with the interesting names of the dearly departed: "Meta Wood died today," she will giggle into my voicemail (which she believes is an actual box somewhere in my apartment where the vocal messages collect). "Sumpter Priddy III," she will say, without introduction, and then hang up.

My mother will read the St. Thomas newsletter front to back, even though it's my father's alma mater. She reads everything that comes from the University of Minnesota, where they both went (my mother to major in Home Economics, my father for medical school), and sends me articles featuring good-looking successful alumni. Perhaps I could track them down on—what do you call it? the Web? That thing on your computer? She reads the AARP newsletter, all of the updates from her investment company, and everything that comes from Lutheran Brotherhood, even though she hasn't been Lutheran since she was in high school. With her bifocals balanced on her nose, she'll devour the hospital newsletter, and news from the Heart Association, the Arboretum, and the League of Women Voters. If something catches her eye, she'll read my father's medical journals. She pours over the materials from the Minneapolis Institute of Art, the Walker, and the Guthrie, and calls to see if I'd like to join her for various exhibits and shows. She dog-ears the Elderhostel catalogue.

My father reads books, but my mother has an appetite for articles, short bursts of information. She has a weakness for advice, aphorisms, pithy phrases, small doses of quotidian wisdom. If books are a meal, my mother loves snacks—just a little something, just enough to fortify you and keep you afloat. She's an inveterate grazer, in that sense, constantly chewing.

And over the years, she has sent me hundreds of clippings. A mother's way, I suppose, of feeding her young. But to me, her offerings were the equivalent of week-old leftovers from the back of the fridge that she was encouraging me to eat up. Because the articles had, for me, this further association: ever since I left home, my mother has been giving me the things she doesn't want anymore: the old, uncomfortable couch; a carpet remnant to use as a rug; a Eureka Mighty Mite portable vacuum cleaner (3.0 peak horsepower) with a broken on/off switch. "You just plug it in and it turns on," she said when she gave it to me. "It's stuck that way, but it works. But also, um, you should be careful," she added, "the cord gets hot, which is not a good sign. Electrically." So as part of my mother's continuous purging, I've been the glad recipient of a vacuum cleaner that might burst into flames, some mugs she bought at an art fair and then decided weren't really her taste, old candleholders, ancient containers of makeup that had been in her bathroom drawer when I was in high school, a shirt from Target that she decided she didn't like, and a sweatshirt that she thought made her "look busty." In other words, if my mother had no use for it, if it didn't work for her, it came to me.

Weren't the articles in that same category? Something she, personally, had no use for? The objects she handed off to me usually came with some brief soliloquy about her early career years, "making do with few resources." It was her way of telling me that on a limited budget, I shouldn't refuse what was free. But surely she also meant that I had few resources in general—financially, emotionally. The articles confirmed this—that my mother was in a better, more stable place: Here, you odd little work-in-progress, they said to me. Here is a cracker, a crumb to nibble on.

My mother had met in ninth grade the man she'd marry. She'd had a brief career as a teacher, living on the beach in California, then married that man and moved back to Minnesota to raise a family. What could she know about my life? Single at forty? Living in an apartment with ancient wiring and downstairs neighbors who chain-smoke in bed, have loud sex, and play video games?

Now I lift the articles out of the dusty boxes and vacuum the piles with the Mighty Mite (which has not yet combusted). Sifting through them, they seem to fall, roughly, into five general categories: Finances, Depression, General Health, Romance, and Miscellaneous. Most of them are from the StarTribune. Some of them are from Reader's Digest, a magazine my mother has never subscribed to, and so I'm picturing her now, boldly ripping articles out of waiting room reading material. Some still have the date, some don't.

"Singles seek romance among bookshelves."

"Resilience: Scientists are exploring the ability of good people to bounce back from bad situations." (Probably sent after one of my breakups.)

"Pillows make a statement about you."

"A bittersweet goodbye to the childhood home." Even though my parents have never moved.

She has clipped several pages from the Vermont Country Store catalogue. They feature black-and-white photos of seemingly simpler times—people laughing and relaxing in the living room, a woman with a gigantic grin on her face standing at a stove—and my mother has tagged them with a fluorescent green Post-It note: *The photos show the atmosphere of the era your dad and I lived in.*

In a *StarTribune* article on depression titled, "Gender gap: neither thinking nor drinking beats the blues," she's highlighted passages: "Women think, and men drink . . . Neither approach is effective against depression."

Here is a small piece, "Confessions of a closet homebody."

The articles I've ignored are seemingly endless:

"What's Your Stress Quotient?"

"Finding a job that fulfills you."

"Eat Smart: Pump up your pantry."

"Tide has turned in dating pool: Men outnumber women."

An article on Gloria Steinem.

An article on a female minister.

An article on creativity in children.

"Calming Jangled Nerves: Six strategies for taming the stress beast." *S—To help you resolve your indecisions—from a loving, caring mother.*

An article on relationship patterns.

"Mind, Body and Soul: The intimate connection between emotional, mental, spiritual and physical health." *S—good article for you.*

"The Enlightenments of Being Alone."

"Becoming Rich in America."

An article on Harry S. Truman, who once said "Don't look back." (He made up his mind and moved on, my mom always says, which is a thing, she adds, that I could learn to do.)

"Power Foods."

There are articles about AIDS, several issues of "Regarding Women" (a newsletter on women's health produced by the hospital where my dad works), and pamphlets galore: pamphlets on contraceptive methods, a pamphlet titled, "A Guide to Progesterone Therapy for Premenstrual Syndrome" (S—*see me about this*), a pamphlet on safe sex, and a pamphlet on safe driving from Shell Oil. The March of Dimes has provided us with "Sexually Transmitted Diseases."

An article on procrastination.

An article on curbing impulse spending.

An article on caring for different sorts of fabrics.

When I was growing up, my mother told me stories about how negative her mother was. "If your grandmother thought I needed to take a bath, she would never say that," my mother once told me. "She'd say, instead, 'Something sure does smell around here.'" My mother grew up trying to translate, to tease from the tangle of her mother's language something straightforward. "Your grandmother was so sharp, so critical," my mother always told me, adding that she'd decided long ago to be the opposite.

I think I must have been, and probably still am, a real mystery to my mother. While she had chosen to go through life as the incarnation of Norman Vincent Peale, I inherited my father's Irish skepticism and a fine sense of Catholic guilt and superstition. Saying something positive invites the negative to shower down upon you. If you say, What a beautiful day!, aren't you inviting clouds? If you say out loud what you're most hoping for, aren't you jinxing it, inviting it not to happen? This sort of precautionary negativity seems to dismay my mother, but I have always thought it to be wise—the last shall be first: if you expect the worst, you can only be surprised and pleased by the average. I see it as optimism in disguise. My mother calls it "The Ernie Larsen School of Stinkin' Thinkin'."

★ ★ ★

"Say Yes to Yourself."

"Confidence is the sexiest attribute of all."

"You remind me of . . . why some types attract." (An article on Bill Clinton's paramours, noting that they all have big hair, big teeth, and big red lips.)

An article by Cokie Roberts on being a working mother.

Articles on getting enough exercise.

An article about a woman potter who lives in Sausalito.

Dear Abby's advice on how to meet someone: volunteer, join the Rotary or Chamber of Commerce, take dancing lessons.

An article on emotional intelligence.

"How to Lose Weight while Boosting Your Energy."

Finding purpose in life.

Finding love.

Saving money.

An ad for a trek in the Andes with news anchor Don Shelby.

An ad from the *Lake Minnetonka Navigator* for a "singles extravaganza" on New Year's Eve (from 1998, too late now to RSVP).

"Hold out for the partner who's right for you."

Free anxiety screenings in Carver County.

"A handy guide to Scandinavian expressions," which answers the timely question, "What does uff da mean?" (According to the article, it is used to "express compassion, empathy or annoyance.")

"How to Thrive after a Rotten Childhood."

Overwhelmed by the confounding amount of advice, and feeling shame at having found, in one box (was I moving when I packed this one?), an oxidized Ghiradelli chocolate bar, a travel-sized bottle of Scope, three packets of instant Folger's, two packets of instant oatmeal, and a wealth of dried-up highlighting markers, I take a break and call my mom.

"It's kind of overwhelming to revisit all this stuff," I say. "Now I know why I've been avoiding it." I tell her about the ancient chocolate bar, the packets of oatmeal (why? why oatmeal? under my desk for four years?). "Why am I like this?" I say to my mom. "Is this genetic? Is it from Dad?"

"Enjoy it," she says. "Celebrate it. It's something unique about you."

"And by unique, you mean disgusting, right?"

I tell her, briefly, about the old journal entries I've found, from a time when I was in a particularly unproductive relationship with a guy who couldn't keep a job and got kicked out of his apartment for not paying rent. My mother never liked him. I'm not sure I did, either, but I dated him for three years, anyway.

"It makes me feel kind of sick to look back at these things," I say. I feel so flawed, so generally hopeless. A forty-year-old woman hoarding oatmeal packets.

"Uh-huh," she says, "Well, that's good then."

"Why is that good?"

"It means you've grown. You've grown out of that place."

I think about that for a second, looking at the television screen, the volume muted. In some movie trailer Will Farrell is combing his armpit hair with a dog brush.

"You know," my mom says, "I remember when I was cleaning things out once, I found some letters that your grandfather had written me. I can't even remember now what they said, but your grandfather had already died, and I found these letters, and I remember the feeling I had. They gave me a new understanding of who he was," she says. "And I appreciated that."

I ask her what her new understanding was.

"Oh, I don't remember," she says. "But I remember that feeling."

I know where my mother is sitting in the house while we're talking. She's at her desk in the kitchen, sitting in the wooden desk chair with wheels. Her League of Women Voters calendar is pinned to the bulletin board in front of her; the dates are marked with birthdays and the anniversaries of deaths, with meetings she's supposed to attend but more often than not skips because she's tired of volunteering, and with the names of snowbird friends to pick up at the airport, their flight numbers and arrival times scribbled in pencil.

While the comfort my mother describes at reading letters from her father seems to have nothing to do with my current discomfort, I begin to hope that maybe when I read the articles I will have that feeling, too. Appreciation. The long view.

"Countdown to a Calmer Lifestyle."
   "Solid marriage can't be built on grounds of passion alone."
   "Low-carb diet is unsafe for most."
   "New keys to a satisfying life discovered." S—*Another good article from a sweet, kind, caring, loving mother!!*
   A recipe for moussaka that I remember asking her to send.
   A Xeroxed poem that begins, "When I'm an old lady, I'll live with my kids . . ." It gives me the shivers.
   Perhaps my favorite find is a Xeroxed copy of an article by former *StarTribune* columnist Syl Jones. The article is titled, "A family gathering is good time to stop the cycle of rejection." There is no date to indicate when the article was published, but my mom has written in the margin, "I'm sending this for some reason. I like Syl Jones (he's almost bald and lives in Excelsior and is multi-talented) and he is a thorough thinker!"

Here's a handout, an anonymous manifesto titled, "As a person I have the right to":
   Be myself.
   Refuse requests without feeling selfish.
   Be competent and proud of my accomplishments.
   Feel and express anger.
   Ask for affection and help (may be turned down, but can ask).
   Be treated as a capable adult.
   Make mistakes—and be responsible for them.
   Change my mind.
   Say "I don't know."
   Say "I don't agree."
   Say "I don't understand."

From another dusty box, I lift quite a large feature article on Kay Redfield, whose book, *An Unquiet Mind*, was then new. My mother has underlined portions of her interview: "'I think in some ways the people who have a depressive view of life probably have a more realistic view,' Jamison says. 'They actually deny less and they see things more accurately than people who go bouncing through life and say everything is wonderful.'"

A conciliation from my preternaturally positive mother? I wish I'd read it earlier.

A few days later, I call my mom. When I ask her what she's going to do today, I hear a heavy sigh. "I'm looking at the kitchen table, well actually, I'm looking at the piles on the kitchen table, which seem about eighteen inches high. The table has disappeared," she says. "It's undiscoverable! We go away for two weeks and the mail piles up like snow."

My mom and dad returned from vacation more than a week ago, which means the piles have been there all this time. Maybe my clutter is partly genetic. Maybe, I begin to think, my mother has struggled more than she admits.

"So, you'll be sorting mail today," I say.

"Maybe I'll take a nap," she says. "Or a shower."

"So what's in those piles?" I ask.

"Mail," she says.

"Yeah, but what else? What'll you be reading today?"

"Well, let's see," she says, letting out another heavy sigh. I can hear her wheeling the office chair closer to the avalanche of paper. There's financial information on the grandkids' college fund, news from the Heart Association, and a Discover Canada catalogue from Elderhostel. "Oh, there's also this conservation magazine," she says, "that's really good. I've been reading an article with really gorgeous iceberg pictures. I clipped those out."

"Are those coming to me?" I say.

"No, those are for me," she says. She goes on to tell me about "The End of the World." "Everything's melting, you know," she says. "The polar bears are dying because they can't get around. Their ice floes," she says, "are too far apart."

★ ★ ★

When I was in high school, I began calling my mother by her first name, Flo. "Oh, Flo," I would say for shock value, "I really need to get laid." I had seen *Bye Bye Birdie*, whose main character called her mother by her first name, and I'd found that run for independence to be appealing. And after a while, calling my mother by her first name became a habit, and, as my therapist pointed out, a distancing mechanism.

"She's not Flo," my therapist said. "You're trying to make the two of you equals, acquaintances. She's your mother. Every child, no matter how old, deserves to have a mother."

I wonder now if not reading the articles has been the equivalent of calling them "Flo." Whatever my mother wanted to teach me, I didn't want to know. Instead of understanding it as nourishment, I understood it as criticism. Each article seemed like a new piece of duct tape, holding a shitty old car together. Here's another strip that will fix you. I wanted to get up and running on my own.

I find a crinkled Sunday circular from Dayton's. Boots on sale. Cashmere sweaters. Dresses for work. My mother has dog-eared the pages and put S next to the outfits she thinks will look good on me.

Another article on curbing impulse spending.

The award for the oldest of the batch seems to go to an article from *Woman's Day*, January 1977, when I was only ten: "First, Love Yourself—You're Worth It!" When had she given me this one?

I exhume a tiny booklet called "The Be-Good-to-Yourself Therapy Book," featuring cartoon drawings of elves, who apparently share our struggles. The elves feel alternatively lonely, ashamed, and nervous. They breathe deeply and try to stay in the moment. (I notice now a little notation on the front: "another elf-help book!")

An article from the December 1998 issue of *Hippocrates*, one of my father's medical journals, on the connection between depression and other diseases like asthma and diabetes. My mother has marked an S next to a few passages, including this one: "The real epidemic in our culture is depression, loneliness, and isolation. . . . When our need for connection is unfulfilled, there are serious consequences not only in quality of life but in quantity of life."

★ ★ ★

As I'm digging, I come across old journals, which I can't resist leafing through, even though the writing—an overly sincere chronicle of myopic self-examination, misguided crushes on unavailable men, and teen angst, I'm sad again today, why do we exist?—often makes me cringe. I make a note to myself to burn these before anyone else sees them.

I fall upon one particular entry, which details the night I was packing to leave for France to study for a semester. It was Christmas break, my junior year in college, and my mother had been following me around the house all night with questions and complaints. "You left the cupboard doors open again. Don't you think you should leave that sweater here for me? When did you get in last night? Excuse me young lady," she said at one point, "but someone took another Diet Coke out of the refrigerator without replacing it. How are we supposed to keep the pop cold that way? Some of us are losing our popularity very quickly around here."

"Mom," I said, "you don't drink your pop cold anyway."

"Well, obviously, I can't. It's a matter of consideration, you know. When you live together as a group of people . . ."

"Jesus, Flo, I'm trying to pack and you're bugging the shit out of me."

My mom burst into tears. "See! See!" she said, "This is why people get divorced! Complete failure to communicate in a rational way. I have a simple complaint, which I'd like to verbalize, and you can't even respond like a mature adult." My mother dabbed her eyes on her sleeve.

"Mom," I said, "It's a goddamn can of pop."

"This is exactly why human communication is doomed to failure," she sobbed. "No one ever has the patience to deal with the little things."

I went downstairs and got my carry-on bag, leaving my mom standing among the piles of clothes in my room.

As I get to the bottom of the second-to-last box, I find a small book, *Good Advice for a Happy Life*. On the title page, my mother has written, *For Shannon on her great, glorious 30th birthday, with love and a few editorial* comments from Mom. Indeed, my mother has freely annotated the small, square book's 374 pages. Underneath Lady Bird Johnson's advice, "Walk away from it until you're stronger. All your problems will be there when you get back, but you'll be better able to cope," my mother has added, Take a nap—troubles are easier to manage. Where Katherine Hepburn has suggested, " . . . as one goes through life, one learns that if you don't paddle your own canoe, you don't move," my mother has scripted, The prince may be a myth. On the page with Robert Frost's quote, "You have freedom when you're easy in your harness," my mother's addition reads: unless your harness is a forty-two double D! On Charlotte Brontë's page, "Life appears to me too short to be spent in nursing animosity or registering wrongs," my mother has added an admonition from my father's first medical partner, a wise old jazz-loving, cigar-smoking, small-town doc named Ted Schimmelpfinig, who has long since passed away. After my mother delivered my older brother, Dr. Schimmelpfinig had come into her recovery room and said, "Well, be glad you're not a dog." Why? she asked. "Because then you'd have to eat the placenta," he answered.

Here she has written: Why get yourself so upset? You then must spend your time getting over it.—Ted Schimmelpfinig.

And then, where Gail Sheehy is quoted as saying, "If we don't change, we don't grow. If we don't grow, we are not really living," my mother has written (in a cursive that I am beginning to see, more and more, is not so different than my own), That is for sure!

Nearing the end of the piles, I find a crumpled-up poem about trusting in life's process, "the slow work of God," which my mother had received at a spiritual growth class. It's about human growth potential and faith, she has written. I think faith in "the process," faith in self, and faith in the wisdom of a higher power who created this wonderful, complicated, interactive world. Do what you wish with it. Love, Mom.

"We should like to skip the intermediate stages," the poem reads, "We are impatient of being on the way to something unknown / something new,/ And yet it is the law of all progress / that it is made by passing through / some stages of instability / And that it may take a very long time."

I used to hate this sort of thing, what I thought of as an amateur poem, a congregation, I thought, of Hallmark feelings, easy aphorisms, the poetry of rainbows and teddy bears, the glittering mystery of unicorns of vague language. But now, digging through all of these boxes, all of this stuff that I've been lugging through life, this handout from a self-help workshop my mother attended sometime in the '80s or early '90s gives me strange comfort.

Another handout, perhaps from the same conference, titled "LET GO," which offers a list of a dozen or so things one might release:

"To 'let go' does not mean to stop caring, it means I cannot do it for someone else.

"To 'let go' is not to nag, scold or argue, but instead to search out my own shortcomings and correct them."

It reminds me of a saying my mother had taped to the kitchen window when I was growing up. She had drawn a picture of a ladybug, and next to it had written, "Thou shalt not bug." I always thought it meant that we should leave her alone while she was cooking, though I found out, in my late twenties, that she had put it up to remind herself not to nag us children. It wasn't the kind of mother she wanted to be. It was a commandment to herself.

Maybe the articles were like that masking-taped message. They meant something to her that I misread. The articles reminded my mother of the past, of things she'd already learned, of adversities to which she'd already adapted; she was passing along these lessons, a sort of Darwinian survival guide. I took them as admonishments, indications that I was a three-legged frog of sorts, a mutant, maladapted creature, and so I threw them in a box, usually only glancing at the titles, not even reading her scribbled notes.

And now, a sheet yellowed around the edges, another Xeroxed page, an excerpt from *Women Who Love Too Much*. My mother has written in pencil, *This is from the book I just finished. I send this to you not cuz I think you're imperfect or cuz I'm trying to improve you. I send it cuz life is tough and I want you to know yourself, to have information and insight upon which*

*you make your decisions and choices in life, cuz I love you a ton and I want you
to live, love and live happily ever after! (Or something like that!) love, Mom.*

If I had read it earlier, would it have helped? Perhaps, as several of the
articles and handouts have pointed out, we understand things only
when we're ready.

I have shredded bags and bags of old checks, tax returns, ancient
phone bills, but now that I've got the articles all in one place, I can't
bear to think of throwing them away. They're a history of sorts, a frag-
mented chronology, notes, and an odd sort of love letter when no one
writes love letters anymore—Here, they say, I care about you, and here
is what I wanted you to know, about me, about you, about the world.
There are diseases and broken hearts and boots on sale at Dayton's.
I love you, they say.

But to me, here is the most surprising part: as I've been skimming
the articles, I've already begun to make piles—for my sister, my
brother, my friends. When I'm done reading the articles, I'll send
them along.

Aftereffects

Carrie Pomeroy

Carrie Pomeroy and her mother in the summer of 1969, when men first landed on the moon

"I'm afraid you think I was a bad mother," my mom confided to me once. We were talking on the phone, years after I'd moved away.

I could hear how much she wanted me to say what's essentially the truth: that she did a wonderful job raising my sister and me.

But I didn't say that. After a long pause, I told her, "It's not that I think you were a bad mother. I just wish you'd had more help from other adults."

My mother's voice was surprised.

"But I didn't need help!" she said. "I had you girls."

As a child, I loved hearing about the doll house, my parents' first home together.

"That house was so tiny," Dad told us, "I had to lean over so I wouldn't bump my head on the ceiling."

As he talked, I tried to picture my parents as I'd seen them in old snapshots: Mom, slim in shorts and a sleeveless shirt, her brown hair in a tidy bouffant, her eyes crinkled with smiles behind pointy cat's-eye glasses. Dad, with shaggy black hair and long sideburns and sleepy, sleepy eyes.

"And we were right next to the railroad tracks," Mom added. "Every time a train went past, the house shook so hard I thought it was going to fall over."

"You must have wondered what you'd gotten yourself into," my dad said to my mom, shaking his head in wonder. "I was flunking out of school when she met me, you know," Dad told my sister Rachel and me.

We knew, all right. We knew how they'd met the summer before Mom's sophomore year of college, how they'd courted long-distance and gotten engaged by Thanksgiving. We knew about how, for love of my mother, my father had buckled down and earned straight As, all while making a living shoveling coal on the steel-mill night shift. It was our favorite fairy tale, the story of how Mom's love and faith had transformed our father.

A successful business executive now, my dad got promoted and transferred so often, Mom barely had time to unpack all the boxes before it was time to pack up again. Illinois, Missouri, Indiana, Ohio, California, Georgia, upstate New York: our homes flashed by like images in a slide show. Still, Mom treated each temporary home as if it were permanent. She painted, wallpapered, put up shelves, hung up pictures, planted marigolds. "If Life Gives You Lemons, Make Lemonade" read a counted cross-stitch sampler Mom had stitched, with a basket overflowing with lemons pictured beneath the words. Wherever we moved, that sampler hung on our kitchen wall, a reminder of the uncomplaining optimism that had gotten our family this far.

When we visited my mom's hometown in southern Illinois, my parents asked if we wanted to drive past the doll house, but we never did go see it. For me, and perhaps for my parents, as well, the doll house had grown into something bigger than a mere house by the railroad tracks. Like the sampler on the kitchen wall, it had become synonymous with our family fable and its crystal-clear moral: With hard work and love, you can overcome all obstacles.

A memory from our house in New York, as vivid to me as if it's happening right now: It's 1978. My parents are practicing the Hustle in our basement, gliding across the smooth cement floor. They're taking disco lessons at the local dance studio, Dad's Christmas gift to Mom, a surprise that made her gasp, hands over her heart.

The Bee Gees coo "I just wanna be your everything" from the stereo. My sister and I sit near the top of the basement steps and peek beneath the wooden railing as our parents dance in and out of sight. We could move closer and get a better look, but it's more fun to spy.

Suddenly, my mom nods at some invisible cue from my father, and the two of them sway apart and then come back together, palms touching, feet mirroring each other's movements. "Hey, hey!" crows my mom with a grin. "We got it!"

I'm not surprised. As far as I can tell, there is nothing my parents can't do. My mom: the funny, cool mom my friends wish could be theirs. My dad: so handsome, with his black hair and olive skin and green, green eyes. When he goes out for a run, my friends' teenaged sisters and college-student aunts crane their necks to watch.

My dad slides one hand slowly down Mom's back and pulls her closer, his fingers dipping toward her rear end. I wonder if they even know my sister and I are watching. Then my mom motions toward Rachel and me with a subtle tilt of her head. She's always aware of us, even when she seems to be focused on something else. Along with my dad, we are the center of her world. She mouths a word at my dad— I can't catch what it is—and arches her eyebrows mischievously. He throws back his head and laughs.

After dinner, Rachel and I sit at the kitchen table finishing our homework while my parents wash the dishes. I glance up from my math textbook. Dad is standing behind Mom at the sink, cuddled up close, his arms crossed over her shoulders. She leans into his embrace, her hands over his. He whispers something in her ear that makes her close her eyes and smile a secret, private smile. I smile, too. Some day, I think, my husband and I will share that kind of closeness. I go back to my homework, still smiling long after I've looked away.

That night when Mom is tucking me in, I ask her what sex feels like. She thinks my question over, nodding to herself.

"When it's with someone you love," she finally says, "it's like someone has flipped a switch, and your whole body comes alive."

The Monday night after Easter, 1981, my sister and I were in the next-door neighbors' basement rumpus room, playing board games, laughing at one another's goofy jokes, accidentally snorting root beer up our noses. The evening passed so quickly, I was shocked to see it was almost ten o'clock when my mom came to pick us up. At the neighbors' front door, I noticed her eyes were red, her eyelids puffy. I shot Mom a questioning look, but she smiled back and reached out to Rachel and me.

"There's my girls," she said.

As we left the neighbors' house, my mom put her arms around my sister's shoulders and mine and said, "I'm afraid I have some very bad news."

Calmly, painstakingly, she recounted what had happened at our house that evening. Dad—he'd been away on a business trip—had come home from the airport hungry, so she'd made him a turkey sandwich from our Easter leftovers. He was eating in the family room while they watched TV. She was lying on the couch, facing away from him, when something small and white flew into her field of vision.

"I turned around and saw that your dad was choking," she told us. The white speck she'd glimpsed was a bit of food flying off the plate he was still clutching in his hands.

She described her attempts to clear his throat, her phone call for help, the ambulance and the paramedics and his ride to the emergency room, with her following in her car.

"The doctors at the hospital did everything they could," she told us as we reached our driveway. I waited to hear that my dad was okay. He had to be okay.

"I'm so sorry, girls," Mom said, "but your daddy died tonight."

My knees buckled.

"No! No!" I screamed, sagging against my mom, scrabbling at her as if I were drowning.

"Shh, shh," she whispered, shepherding Rachel and me toward our door. "Wait until we're in the house."

I tried one more time to make what she'd said not true.

"You're kidding," I cried. "You're kidding."

Three months after my father's funeral, my mother, sister, and I said good-bye to upstate New York and headed for the Midwest in our blue hatchback Chevy, bound for Mom's Illinois hometown. My father's ashes sat on the front passenger seat, packed in a cardboard box.

"We'll take care of Dad after we get settled in," Mom told my sister and me.

Once we'd gotten settled, though, the last thing we wanted to go through was another memorial service. Years passed. Mom told

Rachel and me that we could wait until she died, then bury her and Dad together. Sometimes I wished I had a place to visit my father. Other times, the thought of him in a cemetery surrounded by dead people was more than I could bear.

It's been almost twenty-six years. My dad's ashes still sit on a shelf in my mom's bedroom closet. Twenty-six years, and we still haven't laid that beautiful young man to rest.

My mother found that most people think grief has an expiration date of about six months. When her grief showed every sign of lasting past her allotted six months, people's faces started closing down. They changed the subject.

"You've got to rise above what's happened," my grandmother told Mom, her blue eyes cool, her pink-lipsticked mouth pursed. "For the girls' sake, you've got to move on."

Time to move on. Time to move on. My mother had returned to a place both familiar and unfamiliar, like a dream. She saw people around town she recognized, but she couldn't remember their names. Where there had once been corn fields and stands of oak and maple, there now stood strip malls and gas stations and fast-food joints.

She took my sister and me to Mass at the old brick church where she'd been baptized, confirmed, and married, and found pew upon pew of married couples smiling at each other over their children's stair-step heads. There was no place here for a single mother, as far as she could tell. "If you don't have a husband," my mother remarked dryly, "the women all look at you like you're out to get theirs."

She started college again, working toward the degree she had interrupted to marry Dad and have Rachel and me. She got a part-time job in the marketing department at the mall. Her cross-stitch sampler hung once again on the kitchen wall, its basket overflowing with lemons. As I fell asleep to the sound of her typing her term papers at the dining room table, I reminded myself that my mom was still the same woman I had always thought could do anything.

About three years after Dad's death, my mom's best friend began urging Mom to date.

"You're still young," her friend told her. "I know a nice guy I could fix you up with."

Doing her dutiful best to move on, Mom slipped off her wedding ring and started seeing a tire salesman from the next town over.

"Dad always said he hoped I'd find someone else if anything ever happened to him," Mom told my sister and me, a note of apology in her voice.

Rachel greeted Mom's new man with tremulous smiles. He tried to connect with me, too, loaning me a book about W. C. Fields when he found out I liked old movies. I barely glanced at the book before flipping it aside.

My mother was sympathetic. She just wished I'd try a little harder.

"It's not his fault that Dad died," she told me.

After she and the tire salesman had parted ways, another high-school friend fixed Mom up, this time with a divorced sales rep. Short and paunchy, with a bushy mustache and a nasal voice, he wasn't nearly the dreamboat my dad had been. But he made my mother laugh, and that was enough for her. At the mall, she showed me a white eyelet sundress and commented with a sly smile, "Wouldn't this be nice for a summer wedding?" I felt a chill. I wanted my mom to be happy, sure. But I didn't want her to get married.

I didn't have to worry about it. The sales rep was still hung up on his second wife, a skinny frosted-blonde. He used my open dislike of him as an excuse to hold my mom at a distance. Mom tried to lose weight by fasting, subsisting on herbal tea for days on end, her hands trembling as she lifted the cup to her lips. But she couldn't whittle herself into the petite blonde ex-wife. She and the sales rep broke up, too.

My mother slipped her wedding ring back on.

"I already had Number One," she told Rachel and me. "Why should I settle for anything less?"

A framed black-and-white photo of my father took up residence on her nightstand, a handsome formal portrait of Dad in a suit and tie. I was sad for Mom, yes, but I was also secretly relieved. Dad was back in her bedroom, where he belonged.

★ ★ ★

My mother finished college and started working for a charity across the river in St. Louis. Whenever I visited her at her office, it was obvious to me that she was indispensable. As soon as she walked through the door, her coworkers rushed up to her with questions and problems they knew she'd be able to solve.

Yet Mom was certain she was going to get fired. She regularly did more than her fair share, working nights and weekends, single-handedly stuffing hundreds, even thousands of envelopes for fund-raising campaigns when the volunteers didn't show up. Night after night, she lay awake ticking off mental to-do lists, sure she was forgetting something, sure she was on the verge of some terrible mistake. The worst possible thing had happened to her once. She knew catastrophe could strike again. She worked harder, took on more.

"If I want things done right, I just have to do it myself," Mom often said.

A teenager, I watched my mother and swore I'd never be a slave to my job the way she was. I'd do exactly what I wanted, and if it wasn't fun, I'd walk away and do something else. I conveniently ignored the fact that my sister and I were the reasons Mom couldn't walk away.

I'd do it all differently, I was sure.

I started dating. I sneaked in the house with my boyfriend's smell all over me, my mouth raw from kissing, purple hickeys blooming on my neck. My mother called to me from her dark bedroom and patted the side of her bed for me to sit.

"Have a nice time?" she asked. I could tell she'd been waiting up for me, probably reading one of the gory murder-mysteries she loved. She'd probably flicked off her light as soon as she'd heard my key in the front door.

We were still close enough for me to confide in her. "Sometimes," I admitted, "it's really hard to stop myself from going too far."

"But you do stop yourself, and that's the important thing," my mother said, patting my knee. "You've got too much sense to mess up your life doing something stupid over a boy."

I smelled Oreo cookies on her breath, and suddenly I was swept by a pained and guilty sense of her loneliness. I pictured her standing at the kitchen counter palming cookies into her mouth, filling her emptiness with sweets. I wanted to help my mother, but her sadness felt too big, a pit I could never fill. Her life might be over, I thought with all the fierce melodrama of a sixteen-year-old girl, but that didn't mean mine had to be.

You've got too much sense to do anything stupid, she told me. But I wanted to go too far. I wanted to do something stupid and reckless and see how far from her narrow loneliness I could get.

We bought a house after renting for a few years, a small brick one-story with a cement front stoop. It was a far cry from the spacious homes in fancy new subdivisions where we'd lived with my dad, but it was no doll house, either—a perfectly fine house, just right for the three of us.

"No dishwasher, though," Mom noted ruefully as she showed us our new kitchen.

"You don't need one," I chirped, spreading my arms. "You have us."

Things didn't work out quite so nicely.

Day after day, this was the scene my mom came home to: Dirty dishes all over the living room, with more stacked in the kitchen sink. Bedroom floors carpeted with magazines and dirty clothes. The dining room table a jumble of textbooks and papers and loose-leaf notebooks with no room for us to eat. In the single bathroom we all shared, the mirror and sink were smudged with make-up, the countertop strewn with hair brushes and curling irons and mousse canisters. In our old life, she'd prided herself on the cheery neatness of the many homes our family had shared. Now, except for her own bedroom, there was no escape from the mess.

For a long time, Mom sighed and looked the other way, too tired and discouraged to say anything. After Rachel and I were in bed, she straightened the house, seething inside, telling herself there were no other options because she sure couldn't count on us.

One day, though, she burst into a rage that was unlike anything Rachel and I had ever seen from her. In the past, my mother had disciplined us through the subtlest of gestures: An arched, disapproving eyebrow. A quiet word or two. Now my mother was yelling at us, her gentle face transformed by rage. Standing by the kitchen sink, she snatched a steak knife off the counter and held the serrated blade against her wrist.

"Do you girls understand how close to the edge I am?" she demanded. Her jaw was tight, her eyes wide. "Do you have any idea?"

My sister and I reached out and pleaded with her to put down the knife. She tossed it in the sink, then grabbed her purse and keys and slammed out the door to the garage. We heard her car engine start, the scrape of the garage door, the squeal of her tires on the driveway. By the time we had run to the living room window, Mom was gone.

My sister and I gathered stray dishes and shoved make-up bottles and compacts in the bathroom drawer, working in penitent silence. My heart was pounding, my mouth dry. Would Mom get into an accident? Was she really desperate enough to hurt herself? I couldn't even think the words "kill herself." But I did wonder where Rachel and I would go if something bad happened. Would we live with my Dad's brother, Uncle Mike? Or go to Colorado to live with Mom's sister?

As I scrubbed the kitchen counter, my gaze fell on the lemonade sampler hanging on the kitchen wall. Just try and make lemonade out of this, I thought grimly.

When we heard the garage door, my sister and I glanced at each other, bracing ourselves.

At first Mom wouldn't meet our eyes. With exaggerated care, she set her purse and keys on the counter, her head ducked. Then she looked up. Her eyes were red. Her mouth trembled.

"Oh, girls," she said, reaching for us. "I'm so, so sorry."

We fell into a pattern. For a while, my sister and I did better. But then, over a few days or weeks, we got sloppy again. Things started to slide. Mom exploded, drove away, then came back ready to make up. The messy house now stood for all that had gone wrong in our lives, all the frustration and fear and disappointment, all the grief that hadn't been given its due.

When Mom raged that we were selfish and irresponsible, Rachel agreed: yes, yes, we're all that, we'll do better, we'll do better. I took an almost opposite path; I hardened myself. When Mom reached out to me, I kept my arms crossed tightly over my chest. So you're going to drive away and leave me wondering if you're going to die? I told her with my flat voice and bored eyes. Fine, then. I'll go numb.

"The thing is, if you two really loved me," Mom said during one of our reconciliations, "you'd understand how important a clean house is to me. I feel so out of control in so many other ways. The house is one place I'd like to feel some sense of order."

"It's not that we don't love you, Mom," I replied nonchalantly. "We're just lazy."

My mother opened her mouth to speak, then closed it again. With her fists clenched and her shoulders tight, she stalked into her bedroom instead. My sister eyed me reproachfully: Look what you've done now, right when we were making up. A few seconds later, we heard our mother scream, "Damn you for dying, John! Damn you!" and a crash of shattering glass.

We ran to her room and found Mom kneeling on her floor crying. She'd thrown the framed photo of my father from her nightstand, and the glass in the frame had smashed when the photo hit her bedroom wall. With trembling fingers, Mom was picking up the broken shards.

"Let us do that, Mom," Rachel offered. "Please."

My mother held the photo up to the light.

"Oh, John," she said. "I'm so sorry."

The broken glass had scratched a few faint nicks in the photograph. Mom bought a new frame for it and set it back on her nightstand. But there were always those tiny white scratches on my father's upper lip, like small scars.

My junior year, I started getting college catalogs in the mail. I began plotting my escape.

"You girls are the only thing I live for," my mother often told us. "If it weren't for you, I wouldn't be able to keep going."

Her words tugged at me, holding me fast in that little brick house where I felt as if I were suffocating. With a yearning so keen my heart hurt, I eyed the catalog photos of smiling students chatting under trees.

Maybe Rachel will stay, I thought. Maybe Rachel will stay.

★ ★ ★

She did stay. While Rachel finished high school and then studied theater at the local university, my sister and my mom lived together in the condo Mom had bought from her parents. She and Rachel were like roommates, companionably squabbling, good-naturedly teasing. Their fights never seemed to cut as deep as Mom's and mine did.

I envied the chumminess my mom and sister shared. But driving back to school, I felt as if I could breathe again for the first time in days. I rolled down my car window and whooped into the wind.

At school, I spent my nights listening to punk bands in dank, crowded basements, a plastic cup of Schaeffer beer sweating in my hand, drinking until the world reeled and I had to lie on the ground to keep from falling. I slept with more boys than was really necessary or wise. When I was alone, I sometimes rattled off their names in my head, assuring myself with each one that I was desirable, sexual, alive.

I'm not going to end up lonely and desperate like Mom, I told myself. I got myself free.

Yet in some ways I was just as mistrustful and desperate as I thought she was. Even when I would have preferred to be home with a book, I went out partying, dancing, drinking, afraid my friends would forget me if I wasn't around every night. I put on the bravado of a free spirit who could have sex without getting attached. But I spent more hours than I like to admit waiting for phone calls that didn't come.

My mother turned fifty a few years after I'd headed north to live in Minnesota. She took that milestone birthday as a wake-up call. She got a new job. She hired a personal trainer, and her extra pounds melted into lush hourglass curves. On a roll, she traded in her cantankerous old Chrysler Le Baron for a new Saturn.

Bob, the salesman at the Saturn dealership, was a few years' divorced, with two daughters in their twenties. He and Mom compared notes on what it was like to have your little girls turn into grown women on you.

A few days later, Bob called Mom to check in about the car. Just as she was about to thank him and say good-bye, his voice changed.

"I never do this, I never do this!" he muttered. Then he asked her for a date.

They moved in together less than a year later and got married a few months after that. My sister, assured that Mom would be okay without her, headed to Los Angeles to pursue an acting career.

The first time I visited Mom after Bob had moved in, I was startled by all the signs that my mother's house was no longer hers alone. Bob, a former banker, had brought two framed pictures of foreign currency from his old apartment, and to make him feel at home, Mom had given them a place of honor on the den wall. A stuffed mallard drake presided from the top of the bookcase, clashing with my mom's flowery pastels. In the living room, Bob leaned back in his favorite easy chair, wielding the remote control as if he'd been there all along.

Most startling of all, though, my dad's portrait was no longer at Mom's bedside.

It made sense, of course. But I still felt taken aback. For years, I'd wished my mom would move on so I could plunge into my own life guilt-free. Yet a part of me had wanted her to remain the perpetually grieving widow. As long as she had stayed emotionally married to my father, I could imagine my family intact. Through her suffering, she had kept him alive.

That first year with Bob, she was happier than I'd thought she would ever be again. For years, our phone conversations had been a litany of bad news: the stresses and frustrations of Mom's work, her grief when Rachel broke up with a longtime boyfriend Mom had loved like a son, her continued mourning for Dad. Now her talk was replete with the excursions she and Bob were going on, trips to blues festivals and balloon races and wineries, long bike rides on scenic trails.

Mom and I met up that year on neutral territory, at a cousin's wedding in Kansas. At the reception, she and I danced together to the B-52s' "Love Shack." I wore a navy blue pantsuit with a flared jacket that obscured the shape of my body. At home in St. Paul, I'd hit a rough patch with the man who would later become my husband, and I was uncertain about what lay ahead for us. Haunted by my mom's workaholic ways, I'd resisted a full-time job, but I was just barely getting by piecing together part-time teaching work. Often, I struggled with a nagging suspicion that I wasn't amounting to much.

My mother looked radiant in a slim-fitting, knee-length black skirt and a bright red suit jacket cut to show off her fine new figure. Everyone kept commenting on how great she looked. As she shimmied to the music under flashing lights, aglow in the first rush of a new and unexpected love, I thought, My God. My mother is sexier than I am now.

A few years after marrying Bob, Mom bought a spot in the mausoleum on the edge of town. From a nearby hill, you can see the St. Louis Arch, fifteen miles to the west, where Dad proposed to Mom when they were both twenty years old.

Over the phone, she mentioned wanting to put my dad's ashes to rest at last.

Not yet, I thought, please, not yet. I clutched the phone hard.

"Could you wait until Rachel and I can both be there?" I pleaded. "Please don't do anything without us there, too, okay?"

My mom hesitated. "Sure," she said. "Sure. I can wait."

The next time my sister and I were back in town at the same time, Rachel was pregnant with her first child, and I had my young son with me and was pregnant with my second child. Focused on all the new life, we lost track of burying my father. That was almost two years ago.

"What is it about your family, that you haven't done something about your father's ashes?" a Zen priest I respect asked me when she found out my dad was still in Mom's closet.

I don't know, I told her. I don't know.

But I think I do know. To bury him would be to admit he's not coming back. We've lived this long hoping he might still walk through the door again. How can we give up that hope now?

When I got pregnant for the first time at thirty-three, I was afraid to have a girl. Daughters, I knew from experience, are awfully hard on their mothers. I exulted when the midwife declared, "A boy!" as she lifted my handsome, sturdy firstborn into my outstretched arms.

Three years later, at our second child's birth, my husband was the one who announced the baby's sex.

"A girl," he said in a tone of hushed reverence, wet eyes meeting mine.

"A girl," I repeated quietly, letting the news steal over me, savoring it. With my warm, naked daughter in my arms, I didn't feel afraid. I felt as if someone I'd been missing my whole life had finally arrived.

Ten days after our daughter was born, my husband left on a business trip. Nervous about being on solo parenting duty so soon after the birth, I had asked my mother to fly up from Illinois for a week while he was gone. Once Mom had arrived, though, I deflected her every attempt to pitch in. I thought letting myself lean on her even a little bit would spell surrender: surrender of my independence and adulthood, surrender of the distance I'd put between her sadness and me. When she leaped to change the baby's diaper, I said I'd do it. When she offered to hold the baby while I got my son ready for bed, I waved her away and insisted I could manage. As I headed up the steps with both kids, my mom started putting away the toys my son had left scattered across the living room floor.

I snapped back at her, "You don't have to do that. I can do it later."

She looked up at me from the bottom of the steps, her eyes puzzled, her mouth trembling.

"You asked me up here to help," she said, "but every time I try, you tell me not to. I don't know what I'm supposed to do any more."

The next day, Mom took a different tack: she stopped offering to help me care for the baby and turned her attentions to my house. She tidied the wooden cubbies where we stuff our shoes and hats and gloves. She swept. She wiped down counters. She dusted. I tensed, remembering our old housecleaning battles. I waited for the old criticisms. But Mom said nothing.

One afternoon near the end of her visit, I walked into the kitchen holding my daughter and found Mom on her hands and knees, polishing the floor with an old rag. Most likely she was too afraid of my snappishness to risk asking where we kept our mop.

"Mom," I told her again, "you don't have to do that. You're doing enough already. Really."

Mom sat on her heels and shrugged.

"I get sore if I stay in one place too long," she said. "I feel better if I keep moving."

She never has gotten to stay still for long. All those moves while my dad was alive, and then after he died, no time to grieve: time to move on, time to move on. She had girls to raise, a living to make, a home to maintain. Even now, when she's watching TV with Bob, she's still going several directions at once, jumping up to transfer laundry or unload the dishwasher, flipping through clothing catalogs or home decorating magazines and marking things she thinks my sister or I might like, glancing up to comment about something on the television, her foot restlessly twitching, gum popping between her jaws. I never see her in repose. Never.

She reached up for my kitchen table and hauled herself to her feet, wincing a little. She's almost sixty, but I still think of her as young. It's hard for me to acknowledge that my mom has quite a bit of trouble with her hips, trouble with her knees, trouble with her feet. I call it "trouble," but if I were more honest, I'd call it what it is: pain.

My mom turned away and trudged to the kitchen sink to rinse out her rag. From across the room, my daughter in my arms, I watched my mother from behind. How vulnerable the pale nape of her neck looked, exposed by her short haircut. How vulnerable the tense set of her shoulders, the stiffness of her walk. She had come here to help me, just as I'd asked her to do, her suitcase packed with no-nonsense sweat suits so she could get down on the floor and wrestle and romp with her grandson, so she could scrub my counters and sweep my dust bunnies and kneel beside the tub to give my children their baths. She had come, I'm sure, harboring a faint but unquenchable hope that this time, this time, we might finally be able to reconnect, one mother to another. Yet here I was, responding to her as if we were still stuck in our old brick house, still a young widow and a confused teenager reeling with fresh loss. Here I was, still crossing my arms against my mother's outstretched hands.

My mother turned from the sink to face me again.

"Want me to make us some lunch?" she asked.

I almost waved her away and said, "Oh, I can make it."

But with my daughter's cheek pressed near my heart, I took a small step.

"Sure," I said. "That would be great, Mom. That would be just fine."

Dakota Woman

Susan Power

Mama is born with a hole in her heart, that empty space like a howl for everything sucked away from her Dakota people. At least she is American, born in Fort Yates, North Dakota, in 1925; if she'd come into this world two years earlier she wouldn't be, since the Indian Citizenship Act won't pass until 1924, making our indigenous peoples indigenous in the eyes of federal law. Her mother is educated but poor, so they live in a log house on the Standing Rock Sioux Reservation. And a girl with a hole in her heart needs to keep still, not crawl around on the dusty ground, which is why Mama spends her first three years in a beer keg sawed in two. She watches with intelligent eyes that are black like young fur, unfaded, every political demotion that hits her reservation until there is nothing left but dust and flies and a last buffalo hunt yielding stringy meat. Her parents are leaders and the people come on foot, or in wagons, to argue and plan their way into the future—how do you stitch yourself into next year when you haven't any more beads or sinew or porcupine quills? They argue in Dakota, Lakota, Nakota, because so many bands of a powerful tribe have been thrown together to sink or swim, to fight it out, to conquer one another and divide their hearts into small stones. Mama hears warriors who were young men when they watched Custer die and her uncle who is the last member of the White Horse Society. She is born at the tattered edge of a web and will never forget the complex design we once used to govern ourselves.

Mama's cabin is across the road from Sitting Bull's grave, not the one put up later in Mobridge but the first one his body was lowered into, spread with quicklime to hasten his reduction to history. But she is Dakota, trained to believe that the past is more than ashes, it is in your hands and your tears and your corn soup. So Sitting Bull never dies, not for her or her brothers and sisters or their friends who call him "la la" when they tell him their troubles, "la la" short for "*tunkashila*"—the Lakota word for grandfather. "He is still our grandfather," Mama reminds me after watching HBO's *Bury My Heart at Wounded Knee*. "Poor Dee Brown must be turning in his grave for the mess they made of his book," she says. "Don't believe what they said about our chief."

Mama survives the hole in her heart and the Indian Reorganization Act of 1934. She survives the "Rooshian" teacher who makes his Dakota students listen to Herr Hitler's speeches on the radio. She survives the nuns at St. Joseph's Boarding School, their punishments and grim warnings, how she cards wool for them when she'd rather be reading. She survives the migration of earth, when overworked soil rises from the Great Plains, gritty fields sweeping their way east against the immigrant tide. She survives the Depression and Max Schmeling's defeat of Joe Louis—the reservation favorite, the "Brown Bomber," who represents every other-colored child who presumes to matter. She survives brothers who fight in Korea and her sister the Marine. She survives Relocation and Chicago, where Mayor Daley's police arrest her for sitting in at the BIA. She survives urban Indian politics and the death of a husband, her factory jobs and publishing position at McClurg's, where pallets of books spread before her like the treasures of the world. She survives her anger and disappointments and scalding beauty, and a lost Creek love who sits with her in a nightclub as Billie Holiday trails past with a lush fur coat dragging behind like a child's blanket. She survives her own imagination, complicated as DNA, a diadem of galaxies she wears like a queen—ancient and modern as science fiction. She survives what she knows, what she dreams, what she remembers, what she predicts, what she fears.

Mama is born with a hole in her heart, dense and black as the maw in space. How does it heal itself when wounds are all she knows from 1925 to 1973, from Wounded Knee to Wounded Knee? How does she grow on clumps of peanut butter saved from lunch at school in her linty pockets, pinched off through the hours of a child's day to trounce hunger? How does she contain every American contradiction, old voices and new visions, our lost world which we summon now from Sitting Bull's grave to save our lost world? Somewhere in that hole of Mama's heart is an egg, a red yolk, the daughter gestating in negative space—her missing piece waiting to be born.

Foreign Labor:
Will Be Your Child/Worker

Sun Yung Shin

For almost my entire adult life, I have worked in the field of information technology in some way or another—first in manufacturing, where I documented procedures related to the copying of diskettes for America Online, then in desktop support at one of the largest food goods corporations in the world, then in software development where we had a $2 million contract with the U.S. Navy to build a program to manage their HIV testing database, then in internal service at one of the largest health insurance companies in the world where I helped desktop and server engineers fix problems and perform upgrades for "internal customers."

I have lived through five mergers or acquisitions and have been laid off twice, once while on maternity leave.

I am a child of the Cold War. My own sense of work—of labor—has been profoundly informed by my entry into a post-Reagan work world. Bush, Clinton, Clinton, Bush, Bush. This is the economic empire into which I became an adult and a mother. While I was making nearly $50,000 as a twenty-three-year-old IT consultant, billing $95 an hour, my white American mother was making about $12 an hour as a cook for a daycare. Before that, she was a nanny for a wealthy white family. Before that, she cleaned other white women's houses and was paid in cash.

What does this all have to do with my mother?

What I have been paid to do as an adult, mostly, is work in reproduction—of materials, of documentation, of processes for the standardized use by others. I have always had "customers" whether "internal" or "external." In the mid-1990s it became popular to speak of the various "stakeholders" in our enterprises and projects, regardless of the company's status as private or public. Now that I am an educator in the public school system, there is also talk of our stakeholders, but that is another essay.

American culture is obsessed with reproduction in a subterranean way. It is rarely called reproduction—it is merely our heritage of mass production, perfected by Taylor and Ford and now exported to multinational corporate-owned factories all over the so-called Third World.

While I worked at the food goods company headquarters in downtown Minneapolis, my team facilitated the shutdown (inventorying personal computers, transferring software licenses) of several plants in small-town America—in Wisconsin, Pennsylvania, Tennessee—and oversaw the ramp-up of the plant in Mexico. By now, it is a familiar story to those who have lived it or who have been paying attention, but not familiar in a way that seems to matter to those who work on the fortieth floor of glass buildings, some of whose parents perhaps worked at plants similar to those we shut down. But probably not. Not anymore.

My father worked at a plant—as an account representative selling train parts for Electro Motive—and my mother worked at home. Like many other suburban white mothers in the 1970s and 1980s in America, she raised two children while her husband went to work Monday through Friday. Growing up I felt solidly in the middle of my social peers—I had friends who shared beds with their Italian grandmothers, friends whose parents had heavy accents, friends whose mothers worked at the deli counter, at the aluminum recycling plant, and at the fruit-punch bottling factory. I was neither the most well-off nor the poorest.

Why do I insist on the adjective "white"? Can she not just be my "mother" or a "woman," not a "white woman"?

While I am her first and only daughter, she is my second mother. While to her I am the sister of her son, to my first mother—I do not know how I am related to her other children, or if they exist at all. In one column, the equation of reproduction is known, and in the other, it remains an unsolved mystery, one that is cut off even from the possibility of nostalgia.

I have struggled to understand my history as part of the diaspora of

150   150,000 to 200,000 Korean children sent to Europe and the United States for adoption since the Korean War. I have learned that the way I became the Korean American daughter of my white American mother was through a particular technology: the reproductive technology of adoption.

If I apply the business analysis and flowcharting skills I learned as an IT consultant to my own immigration, I see that my parents commissioned a reproductive project with a group of collaborators—the Holt adoption agency, the U.S. government, the South Korean government, and Eastern Social Welfare. All of these collaborators are known. There are names, dates, and signatures. The origin of the product to be transacted, the manufacturing machine, if you will, remains anonymous. My (Korean) mother.

When I arrived at O'Hare airport on June 16, 1975, approximately thirteen months after my birth, I "took one look at [my white/ American/new/adoptive mother] and screamed." I would not be held by her. I was terrified. Only the man with black hair, the man who was now my new father, could hold me.

I would not be touched by anyone "fair" except for the very pale boy with shiny white-blond hair and bright aqua eyes. He was three and a half years my senior, and he was to be my new brother. His name was David, the man's name was Nicholas, the woman's name was Arlene, and my name was now Claire Nicole.

They tell me that all night long, for six weeks, I screamed in my crib.

I spoke Korean words—*omma, oppa, mul, mamma*—mother, father, water, food—and others, but then learned English quickly.

The technology of my reproduction as a daughter of this white woman was and is called adoption. Although I am one individual, I am the product of a mass production, and an institutionalized and systematic effort to remove infants and children from Korean women (and men), Korean homes, Korean orphanages, and to overwhelmingly white, middle-class homes thousands of miles away. Parental rights and citizenship were both terminated.

Reproductive rights as defined by and struggled for by the white women's movement in the U.S. has largely been about the right to prevent and terminate one's pregnancies, not the right to keep one's own

child from being sent away permanently. It has not been about the
right to be supported by one's society for the labor of mothering.

Quality Control & Perfect Reproducibility:
The Literacy of Business & A (Second) Break with Mother

When I was a technical writer for the diskette reproduction company,
we became certified in the ISO 9000 quality control standards system.
The main goal of my labor was to ensure that all procedures could be
reproduced perfectly, every time, by any individual who could read
English. It was necessary that we decouple knowledge from any one
individual, thereby rendering the flow of goods and services through
our company completely independent of individuality. Those of us in
the office, overwhelmingly a white workforce except for me and two
middle managers (also women, also mothers), made sure that any one
of our floor workers, overwhelmingly black, Latino, and Asian, was
utterly expendable, replaceable. Not even a day's work would be lost if
one worker fell ill, quit, died. Our goal was "continual improvement."
Like many companies in the '80s and '90s, we struggled to transform
from a company that made widgets to a company that provided "service." That was the job where I learned how to use e-mail (for internal
company use at first) and encountered "The Internet." I said good-bye
to DOS commands and hello to globalization. The little oblong gold
sticker on the bottoms of things less frequently said MADE IN KOREA
or MADE IN CHINA and more often was stamped or sewn with MADE
IN INDIA, INDONESIA, VIETNAM, CAMBODIA, or just as often
HECHO EN MEXICO.

That we Korean adoptees were "MADE IN KOREA" has become a
cliché, at least to me and perhaps others of my generation of Korean
immigrants-as-adoptees, the first and second wave, now in our forties
and thirties.

That I was not made in my American mother's body was not so
remarkable to me, or did not signify so much lost, until I became pregnant with my own child. The pregnancy was planned, passionately
though somewhat quickly. Aptly, ironically, I realized I was pregnant
while I was standing in the bathroom at a movie theater—a temple of
reproduction. Gazing into a mirror, another tired trope for adoptees

and for racial self-recognition, and standing in front of rows of bathroom stalls—the place where girls at the prom give birth to their secrets, where other girls vomit up their nourishment, the place to shed and purge.

"What is it like?" my American mother asked me, about my pregnancy.

Though I knew this was not what she was asking, all I could say was, "It's uncomfortable. I'm hot. It's like an oven." I could only focus, with her, on my physical discomfort, not my psychic transformation.

The distance, already significant, between my American mother and me seemed to grow in my mind as my belly swelled with each advancing week. I was reproducing my child, my daughter, in a way foreign to both of us. It was not the way of her labor to bring me into her world as her daughter. Her way was home visits and paperwork and fees and letter writing and waiting.

I wondered if my fertility was an insult to her, or made her revisit the pain of her own infertility. Later I asked her and she said, No, I had come to terms with that before you arrived.

So many things come to term, or we come to them.

As a Westerner, I have been trained to think in terms of compartments, of efficiency, of diagnosis and disease, of problems and how to solve them, then how to make those solutions reproducible. How to keep good records. When we Korean adoptees return to Korea and ask our adoption agencies for our records and are denied them, lied to, or given partial records, we are incensed and confused. We want a utopian form of documentary (or procedural) democracy, a sunshine policy, a Freedom of Information Act. We want to throw off the mantle of shame: we have been taught there is nothing shameful in what we cannot control—our birth, however malformed it was deemed by Korean society then and now.

The New Reproductive Technology:
Still Not Cheap

I am raising my own children, reproduced in the old way, the animal way, in a time in which a woman or a couple of significant means can purchase—or "adopt"—the frozen embryos (viable fertilized human ova) of another couple. Despite being the last and most extreme stop in an array of fertility therapies, it has become commonplace for affluent couples to spend approximately $10,000 a "pop"—per month—for attempted in-vitro fertilization.

This is not only the death of distance but the death of time. I find myself marveling at the ingenuity of science and fearful of our continuing commodification of human life and of the growing chasm of choices between the upper classes and the lower classes in terms of family-making and kinship-maintenance options. I do not object to adoption as an alternate mode of family formation, merely the conditions and privileges that make some bodies (children) more available for migration from (generally) a poor woman with few resources to (generally) a middle-class or wealthy woman with many resources. Often, but not exclusively, this axis is racialized from dark to light, from Southern/Eastern hemisphere to Northern/Western.

I owe my privileged American life to the conquering of distance. I am not wealthy, my American mother is not wealthy, but we live a "First World" existence. Though the computer on which I type this essay runs Windows 98 and was "born" in 1997, it still works to reproduce my language for public consumption, for resale. My American mother (and father) mobilized resources to conquer an ocean and make a permanent intervention in a culture that for thousands of years privileged kinship and lineage. I became her daughter through this reproductive project. Adoption is a technology. I was invented as an American. My Korean mother's part in this transaction I can only guess at, based on historical recovery of other Korean birth mothers' testimony. Many obstacles have been conquered through this technology and there has been joy and despair, lightness and dark. Though my American mother feels grateful and lucky—which is how I am told I should feel—sadly, I often feel merely conquered. I love my American mother but I cannot forget her silent partner. Whether she, my Korean mother, was willing or unwilling, relieved or regretful, I will most likely never discover.

We are taught that technology is rational and transparent and that it exists to make human life better and easier so we can do other things

154   with our lives, rise above our animal origins. Now that technology is so focused on our animal origins—reproduction—what new secrets will brave new generations of daughters and sons seek to unravel? My own story already feels quaint in the face of children of sperm donors seeking out their eight half-siblings, daughters wondering about their egg donors, their gamete mothers. I wish them, and their mothers and fathers, durability of the heart to match the speed of our science.

The Ghost at the Door

Faith Sullivan

My mother had careers and marriages. I lose track of the number of careers, but I remember the number of marriages—six—three times to the same man. She believed, like Auntie Mame, that life was a banquet and she was damned if she was going to miss a thing on the table. From the time I was nine or ten, she was a frenetic butterfly, flickering in and out of my life. A woman of enthusiasms—fast cars, memorable hats, and drinks with funny names—and dauntless affections— friends everywhere—she was not, I'm afraid, a woman of great steadfastness nor perhaps even wisdom. But she had the good sense to see that Grandma's house was the place for me and, later, for my brother.

And Grandma stood at the door, holding it open. Then and always. "Come in, child," she told me on every return, folding me to her.

Grandma's house. It stands even today, at 504 Fifth Street Southeast, Pipestone, Minnesota. Not a ghost house but a clapboard structure with a wraparound sleeping porch where I lay on summer nights those years ago, wrapped in the susurrus of women's voices in the next room. The women are now ghosts.

But I am nurtured by ghosts. Nurtured, inspired, informed by ghosts.

And my ghosts are not finished with me. Through the shifting curtain of time, their voices murmur: Grandma, widowed at fifty-nine when I was twelve; her mother Rosalind and her sister Lily, both widowed young and sharing a house catty-corner across the street; also Lily's daughter Eva, left with four little children when her carpenter husband fell from a tall ladder in the German Lutheran Church.

Eva and her little family lived next door to Great-grandma and Lily, in a house built by the carpenter husband. But now Eva is in the next room, murmuring on the other side of the curtain, with the others.

The cousins, Eva's children and I, breezed in and out of each other's houses, as if they were one. The family had few boundaries. You never knocked and the door was never locked. If you were a child breezing in and out, not infrequently you carried word of Helen Trent or Our Gal Sunday or Ma Perkins, radio soap operas.

Should two or three of the family women be busy picking crab apples from Great-grandma's trees or papering the upstairs hall, unable to listen to their favorite "stories," as they called them, well, someone had to convey the news: "Helen Trent has left Gil, Grandma," Or "Lord Henry sailed for England without Sunday." Whereupon Grandma would stamp her cane on the floor, go misty in the eyes, and deplore, "They never learn."

As if from an old radio, its signal faint, the women's voices float, nattering among themselves about the vagaries of the wealthy and imprudent, those creatures treasured but beyond the reach of sensible women's advice.

Sensible women. I wonder. Hardworking, surely. But could anyone sensible laugh so much? I remember The Girls, grandma's bridge club whose members all belonged to another club as well, a club whose purpose I never really understood, though it seemed to be dessert.

Weeks ahead of her turn to host, Grandma began poring through the Fanny Farmer Cookbook as well as hundreds of tattered and stained scraps of paper stuffed into the Hoosier cupboard in the kitchen, recipes torn from newspapers and magazines. Great-grandma never went near a kitchen, except to get to the bathroom, so Grandma consulted her sister Lily and Lily's daughter Eva, the three of them huddling around the dining room table.

Aunt Lily ventured, "Maybe something with pineapple." She was particularly fond of canned pineapple. "And whipped cream."

"It should be pretty," Eva insisted.

Usually the chosen recipe was so complex—molded and layered in different colors—that Grandma had to prepare it a day or two ahead of time.

During the week prior to The Girls' party, the air in Grandma's house bristled with preparation while we set to cleaning with the Hoover, rag, and scrub pail as if The Girls, upon arrival, would toss down their purses and commence inspecting beneath the cellar stairs, behind the piano, and under the fridge. Table linens, pristine in the buffet drawer, were relaundered and ironed. The good dishes, as dust-free as a fresh bottle of milk, were washed anew. When the day of The Girls arrived, Grandma was flushed and smug, mistress of a house as pure as a newly minted soul.

Dressed in their best georgette or crepe, The Girls trickled in around a quarter to two, trilling their familiar little tunes—"Blanche, you do too much" and "You really shouldn't have" and "How nice the house looks"—the same little tunes Grandma sang at their houses, smiling into their flushed and smug faces. How gay and comforting were The Girls' rituals, a periodic reward for the endless round of good works and toil. From beyond the insubstantial wall of decades, I hear their laughter and feel the throb of their hungers and fears.

The women of my family labored like stevedores, never hiring someone to do what they could learn to do. Money was always tight—each year the same fevered scratching to cover the taxes. Still, we children were not much aware of our poverty. All the women sewed, children's clothes as well as their own, often from flour sacks tricked out with rick-rack or embroidery.

Flour sacks, sprigged with violets or wild roses, also made dish towels and pillow slips. On the old Singer treadle, Grandma ran up bed sheets of unbleached muslin ordered from Monkey Wards. Though the sheets were a little rough and had a thick flat-fell seam down the middle, their very roughness was a strange kind of assurance, especially if you were in bed with cramps, tonsils, or chest trouble.

Except for Great-grandma, who suffered from dropsy, the women rarely phoned for the doctor. No money. Great-grandma traded her handmade quilts for doctor visits. The others, after gathering at the table to consult, "doctored" common and uncommon complaints with home remedies and two or three reliable patent medicines. Poultices and plasters were frequent medicaments.

On Grandma's three-season porch stood a tall green-painted wooden cupboard, a huge old thing filled with herbs and salts and seeds and roots, stored in jars and tiny brown paper bags, all carefully labeled. From this cupboard, Grandma plucked most of our remedies.

And from the cupboard wafted an aroma indescribable—piquant, herbish, medicinal, and foreign. Since you were never supposed to open the cupboard unless sent by Grandma, mystery and possible fatality were undeniably part of the odor.

Because doctors in those days were next to God in the small-town pecking order, and because we rarely called one, I felt a kind of shame about the green cupboard, as if it were an apostasy. Rather than an alliance with nature, it seemed a lapse from grace, and I kept its secrets from anyone outside the family. Today, Grandma would be called an herbalist. In 1600, she'd have been a witch.

My women were economists in the old-fashioned sense of the word—not hoodooists concocting predictions, based on past trends, which six months later prove to be somewhat less reliable than the entrails of chicken hawks, but economists who created much from little.

Whatever stood still long enough to be shot by friends or cousins, the women canned—pheasant, duck, deer, rabbit. And anything that grew in a Minnesota garden or alongside a Minnesota road and wouldn't send you feet-first to the funeral home, they stuffed into a jar—from wild asparagus and ground cherries to horseradish and crab apples.

If it was fruit, embalmed in a Mason jar and eaten from a sauce dish for dessert, along with a slice of homemade angel food cake, Grandma called it "sass." We had apple sass, rhubarb sass, cherry sass, pear sass, and other sasses too numerous to mention.

Condiments? You've no idea: homemade ketchup and mustard, horseradish, pickled onions, pickled beets, pickled apples, watermelon pickles, three kinds (minimum) of dill pickles, gherkins, pickled peaches, and at least six varieties of pickles that have slipped from memory. Through the permeable membrane of years, I smell the heavenly perfume of peaches pickling in clove brine.

By the end of canning season, the women nursed burns up and down their arms from hefting canning racks out of kettles of boiling water. On their wrists, knots called cysts had swollen to the size of jaw breakers, these from peeling and paring and chopping, and tightening jar lids.

But when we all tucked in around Grandma's table or Greatgrandma's, we feasted. And after the feast the women played cards, not in the ladylike way saved for bridge club, but with abandon, pounding the table, throwing up their arms, accusing each other of wicked chicanery, and laughing till they swabbed away tears with hankies.

"Blanche, that's the second time in this hand that you've played the ace of diamonds," Grandma's sister Lily pointed out.

Face washed in milky innocence, Grandma smiled a demure confusion, as simulated as her pearls. "Are you sure?"

They played Lunk or Canasta or Pinochle or Smear—which they pronounced "schmear"—or any faddish nonsense involving a deck of cards. And they played for money. That is, pennies. Where was the fun if something wasn't at stake? Toddling home with an extra fifteen cents in your pocket sent you to bed smiling and humming an old song.

When they didn't play cards after dinner, often they spun out family tales. Never was a family so crammed with saints, sinners, eccentrics, whimsicals, horse thieves, and undiscovered geniuses. The hundredth time that the women dished out the story of Cousin Donald's invention of a virtually gasless engine—the plans stolen by some scoundrel at General Motors (in kahoots with the oil devils), then shelved for eternity—it still inspired fresh sighs and poignant regret: "We'd all be as rich as Rockefeller."

With mystified head-shaking, they recounted the decades-old story of Uncle George, who hightailed it to Montana, never to be heard from again, leaving behind a young wife and child. Dead? Drunk? Living with a floozy? My cousins and I hung upon the scandal stories as limpets cleave to rocks until someone admonished, "Go outside and play," or "Get to that homework."

The best after-dinner entertainment, however, was fortune-telling. Grandma, Eva, Lily, Rosalind—small town oracles—employed tarot cards, tea leaves, coffee grounds, palms, and dream interpretation. They had as many ways of soothsaying as they had varieties of pickles in the fruit cellar. No matter that they had told each other's fortunes the previous night. Fresh fortunes sprang up with the sun each morning.

Such was their reputation for prognostication, that neighbor women and others dropped in day or night to find their destinies in the coffee grounds. "Yoohoo," they called, pushing open the door, "are there coffee grounds?" Sinking onto dining chairs, they pressed, "Will my brother Carl hook up with that frizzy beauty operator from Sioux Falls?" or "I'm praying for a Philco radio. D'ya see it in the cup?"

Cousin Eva, with a nature as fine and soft as babies' hair, worried that the townswomen might be upset by what they heard, so she always assured them, "It's just for fun." Grandma, however, demanded that they pay attention. "You've got to be prepared," she'd tell them. She was saving them from a lot of trouble down the line.

But my women, however slim their purses, never took money for reading cards or palms. If you had a gift, you were supposed to share it. And they were not, after all, gypsies, they would point out.

Now, some religions forbid fortune-telling and, for all I know, the Methodists of that day may have been among them. Nevertheless, the women on that side of the family were all members of the Methodist Ladies Aide, as were many who dropped in for tea and, oh, yes, the tea leaves, if you don't mind. None of them saw anything anti-Christ about pulling aside the curtain of fate. Life was hard. Only a fool would eschew a leg up on the future.

And my women were good at what they did. Days before the accident, my grandmother knew that Eva's husband was going to die. She confided to me one morning that Grandpa had come to her in a dream, warning her. She knew and she hated knowing. Naturally she did not share the dream with Eva until later. You hoped that you were wrong.

That ghosts visited the women is no surprise. Among the staples of family conversation was the story of a woman who had lived next door to Grandma in the small town where Grandpa and Grandma lived in the early days of their marriage—maybe Cottonwood or Woodstock or Trosky. Maddened and ablaze from an exploded kerosene stove, she fled from the house, not thinking to roll on the ground. Not only did her ghost appear in that yard on a number of occasions, a pregnant neighbor who witnessed the woman's flight gave birth to a baby with a wine-color flame across its cheek.

My women—my klatch of mothers—were truth-tellers. If they said that ghosts visited them, ghosts did. After her death, Aunt Lily returned in ectoplasmic form, once to her daughter Eva and another time to one of Eva's sons. Imagine her amazement, she said, to find that the hereafter was a good deal like school, only better. Nothing was compulsory. And Eva, when she visited a daughter and a grandson in the same manner, revealed that the next life was, well, certainly more interesting than the picture Reverend Tuck had painted.

Ghosts come to us in different ways, sometimes murmuring in the next room; sometimes wavering before us, voiceless and grave; and sometimes metaphorically stamping a little foot and announcing, "I'm here."

Grandma does that. She's unpredictable. I'm weeding the garden, showering, driving to the market. I haven't thought of her for several days.

Then, without warning, the air is silver with silent laughter and sweet with Lady Esther face powder. She is not finished with me.

These days, though, it is I who hold the door open for her.

My DocuMama

Anne Ursu

One day about ten years ago, my mother called me with an announcement. "I realized something last night," she said happily. "My mother and my older sister were intellectuals, and all of my life I've felt that I was a failed intellectual. But I'm not a failed intellectual. I'm an artist!"

It would have been difficult to be an artist in that family. My grandparents, Alice and Willard Willis, were quiet, undemonstrative people, and Grandma particularly lived her life in books. She was descended from Mennonites and always seemed constrained. You didn't see them expressing a lot of warmth for each other or for the world—it always seemed locked behind these carefully preserved upstate New York façades. My mother, in contrast, is one of the warmest people you'll ever meet. When I was young she was more reserved, but over the years, perhaps realizing that she didn't have to be her parents, she became more and more open to the world. I never knew that she fancied herself a failed intellectual—she is, after all, a PhD in psychology and very smart—or that she felt bad she did not spend her life immersed in books like her own mother. But when she said she was an artist, I knew instantly she was right.

It all began one Christmas when Mom used her computer to make my brother a gift certificate for a subscription to the *New Yorker*. She wanted it to look like a *New Yorker* cover, and I offhandedly mentioned that you could buy a font that looked like their typeface. She was at a computer store within the hour buying font collections, and that year everyone got intricately-designed, professional-looking gift certificates that Mom had spent hours on.

When I got married a couple of years later, she put together a book—*Anne and John: A Love Story*—as a wedding present. She scanned in photos and documents and told the story of our lives and our courtship. She then made another for my brother and his wife, and a book about my dad for his retirement, and two big scrapbooks for him for a retirement present. "I like to lay things out," she announced cheerfully.

Then she had her epiphany, and suddenly she was not content merely to lay things out anymore. My mother wanted to paint. She immediately signed herself up for classes, turned the attic into a studio, and began to devote her days to art.

"What do you think of Mom being an artist?" I asked my father one day.

"Well," he said slowly, "the other night I woke up because your mother was making noises. I looked over and realized she was singing in her sleep. I thought if you're so happy you're singing in your sleep, something's going right."

Off and on for the next couple of years, my mother painted still lifes. I have one hanging in my living room and no one can believe my mother did it. My brother has another, of a book and a candle so haunting and lovely that I am planning to break into his house and steal it.

As time wore on and she kept doing still lifes, we started trying to convince her to paint something else: "A cat," I would propose. "A portrait," my brother would offer. "A lonely man in a train station," my father would say.

But she wouldn't budge. "This is all I know how to do."

"But why don't you try?"

"This is what I can do."

It was strange to watch my mother set limits on herself, given that she and my father raised us to believe we could do anything we wanted. But, of course, my mother didn't have that; she always felt her mother's critical eye, a steady maternal Superego watching over her.

About a year ago, my mother announced she wanted to make a Ken Burns–style documentary about her parents' experiences during World War II as a family keepsake. My brother and I eyed this prospect with some trepidation; when Mom gets into a project she tends to become rather consumed by it. (We refer to the time she threw the retirement party for my father as "The Year There Was No Christmas.") And indeed she threw herself into it entirely. Suddenly, her office was filled with piles of books and videos. The sound of gunfire and air battles frequently emanated through the house, and we lived our lives to a constant Top Hits of World War II soundtrack, whether coming from the stereo or from my mother herself, unconsciously humming "Boogie Woogie Bugle Boy."

Staying there one night while my husband was out of town, I woke up at 3:00 AM to hear music from the room below. I went downstairs, and Mom was sitting at her desk downloading music from iTunes.

"I couldn't sleep," she breathed, wide-eyed. "I had the best idea!" She had been looking for a way to make a transition into the start of the war—she was going to go from some idyllic pictures of my grandparents' home life right into Pearl Harbor, but didn't know quite how to get there. Until that moment. "I'll play 'Beyond the Blue Horizon,' under these pictures, see?"

I stared at her, uncomprehending.

"How does it end?" she prompted.

This, I knew. "Beyond the Blue Horizon" was one of the lullabies Mom sang most when I was a child. I ran quickly through the lyrics. "My life has only begun. . . . beyond the blue horizon lies a rising sun."

"Rising sun!" she repeated, staring meaningfully at me. "I have footage of sky and then a Japanese fighter coming out of it. Isn't it cool?"

I had to admit it was. "Um, Mom . . . maybe you should go to bed? You can do this in the morning."

"I can't!" she whispered mischievously. "I'm too excited!"

My father called a few months into this project. "Your mother's movie . . ." he said. "I've seen a little bit of it. It's really . . . good."

"It is?"

"Yes. Really, really good."

We never thought it would be. You just don't expect your sixty-three-year-old mother to disappear into her office for six months with a Mac, boxes of photos and letters, and the entire Time-Life World War II video collection and come out with something that should be on PBS. And yet, it should be. It's professional, engaging, and heart wrenching. Using photos, music, home movies, documents, and archival footage, Mom explores her parents' own Love Story against the backdrop of the coming war. We watch as two young, improbably handsome students meet, fall in love, and marry, and in 1939, their daughter Anne, Mom's older sister, is born.

But in the outside world, things are growing dark. War breaks out in Europe, and its shadow looms over America. In September 1940, the secretary of state signs the draft bill, and everything changes. "Dear Daddy, Mother, and Rachel," my grandmother writes in December of that year. "Have I told you all the talk of the draft here? Everyone has a different story and one of them is that all medical men whose numbers come up will be drafted. Willard's number is 581. He expects to get a letter soon. I guess they transfer medical men to the medical reserve as soon as they can, but that takes about six weeks and during the interim they are privates. Can't you see Willard drilling?"

They are able to keep the war at a distance for another year. Willard gets a job at a small practice in Utica, New York, and the young family moves to a pretty white house on Sunnyside Lane. Home-movie footage shows Alice happily reading to a curly-haired, plump-cheeked Anne, and then Anne hurling herself onto her delighted father's lap— the family is so happy, so serene.

And then comes Pearl Harbor.

"The war leaves a dull ache in one's heart," Alice writes in her journal on December 12, 1941. "And apprehension. Perhaps our lovely simple life is over now. How could such things be?" Willard signs up for service a few months later to stay one step ahead of the draft board. They don't know when he'll be called, but they know he's going, and a pall is cast over the white house on Sunnyside Lane. My grandmother's journal entries reflect growing dread:

March 15, 1942
Biggest news lately is that Willard is on the Procurement and Assignment List of first doctors to go to army in this district. It was a terrific blow. . . . If he only stays in this country I won't care if he's a private.

★ ★ ★

April 4, 1942

The things our people say sound as ferocious as the Axis countries. "Nice little show" a British pilot describes a raid on Germany. Sounds like Bruno Mussolini. I suppose you can't wage war without hate. War is hate and murder. We won't see the end of war in my lifetime.

Oh God, I pray Willard is not hurt in the war.

July 15, 1942

Oh, yes, I guess I am pregnant, beginning June 16. I feel fine, except for an empty feeling in the morning sometimes. Let's hope I don't have hemorrhoids and nosebleeds like last time.

That is how the world was introduced to my mother.

There's a picture of the young family at Christmas, just a couple of weeks before Willard was to report to basic training. Three-year old Anne looks wistful, like she knows something is not right, while Willard is clutching her hands and staring at her as if trying to imprint her on his mind forever. A pregnant Alice looks off into space, her face fixed in an expression of loss and dread. Three weeks later, Willard puts his seven-months-pregnant wife and three-year-old daughter on a train bound toward her family while he heads off to basic training. While he's there, my grandmother writes him long, adoring letters, adorned with a thin veneer of cheerfulness, "Do have a good time, my beloved," she tells him, "and be happy. It won't last long."

Of course, it does—Willard will be in the army for twenty months, he will serve in Belgium, England, and France, and when he returns, he will be changed and so will his wife.

My mom was born two months after her father left. When Willard came back he did not know what to do with his spirited new daughter who threw food—a crime to him, after seeing children starve in France. And it may be that neither Alice nor Willard knew quite what to do with each other either.

"I read their letters and I don't know who these people are," my mother said to me once. "They're so warm and loving with each other, I just don't recognize them."

My mother, who would only paint still lifes, who feels too strongly the weight of her limitations, taught herself to make a movie on the computer without a second thought, and it's damn good.

Now, my mother is readying the next installment in the series—the war years. My aunt Jane, who was born in 1948, is transcribing the war letters and is now so involved she wants to go to Europe and see where her father was. Together, the sisters watch footage of soldiers doing basic training, and they weep. "Poor Daddy," my aunt says, her voice cracking.

"The movie is for my grandkids," Mom says, beaming proudly. "I want them to know where they came from. I want them to know my parents."

Through this process, Mom has come to know her parents too. By making the movie, she has brought back the people my grandparents were before war made them shut down from the world, and she understands better who they were afterwards. By making the movie, she has undone some of the damage of war.

I wish I could record Mom making this movie, so my grandkids could get to know her. I would show them everything, the 3:00 AM work sessions because she was too excited to sleep, the office that looked like a World War II archive after a tornado, the strange sounds and lights that came from behind her closed door, the glee that spread across her face as she solved a storytelling problem, the pride she felt showing her product to the family. This is my mother, I would tell future generations. She is a storyteller, she is a memory-keeper, she is a documentarian, she conquers war, she is dear and loving, she embraces the world, and she is limitless. My mother is an artist, and this is the power of art.

Butterfly Cycles

Ka Vang

We stumbled in darkness down the dirt road. Dawn's red rays radiated from the distant horizon, allowing me to see my mother sauntering with my sisters a few steps in front of me. Holding one daughter on each side of her, my mother gripped their tiny hands, as though she was afraid the wind would blow them away. I was unsure about the time, but I was sure everyone was asleep in the tiny town of Belvidere, Illinois.

We lived with my father's younger brother on the edge of town, near County Road G, past a brick Methodist church, past the row of dead elm trees, down a dirt road without a name. My father lived with his first wife and their three children near the Dairy Queen on a paved road with a name in the center of town.

I heard mother's voice first, and then my ears filled with a symphony of cricket cries that had earlier lulled me to sleep.

"Don't make a noise," she whispered as she gently tugged me awake. "Wake up your sisters. I have to pack."

Through half-closed eyes I saw her putting our clothes into plastic Kmart bags.

She acted strange last night when she insisted that we go to bed wearing our next-day clothes.

"Why?" asked Nee, who was three at the time.

"Don't question me," she answered sharply. "Ka, help your younger sisters put their clothes on."

I nodded obediently.

"Even the shoes," she added.

I tied Nee's shoelaces before putting her to sleep on the bed.

"When will I learn to make butterflies?" asked Nee. In order to get my two younger sisters to put on their shoes, I created a story of tying shoelaces as being a way to create butterfly wings. I did not know how to tie shoelaces any way besides making two loops, which I called butterfly wings, and knotting them together. Our mother would not allow us to play outside without shoes, so we had to make butterfly wings and put our shoes on to play outside. Sometimes when we became bored, I made up fantastical worlds with giants and unicorns, but the only way to enter these worlds is with our butterfly-wing shoes.

"Make butterfly wings for me too!" insisted Youa, who was just a year older than Nee. "I don't want to be a caterpillar." Being a caterpillar was punishment for being disobedient, so we couldn't go outside to play or enter our magical worlds if we were caterpillars.

"Can we go outside?" asked Nee. "We have our shoes on. We want to be butterflies."

In a Hmong household, we take off our shoes at the door. In fact, it's one of the first things you are taught as a Hmong: how to eat rice, respect the ancestors, and take your shoes off at the door. All the children slept with our mom in the tiny bedroom on the Salvation Army queen-sized mattress that was just about the same size as the room. On the nights that our father came to see us and slept over, the children slept on the floor. My mother said everything we owned was in the room, because everything else belonged to my uncle and his wife and children. They were kind enough to allow us to live with them, but deliberately cruel when they reminded my mother that she was the lowly second wife, dependent on their kindness to survive. I recalled pleas that led to insults when my mother begged my father to move us into an apartment of our own. Always, he said he couldn't afford to pay the rent on two apartments.

"She's the first wife, and you are the second wife," he always answered. "Know your place."

"At least teach me how to drive," she asked.

He only laughed at her second request.

In the weeks leading up to our night-time flight, my mother stopped asking my father about the apartment. This made my father visit us more.

"Don't waste your time being here with the second wife and her useless daughters," my uncle said during one of my father's visits. "You should be spending time with your sons from the first wife."

There was one thing worse than being a second wife: it was being a second wife with only daughters and no sons. Daughters were not valued because they would grow up to marry a stranger and no longer be a part of the family. All the resources that were given to a daughter would one day benefit another family, another Hmong clan. Also, daughters could not carry the family name.

When my mother and her daughters left the house, we did not steal anything that belonged to my uncle, but we acted like thieves, creeping silently out of our bedroom, down the long hallway, passing my uncle's bedroom where his snores told us he was having a good dream, through the living room and out into night.

I carried the heavy plastic bags, too heavy to be clothes only. I learned years later that in the bags were my mother's dowry presents from her parents, including a silver necklace that weighed about five pounds. When I complained about the bag's heaviness on my tiny arms, she answered, "Be a good girl, and do as I say. That bag and you three daughters are the only things that belong to me."

Sensing my confusion through the darkness, she added, "Don't be scared. We're no longer caterpillars. We are butterflies now."

I didn't know my mother knew about the butterfly stories I told Nee and Youa. As my eyes adjusted to the ebony landscape so I could make out the silhouette of my mother, a strange noise emerged. The noise sounded like a crying cat following us. No, it was not following us. It was ahead of us, at least of me. In the darkness I didn't realize that it was actually my mother weeping. It wasn't until I was older, much older, when my husband asked me for a divorce, that I cried the same way—long, low, almost purring.

My father was a rich and respected man in Laos. Affluent Hmong men in Laos were polygamists, whose numerous wives showed off their status in the community. In America, my father was just another poor refugee.

When my father brought his second wife, my mother, home to his bamboo-and-banana-leaf village after a quick wedding ceremony, his first wife was waiting for them at the door of her hut. The first wife was a chubby woman with dark hairy skin like a coconut shell. But her inside were not sweet; she was bitter. On the day of my parents' wedding, bitterness flowed out of every orifice of her body.

"Did you expect me to welcome you?" she asked with her sausage arms folded as my father and his new wife tried to enter the house. "You are never going to come inside this house or me again."

The villagers converged on the hut to watch the show, which was guaranteed to be more exciting than a bullfight during the New Year festival. The men waited impatiently for the first and second wives to locked horns, while the women giggled, covering their mouths with their hands because it was crude to laugh with their mouths open.

Grinning like a hyena on a full moon, my father let his first wife's words bounce off him. His numerous brothers, who were part of the wedding party, also chuckled. Their contagious laughs spread to the other villagers like a disease until giggles ascended like a line of smoke to the cloudless sky.

My father confessed to my mother that he already had a wife on their way to his village. He waited until they were married and she was far from her village so it would be impossible for her to return there.

"Just think of the second wife as your younger sister," said my father to the first wife, winking at their two sons standing behind her. "She'll help you around the house. I brought her home for you."

"Then she'll share my bed and not yours?" she retorted, pushing her sons back into the dark hut.

"Enough! We are not children," said the village chief, who also happened to be my grandfather. "Step out of the way, daughter-in-law, and let my son enter his house. It belongs to my son. Do you want to be sent back to your clan as a divorcee for disobeying the Vang clan?"

The first wife didn't flinch at his threat. She had her weapons, her sons, the most prized possession in a Hmong family.

"My whole village told me not to marry Vangs, but I didn't listen to them because I fell in love with him."

She pointed accusingly to my father.

"You came to my village to court me! You said my voice was as beautiful as the wind and my skin was as white as pearls."

"Shut up!" he exclaimed, embarrassed that she was exposing their courtship to the village.

"Why do you treat me like an unwanted dog that no longer has any use?" the first wife asked. "I gave you healthy sons."

My father didn't need my mother, but he desired her. To the Hmong, a second or even third wife meant power. Polygamy meant my father was a man, man enough to sleep with several different women and still wake up at dawn to till the fields, feed the ox, and slaughter chickens. He was man enough to father as many children as he wanted and be able to feed them all. He was man enough to run a household of jealous sirens vying for his affection and discipline them when their emotions got out of hand. Men were intelligent beings, and women were livestock meant to be cultivated, sold, and used until they withered with age. When their freshness evaporated, men purchased another piece of meat.

My father, who was western-educated, never saw himself as a polygamist. He thought the practice was crude and demonstrated to Europeans how backwards the Hmong were; but the first wife had become lazy, refusing to cook and play hostess for him. For an important man such as my father, the first wife's disobedience was unacceptable. A second wife was needed to fulfill all the duties the first wife could not.

"If you had done your duties, a second wife would not be needed!"

"Lie," she retorted. "You couldn't resist a younger woman. Divorce me!"

"Why would I do that?"

· My father did not want to lose his precious sons if there was a divorce.

The first wife didn't see the villagers' leering eyes or hear their ridicule. Through her tears, she focused on a dew drop dripping off a leaf like a pearl from the mammoth ginger tree nearby. The pearl disappeared when it hit the soggy road. The little girl left her body and was replaced with a woman—a vengeful woman.

"Stop crying. You sound like a pig being sacrificed to our ancestors," said her annoyed husband. "You're upsetting my sons."

She tried saying something, but choked on her tears. Her shaking hand rose and pointed accusingly at my father again.

"You are scaring my sons," he screamed, stepping forward with his fist clutched so tightly that his knuckles turned white. But my grandfather blocked his way.

"We have shown enough ugliness in our hearts to the world today. Whatever you want to say and do to her, you can do in private," whispered the village chief to his son's ears. "Let her disgrace herself and her clan with this public display. In the end, you will have your way. You are the man."

"I will break your bones like I broke your heart," he calmly told the first wife, and then he chuckled like a hungry hyena raking over his victim.

"It will not be the first time you beat me."

My mother shook her head in disbelief. Maybe he would hit the first wife and not her, but she was wrong.

"Enough! I need rest."

My father grabbed my mother's hand and the two of them prepared to go past the first wife into the hut.

"Rest? Is that what they call sex nowadays?" blasted the first wife, shoving her sons back into the bamboo house, before closing the door, and locking them inside. She picked a green camouflage army bag resting next to the doorway.

"Where did you get the bag?" inquired my father. "Did you whore yourself to the Americans to get the bag?"

"While you were out finding another wife, I went to Americans for rice. Instead I got this!" she said, picking up the bag and slinging it on her shoulders.

The first wife pulled a grenade from the bag, took the pin out, and flung it at my parents. The villagers scattered like a pile of leaves being blown apart by a gust of menacing monsoon wind. Some of the villagers screamed for the newlyweds to run, while others yelled, "Jump!"

That is exactly what they did. My father and mother leaped backwards, tripping onto their backs as the grenade exploded on the ground in front of them. Dust and dirt erupted into the air. The explosive carved a crater in the soil at the tip of their feet.

"Mother, please don't kill Father," pleaded the first wife's sons, who had opened the door just in time to witness their father's attempted murder. "Please don't kill Father!"

"Shut up, you little dogs!" she shouted through the commotion. "He is no longer alive to us. He is no longer alive to us."

She repeated these words as she yanked a second grenade pin with her teeth, tasting the pin as though it was an aphrodisiac before hurling it towards the newlyweds, who had just gotten back on their feet. They bounded backwards again, and this time the grenade landed on the very spot where they had fallen moments before. Dirt flew into their eyes, blinding them, and into their mouths, making them choke.

"You are a pig. Eat mud like a pig," the first wife shouted, reaching into the bag for another grenade. Some of the people who ran to the edge of the village and were now safe from the first wife's wrath began to laugh at my father and his two wives. Their laughter and other cries created from the chaos sounded like a dying elephant wheezing in pain.

"As soon as I take care of you, I will finish off your children, so there will be nothing left of you on this earth."

The villagers gasped in unison at her threat. Their horror did not stop the first wife from throwing another grenade at her husband and the second wife. The newlyweds leaped again to escape another grenade and fell in a filthy pigpen.

"Stop! Stop! Stop!" screamed an old Hmong woman, emerging out of the jungle's green curtain. Her voice stunned the first wife so the grenade in her hand slipped, making a loud thump when it landed on her feet. The bag slipped from her shoulders and opened when it hit the dusty red earth. A dozen grenades rolled out.

The old woman was the first wife's mother from the village on the other side of the mountain. She had heard that her son-in-law had taken a second wife and knew her temperamental daughter would react foolishly.

The sagging woman, with the earth pulling down her droopy breasts, face, and stomach, hugged her daughter.

"This is not the way to handle a second wife," she whispered to the first wife. "We will put a curse on her so she only has daughters."

Later that night as my father and mother, bodies sweaty and intertwined, created me in a bamboo-and-banana-leaf hut, the first wife and her mother brewed a curse in a cauldron.

The shamans my mother consulted told her the curse must be why she conceived only daughters. She repeatedly saw shamans, herbalists, and fortune tellers for help conceiving sons—in Laos, in the dirty refugee camp in Thailand, and after we finally got to Belvidere in 1985, when I was five. My mother made $3.75 an hour cleaning motel rooms at a dingy Norman Bates–style motel off the Interstate, and almost every penny she earned went to the cause. She paid more attention to her imaginary-not-born-yet son than to her daughters, and as the oldest I was expected to be the mother when she became disinterested in us. But the shamans all told her the same thing: you are cursed by the first wife. Did any of them see in their magic eggs, teacups, and trances that my mother planned to leave my father?

The night we ran away, she was playing the mother role, deciding our fates. We walked quite a distance before a woman in a metallic gold Chevy pulled over and offered us a ride. I didn't know who she was, but my mother seemed familiar with her. Maybe she was just a kindly stranger who wanted to help out a woman with her three children in the middle of the night. To this day, I still don't know who that woman was or even if my mother knew her.

She dropped us off at the Greyhound bus station near the Dairy Queen and the apartment where my father was sleeping soundly with his other family. No one bothered looking at us when we entered the one-room bus station that looked like it had been frozen in the 1950s. Even the man who sold us our bus tickets looked like he belonged in a Norman Rockwell painting. The people and the room were all colored in soft browns, whites, and blues: the browns of the faded wooden benches and floor, the pale white faces waiting for their buses to come in, the soft blues of the wall and even softer blue morning sky beyond the windows. Only the prune-faced man sleeping on the wooden bench, covered with yesterday's newspaper like it was a comfortable blanket, looked like he didn't belong.

We were not painted that day with soft colors; instead our bodies and faces were a hard jaundiced yellow, and our black hair resembled the color of crow's feathers. We sat on the only other wooden bench in the station. I looked at it with its scratches, dents, and names carved into its pieces. The bench reminded me of my mother, used and abused, yet she and the bench's pieces were still solid, unwilling to be broken by life's hardness.

"I want Smurfs," declared Youa, suddenly remembering that it was Saturday.

"I want King Vitamin," insisted Nee. King Vitamin was the free cereal that was given to us at the market when we went to get our government cheese and milk.

"Let's go watch cartoons," I said, hoping to distract the two of them so they wouldn't ask for other things. I knew questions made my mother nervous because she didn't have the answers for them.

We sat on the wooden bench and forgot about our night-time flight, engrossed in the lives of Smurfs, Superman, and Captain Kangaroo. At first my mother paced the bus station and nervously looked outside as though she expected my father to show up. Did she want him to show up? After a while she sat next to us and watched cartoons. We sat through four thirty-minute cartoon shows and countless cereal commercials until the man behind the counter walked towards us.

"Ma'am, your bus for Chicago is leavin' any minute now!" he screamed. "Didn't you hear me make the announcement?"

My mother answered him by nodding her head since she didn't understand a word he said. We had only been in the country for a year, so her English was just as good as my kindergarten-level English.

"Chicago is a big terminal; it's not like Belvidere, but just show them your ticket with the final destination of Sheboygan, Wisconsin," he said. "Good luck, Lady."

"Let's go," she said grabbing Nee and Youa as she did before.

I couldn't move.

"Let's go, Ka!" she yelled when she noticed I was not coming with her. "I can't carry all three of you."

My eyes stayed glued to the television set. I pretended not to hear her.

"I can't do this without you," she said. "I need you to carry the bags. Be a good girl and help your mother."

I was through being the obedient oldest daughter, just as she was sick and tired of being the disrespected second wife. We were both going to break out of our roles.

"Lady, the bus is going to leave without you," announced the clerk.

Although my mother didn't know his exact words, she understood the meaning.

"Your father doesn't love you," she declared. "He has another family, so you have to come with me."

My eyes never left the television set. She threw her hand up in the air as though she was asking the heavens to help, then she kneeled down so we were eye to eye.

"Your father doesn't love you because you are a girl," she said. I felt as though cold icy hands gripped my heart and began to squeeze it until I was unable to breathe. My relatives had told me that my father didn't love us because of our gender, but I never believed them until now. My mother never lied to me before, so why would she lie about this? But I wasn't mad at my father for not loving me. I was mad at my mother for confirming the truth. I was definitely not going with her.

When the truth didn't work, she used a different strategy: she offered me my very own Barbie doll. Nee, Youa, and I had to share a three-year-old Malibu Barbie doll with a missing right arm (it was ripped off when Nee and Youa fought over it), blonde Mohawk (I gave her an extreme hair cut I saw in a magazine), and shredded legs (no one owed up to being the cause). Next my mother offered me candy. My six-year-old mind couldn't be bribed. I didn't want to leave Belvidere, not because I loved my father more than her. But somehow I thought my mother was being a coward by running away. She should have stayed and fought for my father against the first wife. She should have fought for people to respect her. I never wanted to be a coward like her, running away from my problems instead of facing them.

"Help me," my mother muttered in Hmong, then English, to the clerk.

He picked me up like I was a doll. I didn't kick, scream, or cry;

instead I made my body stiff and heavy so he would have a hard time carrying me.

I couldn't accept that we ran away from my father until we arrived in Sheboygan where my mother had relatives. We stayed with her family for three months, until my father came and got us. I don't know why she went back to him, since she made such an effort to get away in the first place. A year after we returned to my father, we ran away again from him. By this time my mother had her driver's license and we lived in our own apartment, but she was still the second wife without any sons. In a beat-up station wagon, she drove us back to Sheboygan. During the journey, mother reminded me of the station wagon, with its broken engine, torn seat covers, black fumes spurting out of the muffler; her will to reach her desired destination overcame her weaknesses. The second time we stayed almost two years. I had forgotten my father's face. When he visited us and offered me a Snickers as I played marbles at the playground, I turned the offer down because my mother told me not to accept candy from strangers. She ran away from him four times and took us with her each time.

Those experiences of running away with my mother as a child influenced my adult relationships. I swore that I would not run away from a relationship, even a bad one. Maybe that is why it took me five years to leave a bad relationship in my early twenties. I didn't want to be like my mother, someone who thought running away was the answer to life's obstacles. I hated it even more that she always returned, someone who had no will to see her actions through. When I was through with a relationship, I never looked back.

"Can you help me up the steps?" I asked my husband of eight years after he returned from a short business trip. "I know it's only a couple of steps into our home, but either you help or I'm crawling."

While he was gone, I had fallen and torn three ligaments in my left ankle. At first I wasn't sure if I saw it correctly, but my husband rolled his eyes at my request. Then, he dragged me up the steps with the same tenderness that Jimmy Stewart showed dragging Kim Novak up the mission's stairs as he was about to murder her in *Vertigo*. Biting my lips from the pain until I tasted blood, I searched my husband's eyes for clues to his cruel behavior, but I saw only venom.

"I want a divorce," hissed my husband that night in bed.

My first reaction was disbelief: after all, we had problems in our imperfect relationship, yet we never mentioned the D-word. After eight years of marriage, our relationship slowly became predictable, even boring. My second reaction was that he was mad at me for spraining my ankle again and didn't want to take care of me. My last reaction was about my weight. I blamed myself for gaining sixty pounds since we married. That was the reason he no longer wanted to have sex with me and the real reason he was divorcing me.

"I'm not divorcing you because of those reasons," he answered. "I just don't have that gooey feeling inside my heart for you any longer."

Gooey feeling?

"I'm looking for the love of my life!" he added.

I thought I was the love of his life; at least that is what he told me when we married. I felt as though he had ripped my heart out of my chest and started playing hockey with it. A few times in our relationship, when our arguments became heated, he had disappeared for a few hours, a few days, but he always returned home. And I always took him back. It wasn't until recently that I realized my husband was a lot like my mother. Even though I spent my whole life trying not to be like my mother in relationships, I married a man just like her.

"Why do you leave and come back?" I asked him once after he disappeared for three nights and on the fourth day showed up for breakfast, acting as though nothing had happened.

"It's in my nature, baby," he repeated several times, trying to understand it himself.

A week after his divorce announcement, I left for a two-week business trip to San Francisco. While I was away, we communicated only through formal e-mails with subject lines like Arrived safely in San Fran, Bills paid for the month, Pick up dry cleaning on Tuesday. But in one of those e-mails, he agreed to pick me up from the airport.

"Hey, it's me!" I screamed into my husband's cell phone voicemail over the airport noise when I returned. "My flight's landed, and I am at the luggage claim waiting for you to pick me up."

It was my fourth message. A feeling of dread crept over me when I called him the fifth time, but I still lied to myself and made up excuses: his cell phone wasn't charged up so he couldn't get my calls, or he was called into work for an emergency and had no way of letting me know, or got into an accident on his way to the airport to pick me up. The last excuse was the most romantic one, and I think I got it from a movie.

"I'll catch a cab," I spoke after the beep during my sixth call. "I love you and can't wait to see you again."

I opened the door, feeling relieved to be home after being gone for fourteen days. I knew immediately he was gone. His books, CDs, and even his hermit crabs were still where they belong. The only thing missing was him. On the computer was a yellow Post-It note with the words: Divorce.

I unpacked and tidied the house. It wasn't until I washed the dirty dishes and couldn't see through the tears that I realized I was crying. I was crying the same way my mother cried that early morning we left my father for the first time: long, low, almost purring. That is when I realized that in relationships whether you are the one who runs away or gets left behind, breaking up is painful.

I wondered if my soon-to-be former husband would be like my mother and come back. Would I be like my father and chase after him? The thought that my husband and I had the same relationship as my parents immediately dried my eyes. Instead, I laughed. It was a hearty laughter that came from the pit of my belly, shocking me with its power.

I went over to the closet and got my oldest pair of sneakers. I sat down and made two big loops like butterfly wings and knotted them together. When I walked out the door, I felt like a butterfly emerging from her caterpillar cocoon, ready to take flight. With my wings I was going to explore a magical new world.

Tough Love

Wang Ping

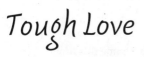

From the Tiger Leaping Gorge on the Golden Sand River, I call my
mother.

"Hello?"

"Are you in Shanghai now? Are you coming home this time?"

"I'll be in Shanghai tomorrow morning and fly back to Minnesota
the next day. I have nothing planned except for a visit to Chongming
Island. Have you been there? It's an amazing place. We can meet at the
airport at 10:00 and take a cab to the ferry. We can hang out on the
island and eat hairy crabs. It's not the season, but I'll find some for
you."

Mother loves Chongming hairy crabs. A brief silence, then she says,
"See you tomorrow."

"Happy New Year, Mother," I say. But she's gone.

I begin to descend the steep mountain road. I must reach the ferry
and cross the river before sunset, then climb to the mountain top
where a four-wheel truck is waiting to take me back to Lijiang Airport
for my early morning flight. It's going to be a long journey.

Tomorrow Mother and I will meet again. We parted in New York
ten years ago, angry with each other, and I thought I'd never see her
again. I thought I finally listened to my sister's warning: Mother is a
tiger, and I'm a chicken. The farther I'm away from her, the safer
I feel.

I've wanted to talk to my mother all my life. I fantasize us sitting close,
my head on her shoulder, and we chat, laugh, and cry like a normal
mother and daughter. I've got my entire life bottled up inside—my
desire to love and be loved. But whenever I face her, I'm tongue-tied.

"Why do you pull a long face as if someone wronged you?" my late

Shanghai grandma would chide. "You scuffle and scowl like an orphan, and you'll end up like one. Smile and talk sweet if you want to be loved."

I tried. I pulled my mouth from ear to ear, a smile like Mother's that conquered the world. After a few hours' practice, my father slapped me on the head and told me to "cut out the monkey grimace." So I picked up singing. "Just forget it," shouted my father. "No one can sing like your mother except for your sister." True, Mother was known on the island as the queen of beauty, fashion, and wit. When she was not around, the house felt empty, and Father moved listlessly as if he had lost his soul. When she came home, smiling with her pearly teeth shining in the sunset, her white and black polka-dot dress billowing like a flower, Father's eyes lit up. The whole navy compound lit up.

Mother was eighteen when she met my father in Shanghai in 1956. Born in a poor peasant family, he ran away at sixteen to join Mao's army, fighting the Japanese, then the Guomindang Nationalists. He rose from an illiterate peasant boy to a battalion commander, then captain of a minesweeping ship in the East China Sea. My mother had just graduated from high school and started teaching. It was love at first sight, but his marriage proposal was met with vehement opposition. My mother's mother called him a country bumpkin. My father's mother called my mother a husband stealer.

Back at home in Shandong, my father had a fiancée, a peasant girl picked by my grandma. She was hoping for a grandson when my father turned sixteen. But he ran away instead, and the girl moved in to help my grandma in the house and fields. After twelve years of waiting, she got a letter from my father asking her to dissolve the arranged engagement. She vowed that she would stay home and take care of her aging would-be in-law for the rest of her life—the only choice for a twenty-nine-year-old spinster at the time. My grandma, who had never traveled away from her village, took three buses and a two-day boat ride to Shanghai to plead with her son to marry the good girl at home. When he refused, she went to his boss. Perhaps his adultery would get him dismissed from the Navy? There she met her future in-law, who was screaming at the navy commander that his young captain had raped her underage daughter and got her pregnant.

The two ladies had a spitfight that ended with scratched faces and torn hair in the office of my father's boss.

Under normal circumstances, my father would have been discharged with dishonor. An engagement, arranged or voluntary, was a commitment. But Red China was young and people worshiped the Communist Party with religious fervor. Every girl wanted to date a People's Liberation Army soldier decorated with medals, and many officers, taking advantage of China's new marriage law, started divorcing their old wives back home, causing disruptions in the Communist Party's old base in the north. The army finally issued an edict that soldiers must carry out the revolutionary morality by remaining faithful to their lifelong companions. But due to revolutionary demands, officers above the rank of battalion commander could get a divorce and remarry with the Party's permission.

My father was one of those lucky officers. At the age of twenty-seven, he married a Shanghai girl eight years younger, who loved to sing, dance, laugh, and have sex.

I was their first-born, an ugly, awkward child. "It must be from your wet-nurse's milk," my mother often said. A month after my birth, she went back to teaching, and my grandma hired a peasant woman to breast-feed me. "You're just like her, quiet and stubborn, and dumb like a cow." I broke bowls, burned rice, forgot to sweep the corners or mop under the bed. I couldn't bargain at the market or cut in lines to get meat, tofu, and other rationed goods. My mother would hit me with a special bamboo stick she kept behind the door. She hit all of her four kids, but somehow I really fired her temper. I was lazy, sullen, stubborn, a dead ghost, an abacus that moved only when pushed around. I dreaded her smile. It was the star that lit my father's eyes, but for me, it was the snake's bite.

"Your mother is a tigress," my Shandong grandma would mutter. "She's devoured your father and is devouring all of us."

Before I turned fifteen, I secretly moved my city residency registration to the countryside, a suicidal act at that time. Once a peasant, forever a peasant. The chance to return to the city was almost zero. But I had to get away. I had tried to join the army, the only chance for young people to get a job. I told the recruiter I was eighteen, even though I was fourteen and looked like twelve. The nurse measured my pulse and told me to go home. I glanced at the chart. My pulse was 180 a minute. I wasn't surprised. My heart had been burning with the desire for college. It was the wildest of all wild dreams. I had no formal education. The Cultural Revolution started when I was a second-grader. School was closed, then reopened, but we only studied Maoism until we graduated from middle school. I had no math, chemistry, physics, geography, or history. But it didn't stop me from dreaming. College had just reopened that year and started admitting three kinds of people: soldiers, workers, and peasants. Since I had no means to become a soldier or worker, I became a peasant, so I could be sent to college by the People's Commune as a re-educated youth. My chance was one in a million. But it was my only chance. I would never be beautiful or charismatic like my mother, but I would have a college degree.

I got one from Beijing University, after twelve years working in the fields and schools, then two master's degrees in New York, then a PhD, while writing poetry and novels on the side. I should have been happy, and I was, for about a day, a week before I became restless again and my eyes wandered off to the next goal. Finally my shrink said, "Why don't you spend some time with your mother? Just talk to her, hold her hands, and cook together. Create an atmosphere where you could be a daughter."

So I got a sublet in the East Village and invited Mother. She would stay with me for three months, enjoy a blissful mother-daughter reunion, and I'd be whole again, just like the days in the womb.

"Are you sure you want to do this?" my sister called from Germany. "I have consulted fortune tellers, and each one of them said it would end badly. You two are not meant for each other."

I said I had to try this one more time.

"Try not to kill each other," she said, and hung up.

In the winter of 1996, I picked up Mother at JFK. I hadn't seen her for seven years, but we greeted each other casually, as if we lived together. She had aged and put on some weight but still walked with vigor toward the long taxi line. Even in a foreign land, she knew where to go. I followed with her baggage cart.

"Your dad is gone almost seven years. Now I'm ready to date," she said in the cab. "Lots of men have been running after me. But I have no appetite. Your dad was an ocean that made all other men dirty puddles. And who will ever hold me up that high? But I heard Americans are different. They love Asian women. They treat them like queens."

"So you want to date Americans only?"

She laughed. "If you put it that way, yes."

"I know a lot of Americans, poets, writers, or students, most of them married, and the rest have no jobs and live in studio apartments infested with rats."

"You mean you've squandered twelve years on poets and students only, and you haven't built a pool of prospective men for your future? You're heading toward forty-something, not young anymore. When are you going to get serious about life?" she raised her voice.

"I've been writing my dissertation, Mom. I just got two books published, and a third coming out."

She waved her hand. "Well, poets are for the young and romantic. I'm almost sixty, need to be practical. Don't you know anyone who actually has a job?"

"I do. Dr. Zhang."

"How much does he make a month? What kind of a doctor? No gynecologist, please. I don't want someone who peeks into vaginas every day."

"He does acupressure. Strong hands that can break bones. His treatment hurts like hell, but you feel like a newborn afterwards. Imagine all the free treatments you'll get."

Her lips pulled down. "You mean he gives massages for a living? You want your mother to date a duck?"

"He's not a duck."

"A duck for a man is a chicken for a woman. Where have you been all these years? Duck means gigolo as chicken means hooker, the lowest of the low!"

"He's not a gigolo, Mom, he's a masseuse, no, an acupressure doctor, a well-respected trade. This is America. A masseuse or hair dresser is not a synonym for gigolo or hooker. Besides, Dr. Zhang is almost sixty."

"Call him whatever you want, but he's a massage man. How much did you say he brings home every month?"

"I don't know. I pay him thirty dollars a shot. If he has ten patients a day, that'll be three hundred."

"Set me up, then," she said. "Remember, my visa expires in three months."

Now I got worried. Dr. Zhang was not only my friend but also my painkiller. Once a week, he came to my apartment, loosening my stiff body with his steely hands. When I screamed in pain, he just smiled his Buddha smile and said, "A little pain is good for the heart." He told me stories about his life in China, Taiwan, and New York: married three times, had many girlfriends, but none worked out. Women only wanted three things from him: money, green card, and free massage.

"I guess I don't have luck with them," he smiled. "But at least I have health."

Would he have better luck with my mother? According to my sister, there was nothing but emptiness in our mother's zodiac. Whoever lived with her was sure to die, like our father, or go limp, like our brother. She was not supposed to have a husband, not supposed to have kids at all. I asked if it meant we'd all die young or have bad luck for the rest of our lives.

"It means our mother has only the empty names of wife and mother, but none of the benefits," my sister snapped. "She's destined to be alone."

That's exactly what Mother complained about: she had worked like a horse, yet still pinched pennies to get by in her old age.

What if she didn't like Dr. Zhang? What if she chewed him up the way she chewed my father alive? If things went bad, I'd lose Dr. Zhang. Maybe he had a way to please her. Maybe his intrepid fingers would loosen her up and break her down.

I made an elaborate dinner for them. Mother was polite and proper, talking about her life as the wife of a high-ranking officer, a popular teacher and singer. Dr. Zhang sweated and popped his knuckles. Without his homemade baby-blue doctor's uniform, he looked out of place.

I thought the dinner had failed, but a few days later, Mother announced she was going on a bus tour to Niagara Falls. I asked if she needed any more money; she winked and said everything was taken care of. I was shocked. She had never said "no" to money. In her mind, I could never give enough for all the pains she had gone through. Three days after her arrival in New York, I wrote a four-hundred-dollar check out of my student stipend, along with a registration form for a bus tour to D.C., Virginia, and Philadelphia. I needed to buy some time alone to write my dissertation. When I was working at my desk, she'd sit next to me drinking tea and chatting whenever she liked.

"Can't you take a break from the books," she'd say. "They don't really make you smarter or richer, you know."

She would go quiet for five minutes after my tearful plea, then start again. "The screen will make you go blind, and the radiation will shrivel your breasts, make you lose hair and eyebrows. Then you'll have no hope ever to find a date, let alone a husband."

She had pocketed the check and showed no sign of leaving after a week passed by. When I asked if she had signed up with Golden Luck Travel, she said she had put the check in her savings account. "Tour bus is not for me. I'd rather die than spend a week with a group of quacking old ladies."

What made her go this time?

"Have you seen Dr. Zhang lately?" I asked.

She smiled. "He might turn out to be a real gentleman. We'll see."

I called Dr. Zhang. He admitted they had hung out a few times in parks and restaurants. "Hope you don't mind I take your mother away for a few days."

"Take her as long as you want, Dr. Zhang."

The first day she was gone, I couldn't write a word. I missed her terribly, though I wished she'd be away longer, three weeks instead of three days. Perhaps she and Dr. Zhang would marry quickly. On the third day, when I finally wrote a paragraph on the pain of footbinding, I heard stomping footsteps.

"What a monster you have introduced me to!" she cried as she burst in.

"Monster?" I murmured and turned to her with a stiff neck.

"A sex fiend, worse than your father," she sang, cheeks flushed like a crazed girl.

I dodged her eyes. How could I dampen her urge to talk about father's virility this time? For the past three weeks, she had been telling me stories about their sex life in graphic detail. When I begged her to stop, she shouted, "What are you ashamed of? Your father was a man. He wanted me every day, twice, three times a day. But I was too young to appreciate him, and too busy with four kids and a demanding job. I don't know why he started drinking and smoking in his late forties. I guess he never got the promotions he deserved in the navy, and the five-year-exile in the deep mountains really got him. He came home as a wreck, two-thirds of his stomach cut off, Hepatitis C, and both eardrums broken. Depression or deformation, his desire for me never waned."

"How was Viagra—excuse me, Niagara, Mother?" I asked quickly.

"Good, good. I would have enjoyed it more had I not been so tired. Dr. Zhang kept me up all night long."

"Oh!"

"Do you know why he had three divorces? They couldn't keep up with him, those poor women. After he came to New York, he got wild, living with three women from the mainland. They had two queen-sized mattresses on the floor, and had orgies day and night."

"Did you stop at the casino, Mother? Did you play slot machines?"

She looked annoyed. "I don't care for gambling. I thought you knew."

"What about the glass factory, the most famous one in America?"

"Not bad. I wanted to buy some souvenirs, but the tour guide threatened to leave without me. That little bitch! She had the nerve to ask for a tip at the end of the tour."

"So he's a real gentleman, then."

"A gentleman on the surface, a sex fiend in the bones. Our first night in the hotel . . ."

"What did you talk about on the bus, Mother?" I shouted.

"Ah, I asked him how much he got in the bank as soon as we boarded the bus. Don't give me this face, Daughter. It's good to get the business cleared before you start a romance. He looked frazzled, but kept a good front. He has fifty thousand saved in his retirement plan. That would last less than a year, I said. He laughed and explained he had no debt, no mortgage payment on his two-bedroom condo in Flushing, and he was making good money doing acupressure, about two thousand a month, cash. I asked him what one could do in New York with two thousand a month."

"A lot," I burst out, "especially if you don't have to pay rent or mortgage."

She looked at me. "Your mother is too old to live like you, pinching pennies like a miser."

"With two thousand a month, you don't have to pinch pennies, Mom."

"That's what he said, but I know better. I've been walking around in Manhattan, Central Park, and Upper East Side. Two thousand wouldn't last a week. Your mother may not speak English, but she's not stupid."

I stared at her, speechless. What kind of husband was she looking for? And how did she get to those fancy places from the East Village? Bus, subway, taxi, or simply walking? I'd taken her to Chinatown only once to open a savings account for her. Thinking she'd be terrified of the underground maze like most new immigrants, I had showed her around my neighborhood so she could walk to parks.

"You're not supposed to ask people how much they make, Mother," I finally said. "It's America, not China."

"Dr. Zhang is Chinese, not American. He didn't seem to mind at all. In fact, he immediately suggested I should meet a patient of his, a retired congressman from Taiwan. He's a bit old, a bit fragile, but loaded with money."

"And you still spent two nights with Dr. Zhang?"

"This is America, not China!" She laughed at her own quick wit. "Besides, I didn't let him touch me. Oh no! I practice chi gong. Sex will weaken my chi."

"But you said he's a sex fiend who kept you up all night long."

"You are obsessed with sex, aren't you? What made you think that two people spending a night in the same room have to sleep together?"

"But you did sleep together, two nights in a row, and it's only logical to come to that conclusion since you mentioned he's a sex fiend who kept you up all night long."

"We just talked about sex, okay? He told me his stories and I told him about your father and my lovers."

My chest tightened. My mother had quite a few male friends when Father was in exile. One of them, Uncle Qi, was good-looking and friendly. A bit too friendly. When Father returned home, he made a big stink about Mother's relationship with Uncle Qi. My sister mentioned several times that he would have been promoted to a much higher rank if not for Mother's affairs with her husband's assistants.

"You know what really killed your father?" mother asked, her face two inches away from mine.

"What?" I jumped.

"Not enough sex. In his last two years, I was fed up by his lust. So I kicked him out of the bedroom. Had I known that all the fire had no outlet and started to burn his liver. Yeah, the fire singed his mind. Once he cooked a chicken and hid it under the bed. When I saw the half-eaten chicken, I sprayed it with mosquito spray. He broke my heart, you know. The old man had always saved the best morsel of food for me, the best everything. I don't know what happened—he didn't leave me a penny in his will. All his pension, military benefits, and insurance went to your sister. What a slap in the face! We were husband and wife for over thirty years."

I suggested that DDT might have caused the cancer.

"Nonsense! I sprayed just a little, not even enough to kill a mosquito. I just wanted to wake him up from his drunken stupor. It's the drinking and smoking that killed him, not DDT."

"I thought it was the lack of sex."

"That too," she laughed again. "That's why I can't go with Dr. Zhang. He'll kill me, like your father. I've had more than enough sex for my lifetime. Now I must preserve my chi, and you should do the same, my daughter. You've been squandering your precious youth. Had you just concentrated on your work and on one man, you'd have finished your PhD, got married, and had a bunch of kids. Now you're almost forty, still a poor student living in a dungeon. When are you ever going to do something real? Like helping me with my patients? By the way, I need the apartment for a week, starting tomorrow. I'll treat a boy with brain cancer from Canada. You can hang around if you have nothing better to do. Perhaps you can be my assistant. Together we can make a lot of money. I'll buy a building, one floor for my business, the other for renting."

"Mom, you just told me to finish my dissertation so I won't be a pathetic student forever."

"Never mind, then, thou art a rotten log that can't be carved. By the way, I consulted the Book of Change a few times for you. If you don't get married before you turn forty, you won't have another chance till you reach sixty."

I'm climbing the "Sky Ladder." The ladder, made of steel cable with wooden rungs, hangs on the cliff like a snake. Why am I here on this high mountain where nothing grows but giant rocks? To see the origin of Chinese sturgeon. These noble creatures are doomed because of the pollution and dams that block their way home to the Gold Sand River, where they mate and spawn and raise their young before returning to the sea. This has been their way of life for millions of years, since before the dinosaurs. They hurl themselves against the concrete over and over until they die, refusing to settle behind the dam, the new home man has created for them.

Below me, the ferryboat bobs across the riverbank like driftwood, and its owner, Mr. Chen, squats on a rock, smaller than an ant. The silk ribbon of the Golden Sand River flows by, seemingly gentle and quiet. But I know it roars, rushing through the narrow gorge with a power that moves mountains. I know because I've been here three times, flying across the Pacific to Shanghai, from Shanghai to Chengdu, taking the train and truck to the Golden Sand River, the Upper Yangtze. Of all the great places on earth, why am I drawn to this place? Is it the river? The sturgeon? Or just my stubbornness? I look up but cannot see the end of the ladder. I'm terrified of heights. Once I climbed a tree to rescue a hen, and we both got stuck on the top. Mother put a ladder under my feet. Just look ahead, one rung at a time, she ordered. An eagle soars above me, so close I can easily grab its

talons and take a ride in the sky. There is nothing to stop me from div-
ing into the sky.

But Mother is waiting in Shanghai. We'll go to the island, the end of
this mighty river and beginning of the sea. We're going to talk.

I focus, one rung at a time.

The day Mother arrived in New York, I started pissing blood. Mother
scraped my spine with a rhino horn till purple blisters popped up. She
ordered me to close my eyes, my palms in front of my chest. "Fingers
grow longer, longer, now shrink shorter, shorter, shorter," she
chanted. When my fingers refused to obey, she got angry. "You won't
tell me but I know you've killed three fetuses, all boys! Don't stare at
me like this. You can fool others but not me. I'm your mother."

After the trip to Niagara Falls, Dr. Zhang arranged for her to meet
the retired congressman from Taiwan. It lasted only fifteen minutes.
She told the old man and his daughter that she had no intention to be
a nurse or a maid, nor did she like to be house-bound. She was a free
spirit, traveling the world to practice chi and treat the sick. Dr. Zhang
was very apologetic, both to me and the congressman's daughter.
Mother was upset because she had spent fifty dollars on a dress to
meet the old man. Later, she joined a club named Oriental Fox and
Western Stud and spent two hundred dollars on Global Harmony,
a translation machine, for her very first date with a retired engineer
from New Jersey. She left in jubilation, telling me not to stay up waiting for her return. By 10:00 PM, she came home, looking depressed.
After much prodding, she said, "American men are cheap!" It
occurred to me immediately that I had forgotten to warn her of the
"go Dutch" custom.

Although her dating business dwindled, her treatment service flour-
ished. Some of my friends returned for more chi healing after she
made their fingers grow and shrink. They found her laughter infec-
tious, her communication with her body very amusing, and she only
charged them ten dollars. One poet saw her twice a week until he had
an enormous seizure on the kitchen floor, and my mother revived him
by digging her nail into his renzhong, the acupuncture spot under his
nose. She remained calm throughout the emergency, but later I heard

her tossing around all night. The next day, she got up early and went to Chinatown. At supper, she announced that she was tired of giving her precious chi to lunatics at such a low price. She wanted to do something else. She had just found a job teaching three kids Chinese, math, and music in Kansas City. Two thousand a month, cash, plus food and lodging and one-way bus fare.

I wept and pleaded. How could she travel to the middle of nowhere with no English, no friends? What if the family treated her badly?

"No need to cry," she said. "I must leave for your good and my own good. We're not meant to be together. Our energies clash. Besides, I need to make some money to buy an apartment in Shanghai. I'm tired of being treated as a country bumpkin by my mother and sisters. And I want to see more of America, especially the Midwest. I saw a painting once, a house floating in tall grass, like a boat in a golden sea. I learned it was prairie, once an ocean, then ruled by buffalos. I want to see the place. I know you can't pay for my flight, so I'll travel by Greyhound. Don't worry. If I could handle the East Village, other places will be a piece of cake. Besides, I have my Global Harmony. Together, we'll go around America. I'm fed up with this dump, worse than Shanghai. No good for people like me, or you. You should finish your dissertation so you can get a job somewhere. Your hair is turning gray. Time to quit hiding in college and New York."

Mr. Chen greets me like an old friend, but he insists that I pay before the crossing. He trusts me, he says, but since he raised the fee to keep up with his costs, some clients have refused to pay after crossing back. The sun is setting, casting a deep blue shadow on the yellow water. Mr. Chen tells me to sit still. Under the quiet surface, the river runs with strong currents and whirlpools.

After the crossing, we start climbing back to the mountaintop. Mr. Chen walks on the blue slab steps he spent five years paving, pulling weeds and kicking a rock off the road here and there, his small body steady against the impossibly high mountain. He has borrowed two hundred thousand yuan to open the new ferry on the river and is losing money every day. Why did he do this? Why is he still doing this? I want to ask but keep quiet. Certain things can't be explained, like the sturgeon's instinct to go home, like my need to come here. My sack is getting heavy. It has a bottle of water, a camera, a package of Wisconsin ginseng, and *The Magic Whip*, my latest book. I've carried it across the ocean, hiked with it along the river, up and down, down and up.

I started writing to talk to my mother across the ocean. I wrote in English, so that she wouldn't be able to read it. When my first book came out, I sent her a copy. Finally, her dumb child had done something with her dim wits. She wrote back fast. "Ungrateful beast, is this how you thank your mother who sacrificed everything to raise you through difficult years and made sure you never lacked anything?"

My shrinks believe my mother has borderline personality disorder. They lend me books, but the more I read them, the less I feel assured. It seems that I have more borderline personality symptoms than my mother. To be born in a period of such turbulence and change, who would not be borderline? Between my mother and me, we've gone through the Japanese invasion, the civil war, the Mao era—riddled with the Land Reform, the Great Leap Forward, and the Cultural Revolution—and now the economic reform that is uprooting China's five-thousand-year-old tradition.

Sometimes I wonder what would have happened if she lived in my era, had my opportunities. Would she be happier?

After she returned home from America, she bought a two-bedroom condo in Taiwan Village, a three-hour bus ride from Shanghai. She had wanted an apartment in the city but couldn't afford it. There she lived with her granddaughter, helping her with homework and training her to become a pianist. She continued to practice chi, joined a cyclist club, and started teaching singing to a group of retirees who call her Professor Shen. Last year, however, she had two major operations. For years, her uterus had dropped through her vagina. When she could no longer control her bladder and had to wear a diaper, she went to the doctor, and they immediately took out her uterus and every other reproductive organ, including half of her damaged bladder. I called her hospital, our first conversation since New York.

"Ah, the operation was a great success," she laughed on the phone. "I won't need to wear diapers anymore, thank heavens. My doctor is super kind and skillful. He knows your father, too. So are the nurses.

Two of them wanted to be my goddaughters. I have over a hundred adopted children all over China. I heard you've left New York and have two kids. Good for you."

Soon after she went home, she fell off her bike and broke her hip. She got herself on two long-distance buses and went to her trusted doctor again on the island. This time, she had to stay in bed for three months until the crushed hip healed completely. "It's killing me. I can't move, can't eat. Lost fifty pounds. You should see the loose skin on my stomach. Your mother is getting old," she said on the phone, laughing. Then she started counting the days for her recovery until she could go back home. "People there love me. They can't wait for me to start teaching choir again. They hate the substitute. We're planning a ten-thousand-mile bike tour to Xinjiang and Mongolia for the sixty-year-olds. You think we can make it? Of course we can. By the way, the operation and hospital fees are twenty thousand yuan. Send me the money as soon as possible."

The Magic Whip weighs like a mountain on me. Should I give it to her tomorrow?

She sees me first and starts walking—with a cane. So it's not a lie to extract money from me, as my sister hinted, and she still has seven nails to hold her hip together. How did she get herself on the bus? How did she travel across America with no English? How did she go through her life with such laughter? I watch her come towards me, aged and shrunk, yet her eyes still shine. She breaks into a smile.

"You look good and strong, my child," she says.

My heart quivers. I'm not used to seeing her wrinkles. Not used to hearing her praise.

"We'll find hairy crabs on the island, Mother. It's not the season, but I'll find some for you." This is all I can do—repeating myself like a dumb child.

She laughs, gutsy, loud, and wild.

The January wind comes hard from the ocean. We stand on the bank, watching the wetland stretch into the horizon. The watch deck seems afloat over the sea of rustling reeds. The island, rising above the water in the late eighth century from the Yangtze sediment, is Asia's

largest resting ground for migrating birds between Siberia and
Alaska. The water here is the estuary for Chinese sturgeon. It is the
end of the Yangtze, the beginning of the sea.

"How are the kids?"

"They're growing big, too fast."

"I know. How's Minnesota?"

"Good. It seems to be the right place."

"I know."

It occurs to me that she already knew ten years ago, before I even
heard of the state. As she nannied her way through America, a month
in Philadelphia, another in Michigan, Ohio, Alabama, she would send
me a postcard from each different place. Her last one was from the
Blue Mound, Minnesota. Across the golden prairie, she wrote: "Once
an ocean, always an ocean. Here, we'll meet again, someday."

I remembered pondering over the image and words. I kept that
card, however, and took it with me to Minnesota. It's all coming back,
with the light of forty-nine years of our lives together and apart.

She's been trying to talk to me since then, since the day I was born.

An eagle swoops down from the sky, startling flocks of birds out of
the dry reeds.

I take out the ginseng and *The Magic Whip*. "For you, Mother."

She traces the lips on the high-gloss cover, the fingers braiding hair
into a million whips, a million wings. We have the same hands: rough,
stubby, and stubborn.

"I carried you an extra month in my stomach," Mother says. "When
you came out, you had a full head of shining hair, dark like eagle feathers. And I knew you'd fly far. I knew I had to train you hard."

The salty wind blows again, sending rusty reeds this way, that way.
Each stem broadcasts my gratitude. She hears it. Tears roll down her
face.

"Forgive me, Baby, your mother is getting old."

My Good Bad Luck

Susan Steger Welsh

It was one of those middle-of-the-night conversations that feels like a dream in the morning: my parents coming into our bedroom to wake me and my younger sister in our bunk beds—Dad with a bandage on his cheek, Mom on crutches. Tears and hugs and something about an accident, headlights straight at them in the rain, an ambulance, the hospital. But in the morning the proof of our almost-orphanhood stood parked in the garage: the accordion hood of the car, the blessed seatbelts crossed like hands in the lap of the front seat.

I was perhaps ten years old. The only mothers I knew who died were in fairy tales, and even then, everything somehow turned out all right.

It was July 25, 1977—one week shy of my twenty-fourth birthday— that my mother went in for surgery for what the doctors thought was inflammation in her intestine.

I hadn't even gone to the hospital. It didn't seem like it was going to be a big thing. But when the phone on my desk in the KSTP TV newsroom rang that day, it was my father calling from the hospital to tell me that when they opened her up they found cancer. It was everywhere from rib cage to pelvis, too much to remove.

"You're kidding," I said, as if he could be. I hung up and thought, What do I do now?

My mother was nobody's fool. Even groggy, coming out of the anesthesia, she knew something was up when she saw me there. "What are you doing here?" she wanted to know. "Aren't you supposed to be at work?"

I suspect my mother had had a foreboding that something was seriously wrong. She had been having a lot of abdominal pain and was losing weight without trying. She had been afraid to have the surgery.

My dad was urging her to do it, get it taken it care of and get back to normal. Suddenly, normal was a snuffed candle. We didn't know if she'd even come home from the hospital. Was it going to be days? Months? How much time did we have?

The diagnosis was metastatic leiomyosarcoma, a rare type of cancer that attacks the lining of internal organs. We had never heard of it.

She turned fifty-two three weeks later, in the hospital. We brought in the slide projector and a big screen for a family slide show. We couldn't give her a future so we gave her the past: all four of us kids in pajamas on a series of Christmas mornings, at birthday parties with cakes and hats and balloons, dressed in Halloween costumes as drum majorette, train conductor, princess. All of us smiling: her in red lipstick, my dad with a full head of hair.

This was the mom I wanted to remember, the one who read us Uncle Remus stories, doing all the voices. The one who laughed at Bullwinkle cartoons and played Mahalia Jackson spirituals on our hi-fi in the living room. The one who treasured our childhood artwork, filing it in her kitchen desk drawer. My mother took us to the symphony, the theater, and the library. She read cookbooks in bed and threw fabulous dinner parties, her table set with china and silver. At our house, the drapes were vacuumed and the walls were scrubbed. She taught me how to throw parties, clip coupons, knit sweaters, iron dress shirts, mend pantyhose, and darn socks.

Another lesson she preached, over and over again, was how lucky I was. Lucky to have a sister (she had only brothers), lucky to grow up with a big yard and a pond (she grew up on a city lot in Detroit), lucky to have thick hair (hers was thin), lucky to have such a good daddy.

There were few stories about her own father, a stern man who objected to my mother's choice of husband on the grounds that he wasn't Polish. My grandfather was a physician who was too proud, Mom told me, to ask for the fees his patients couldn't afford during the Depression. "On Saturdays he'd sit silently out on the porch, listening to baseball on the radio, smoking a cigar," she told me. "I hate the smell of cigars."

My mother's mother, my Polish Busia, was a strong woman, the kind they described in those days as "wearing the pants in the family."

On her first visit to St. Paul, she tried to give my father driving instructions from the back seat, until my Dad finally pulled over and asked if she wanted to take the wheel. She didn't drive.

Mom herself drove as little as possible; never in bad weather and always with one foot on the gas and one on the brake.

She painted delicate watercolors, a striking contrast to the bold oils my father produced when they took painting classes together. I often thought you could look at their paintings and see immediately how it was with them, the introvert and the extrovert; how differently they approached the blank canvas of the world. "Oil painting is easy," she told me once. "If you make a mistake, you just let it dry and paint over it. With watercolor, every brush stroke is permanent. One mistake ruins the whole thing."

When they offered to pay for painting lessons for me, I chose oil painting.

There was a decision to start chemotherapy, a more brutal treatment in those days than it is now. Mom withstood only one round. There was no hope of a cure, in any event. Since the hospital wouldn't keep her if she wasn't receiving treatment, we brought her home to White Bear Lake. Dad was trying to keep things going at his office, so I took my vacation time and moved home to tend Mom and run the house. I cooked and did the laundry. I doled out the pain pills separated into plastic trays on the kitchen table. I washed her hair, which came out in my hands. We didn't have a bell, so we gave her a pot to bang if she wanted something and I was out of the room. When she got tired of being in bed, I'd help her out to the living room, where she sat in my father's easy chair and listened to me working in the kitchen. One day I was mopping the floor.

"I don't think you understand," she called out, clearly irritated. "I'm dying. You know how that floor should be done." As if to say, Haven't I taught you anything?

Dying was God's will, something she could accept. But not a daughter who would use a mop rather than scrub a floor properly on her hands and knees.

The weeks that followed are a blur. I had to go back to work, and she didn't want strangers coming into her house. Half a dozen of her friends each took one morning a week to stay with her, and Dad took over after lunch. Mom was never well enough to go out, and there was a lot of pain. But she had visitors, at home and then again in the hospital when she grew worse and was readmitted. Her brothers came from Detroit to say good-bye. My sister and brothers and Dad and I rotated in and out, sitting for hours at her bedside. Mom warned my Dad not to spoil my fifteen-year-old brother, the only one of us still living at home. She assured Dad he wouldn't be alone; that women would be coming out of the woodwork to console him.

We talked often about heaven. She told me that she was eager to see her firstborn, the baby who died of hydrocephalus at eight months. She prayed with ferocity: Holy Mary, Mother of God. Help us now and at the hour of our death. I mean it. Amen.

Another time she asked me, "Was I a good person?"

Our last conversation, if you can call it that, was in the hospital, the day before she died. She was on her side, curled up in the fetal position. The quiz show audience was applauding from the television bolted high on the wall. My mom asked me what she'd won.

Why didn't the nurses tell us it was close to the end? Surely they knew how death moves in. We would have stayed by her side. This time the phone call came to my apartment. It was before dawn on October 4, my dad telling me it was over.

Then came the year of learning to cook the turkey. The year of crying in the car.

When my sister and I split up the things our Dad didn't know what to do with, I got my mother's engagement and wedding rings, a pair of silver candlesticks, her cookbooks, several tablecloths, some silk scarves, and an oil painting she loved. The lamp from her bedside, with its base of porcelain birds, one with a broken tail. A half-finished cabled sweater she was knitting when she got sick, still on the needles. The fern from her hospital room. Today, thirty-plus years later, it unfurls new fronds in my living room window.

I also kept, coiled tightly inside me, the small animal of my fear, whispering: No guarantees. Don't waste time. I did some research, but there wasn't much literature about leiomyosarcoma; it was too rare. My uncle, an internist, confirmed what scant information I could find: no strong evidence of a genetic link had been established.

Still.

There is a way the daughter studies the mother and takes the lessons personally. Whether the lesson she takes away is Do Like This, or Do Not Do Like This, it has an extraordinarily powerful hold. I felt connected to my mother biologically, if not temperamentally. And her body had betrayed her. Mine, I concluded, required close supervision. I became conscientious, religious even, about checkups. I went early and often for mammograms and Pap smears, any test they had that might give you a running start on cancer.

Does fear make you watchful, so that you can see the danger and save yourself? Or does fear chain you inexorably to the object of your fear, pulling it towards you?

Yes.

I am discussing this with a longtime friend. What does she think?

"Well," she says, "you always have been paranoid."

True enough. In my late thirties, a questionable Pap smear threw me into a state of panic. My daughter is so young, I thought, she won't even remember me if I die now. I decided to hold off buying the new suit I wanted until after the follow-up tests the doctor ordered. When the all clear came, I was flooded with gratitude: spared!

Sometimes I take those quizzes that tell you your "real" age, based on your answers about health habits, and the ones that predict how long you'll live. I award myself points for the basics: I wear my seat belt, don't smoke, get enough exercise and maintain normal weight. I bless the grandparents who lived into their late eighties and nineties, pushing my score to 99. I say to my husband, "I figure I'll either die young, like my mother, or live to be really old. Maybe one hundred."

This irritates him. He hates it when I talk about death, specifically, mine or his. "What about average?" he asks. "Does average ever occur to you?"

Honestly? No.

The birthday that looms as the breakpoint is the fifty-second, as if by making it past the age of my mother's death, I'll have broken the curse. Intellectually I recognize how utterly illogical this is. Emotionally I cling to the idea that once I outlive her, I'll be in the clear.

Of course, cancer doesn't wait that long to enter my life again.

When I am forty-five, and my good friend and next-door neighbor is forty-five, she is diagnosed with metastatic ovarian cancer. When she is weak from surgery, I help throw her daughter's high-school graduation open house. When she shaves her head after the second chemotherapy, I bring over my best scarves and hats. That summer her husband rents scaffolding, and methodically paints their house, covering the color she's hated for years. Months go by and I imagine my friend sleeping, water rising around her bed as a long line of us pass sandbags. When the doctors finally announce there's nothing else they can do, I sit with her and she asks me, "What do I do next? What do I do now?"

It was like watching my mother die all over again, only in slow motion. Technically, my mother died of pneumonia; fluid slowly filled her lungs. My friend starved to death, the cancer growing up like a fist around her stomach. Her husband knocked on our door the night she died, but my husband and I had gone out. We returned late to find their windows ablaze, revealing men in dark overcoats moving about the first floor. A hearse was parked outside. Silently we went to huddle with her husband and children on the sidewalk as they took her thin body out, put it in the hearse, and drove away.

That was a Saturday night, exactly one year from the date of her diagnosis. The next day was Mother's Day.

The year my friend was sick was the year two pine trees in our front yard suddenly dropped all their needles and died.

It was the year I heard a voice one dawn as I emerged from sleep, a voice that said, What is going to happen has begun.

It was the year I got what my mother never did: early warning.

It began with that sick feeling you get when they tell you not to get dressed yet; they want to do the mammogram over again. There was a breast biopsy, and six months later, another. The machine they used to collect the tissue sounded like a staple gun. The doctor called me at home to say that the tissue sample was benign—no cancer—but they did find some abnormal cells that could head in that direction. Not cancer but a risk factor for cancer. In technical terms, a nondeterminant precursor, which I took to mean, Nothing has been determined, but you are cursed. I felt that small animal inside me stir. I named it My Good Bad Luck.

Now I was on the high risk watch list. I started seeing an oncologist, who prescribed preventive medication. I ate more fruit and vegetables, drank less wine. One time the oncologist's bill erroneously listed a chemotherapy treatment. When I went in to the office to straighten it out, I heard my voice say, way too loudly for a waiting room, "This is a mistake. I do not have cancer."

The spring before I turned fifty I had a digital mammogram, and the doctor showed me the image.

"Where?" I asked, leaning in to study the moonscape on the screen. "I don't see it."

He pointed to the upper right hand corner, a tiny spray of pinpricks, like stars from another galaxy.

The doctor ordered an ultrasound, an MRI and another biopsy, just to be sure. This dragged on for weeks. A bad feeling was beginning to accumulate in my stomach. It was taking a long time to get the results from this latest biopsy, and my husband tried to reassure me. "They just haven't gotten to it," he said.

"No," I responded. "They can't decide. They're sending it to more pathologists, who are squinting at the tiny cells and saying, 'I don't know—what do you think?'"

When we finally went in to see the doctor, he said, "Well, this time they're calling it. It's DCIS—ductal carcinoma in situ. You have a decision to make. There is no rush, but you need to do something."

DCIS is classified as Stage 0 breast cancer, the stages being a way to describe how the cancer has grown and spread from the original site; Stage IV is the most advanced. In situ means it's just sitting there; it hasn't even laced up its shoes yet. Is it even really cancer, if it's not going anywhere? Will it ever launch? Maybe. Maybe not. There is no way to know. Although at Stage 0 there is no lump, I am offered a lumpectomy. I imagine the surgeon hunting for those tiny pinpricks.

What if he doesn't get them all? Radiation is the usual cleanup, but the DCIS is on the left side: Do I want intense radiation pointed at my heart muscle? Do I survive this and wind up with heart complications in ten years, or in fifteen? And what about those suspicious cells on the right side—what were they plotting?

I am given a choice. It is not a pretty choice. Both the oncologist and the surgeon use the term "surgical cure." Cure is a good word. Cure means Gone and Won't Come Back. Cure means no radiation, no chemotherapy.

Cure also means I surrender my breasts.

"You're taking this well," the surgeon says.

It is a very surreal situation in which to find oneself. Part of me is researching logically, poring over Dr. Susan Love's Breast Book, wading through articles on the internet, flinching at graphic photos of mastectomy patients and reconstructions, talking to other women. Part of me is shrieking: You want to cut WHAT?

I think about my mother, and about my friend, how their cancers gnawed them back to skeleton and soul. Why would I risk the possibility of some malignant cells escaping into the rest of my body? I picture the uncertainty, the fear, hovering like a cloud just outside my peripheral vision for years. It doesn't take long for my husband and me to agree: The breasts go. I stay.

This is My Good Bad Luck.

I discover that my diagnosis enrolls me in a vast club—a club nobody wants to join, but one whose members will do almost anything for you. I find myself driving around town to see women I'd never met, so they can show me what I'm in for. One shares a photo taken before the surgery. She keeps it in her dresser drawer.

I begin to think of the surgery as stepping off a cliff into the arms of a medical team that will mutilate, and then remake, my body. I dread all the questions, having to explain my decision to everyone who cares about me, over and over again. I can see they feel sorry for me. They keep telling me how brave I am, but I'm not thinking about courage. What I'm thinking is, surgical cure. I'm thinking, I am not my mother. I am thinking about the wan, exhausted people I've seen in the oncologist's chemotherapy infusion room. I imagine asking how many of them would trade places with me, and all their IV-taped arms going up.

In the weeks I am waiting for the surgery, I have a horrible dream. It takes place back in my father's house, where I grew up. My mother is upstairs in the kitchen with a dark-haired girl—me or my daughter, I can't say. Downstairs I open the door to my old bedroom and discover someone emaciated, near death. I am horrified: How could my mother let this happen? I am torn by the desire to protect her, but I know that if I get help immediately, there is still time to save this person. I go get help.

I contemplate this dream and what the Jungians say for a long time: that in the drama of the dream, it is the dreamer who plays all the parts. I am the mother and the girl; the person in danger, and the person who saves.

When it's all over, and the pathology report comes back all clear—sentinel lymph nodes clean, no invasive cancer found anywhere—I think, I've cut a deal.

On the bookshelf in my living room is a fat, 400-plus-page collection of fairy tales, folk tales, fables, and myths from around the world. It was a gift from my mother. Inside the cover my name is written in childish cursive, along with our address and phone number from a time when 4–2–9 was GArden 9. The illustrations are sparse, simple line drawings. The stories are full of clever animals, purses of gold, kingdoms to be won, witches, beautiful princesses, fantastic spells, and, here and there, a mother who dies. Her children wander, or are made to work as servants, or get banished beyond the gates, sometimes for years, before they are saved and restored to good fortune. Somehow, everything turns out all right. I love this book. I plan to read it to my as-yet-unborn grandchildren.

The morning of my fifty-second birthday I rise at dawn, while the house is still quiet. There'd been a heat spell, so the rain that starts to fall feels like a blessing. I look up from my desk to see hundreds of tiny drops clinging to the needles on the spruce tree we planted for our son's baptism. Each one a tiny crystal throwing off light. Each one a brilliant piece of luck.

Riding Shotgun for Stanley Home Products

Morgan Grayce Willow

Ruby Fleenor 1937

It's nearly ten o'clock on an early October night in 1964. My mother and I are on County Road T64 headed south. We left the small, northern Iowa town of Grafton about thirty-five minutes ago; we have just a little over five miles to go. I struggle to keep my eyes open. The geometry homework due tomorrow nags at the back of my mind. I'll have to do it on the fifteen-mile bus ride to school in the morning. I long to rest my head against the scratchy, dull green upholstery of the 1956 Ford. Instead, I look at the narrow strip of gravel between the blacktop and the steep ditch and calculate our rate of speed, the angle of incline, and the impact should my mother fall asleep at the wheel. It's my job to keep Ruby awake on these long, late drives home.

At the other end of the front seat, Mom grips the wheel with both hands, looks straight into the swath of light the headlamps push out ahead. She has probably been up since before dawn. I am trying to think of something to say, to start a conversation.

We are coming back from a Stanley Home Products house party where Ruby has laid out and demonstrated her wares. Town- and farmwives have gathered to shop for spot removers, Lady Catherine hairbrushes, rat-tail combs, Slim Line brooms, Aquilawn delicate fabric detergent, and Stanley Degreaser, a popular new product which easily cleans even the most stubborn cast-iron pot. In addition, Stanley has recently expanded its skin-care products into a full-blown cosmetics line, adding another role for me on these junkets. I am Mom's model. I sit in the middle of the circle while she demonstrates base foundation, subtle shades of blush, light blue to charcoal gray eye shadow. My eyelashes feel sticky from the mascara we've applied to dramatize my dark eyes for the ladies. Before I go to bed, I will use Stanley's cold cream to remove all this. I am not allowed to wear this much makeup to school.

Like most farm wives, Mom had tried raising chickens, the egg money hers to use for buying fabric to make bright Easter dresses for my sister and me, or a fine new rosary blessed by the Holy Father especially for her. But she hated the hens, their snappish pecking, their constant clucking, butchering and dressing them out when their egg-laying bodies were spent. The only way to turn a profit on the messy work of raising chickens was to invest even more money and time in them. Stanley Home Products held out the promise of good money from cleaner work. By the time we are making the drive through the moonless autumn night, Mom has "had her cases" a couple of years. She's beginning to build a strong customer base and bring in the extra money she'd hoped for. She gets a substantial discount on all the products she buys for our use, from brushes to spatulas to dust pans. Her crimson lipstick came with the sample case, and, as a Stanley Home Products Demonstrator, she can get off the farm and out to visit with other ladies who are equally eager for the social gathering disguised as a practical way to shop.

I blink myself out of a doze and immediately check the distance between bumper and ditch. We're just a few yards past the driveway to the Fox's place, the last landmark I recall seeing. Reassured that I haven't slept more than a few seconds, I shift on my end of the bench seat. "Think they'll start corn picking soon?"

She nods, then says, "Don't worry. We're almost home."

I come by my reticence naturally. By Dr. Huber's calculations, I was to have been a Leo. Ruby, however, informed him that, "This baby will be a girl, and she will be born on my birthday." And so it happened that I was born on September 4, 1949, the day my mother turned thirty. Like her, I am a Virgo.

Virgos are known for their reserve. Ruby was no exception. She rarely talked about herself and, if asked, flat-out refused to tell more than the bare facts about her life. We knew that she was third-born in a family of seven: Mary Belle, Roy, Ruby, Zola, Ruth, Hazel, and Betty. We knew she grew up on a farm near David, Iowa, a village that exists vividly in the history and lore of Mitchell County but no longer on its road maps. We knew she graduated from Little Cedar High School in

1936. We also knew—but only because we came across a team photo—that, short as she was, she played guard on the girls' basketball team. This would have been under the old half-court rules, when there were six players per team and neither guards nor forwards were allowed to cross the center line. She earned a gold-plated basketball pendant, in lieu of a letter, for her participation. This, like the village and the school, has long since vanished.

We do have one story. On a blustery November day, Mom and her sisters managed to convince Grandpa to give them a ride in the buggy to the schoolhouse a mile or so away. It would have been out of the ordinary for him to do this, so perhaps he needed to hitch up and go into town a couple miles beyond the schoolhouse for some other reason. About the details, Mom's version differs from Aunt Betty's. In both tellings, however, they were barely a quarter of a mile down the road when the mare spooked and bolted. Startled, Grandpa lost his grip on the reins. The horse—which my mother only ever referred to as The Runaway—galloped as fast as she could to get away from her perceived predator. Grandpa was powerless to stop the jostling and tossing of the girls on the hard buggy bench as they clung to each other and the rough, splintery edge. They finally came to an equally abrupt, jarring halt, the carriage aslant at the edge of the ditch where the wheel had slid and stuck. It was sheer luck, a miracle, that they hadn't turned over or been flung from the buggy—or that the poor, lathered-up beast hadn't broken her leg. An axle could be fixed; a horse's leg could not.

How much did I fill in for what my mother wouldn't say? I'm not sure. In the absence of story, I have been known to make things up. One sure fact, however, is Mom's persistent refusal to allow us to raise horses on our farm. No matter how much we begged and pleaded for even a pony, her reply was always the same: "Nobody needs horses to farm any more." If we were to ride, it would be on the back of someone else's horse. Our farm, like most around us, would raise only animals that could be of use, either for food or income. Even the barn cats earned their keep by keeping the rat population down in the grain bins and hay loft. The only exception to the rule was the farm dog, though the best in the long succession of dogs was always remembered for its ability to guard gates and help herd cows from one pasture to another.

Ruby had good reason to want a daughter. By 1949, she'd had four babies, all of them boys. Even my brothers were glad I came along; before me, they not only had to haul water in from the well house, but also heat it and actually wash the dishes. Their rightful place, of course, was in the fields. My birth released them into their true identities. As soon as I was big enough to stand on a stool at the kitchen table, my arms were immersed in warm, sudsy water in the large enameled dishpan. Mom tested and adjusted the water, adding hot from the large tea kettle warming on the wood stove, or dipping cool water from the drinking pail to bring the temperature down. Until I grew tall enough to empty the dishpan outside all by myself, one of the Big Boys still had to help with that chore, but they had much to do outside the house. Mom needed all the help she could get inside, and I was it. By the time my sister came along two years later, I was old enough to believe that she'd been born to help me work.

We played when we could, of course. Our favorite game was dress-up. In the back of our bedroom closet, we kept a box chock full of hand-me-downs: faded, floral-patterned housedresses Mom no longer wore and older, sheer fabrics from Grandma Weber's wardrobe, seams frayed under the arms, hems coming undone. And shoes. Three-inch pumps with broken-down backs and slope-worn heels, no longer wearable to church, or even card club. Grandma Fleenor's old mule slippers. And, the best prize of all, Mom's glittery silver wedding shoes. Wrapped in tissue and stored in a separate shoe box, these open-toed, one-inch heels demanded special care and attention. We were allowed to play with them only if we promised to be careful.

We push our small feet forward under the silver, mesh bow until our own small toes poke through. We walk stiff-legged, half gliding, half stepping, trying to prevent the heavy clomp the heels make on the floorboards when the back part of the shoe rebounds between our short feet and the floor. We soon forget that Mom is napping downstairs, that we've promised to play quietly. We put long dresses on over our summer skirts and wrap brightly colored nylon scarves around ourselves—two, three times—fashioning belts that will hold the hems up at our ankles. We don hats from Easters past, now misshapen, their netting torn, fabric flowers crushed and drooping. They slide down over an eye, so we tilt our heads back to see, still holding our skirts up. We pretend to be Miss Kitty stepping across the muddy Dodge City street on the arm of Marshall Dillon. We clomp around the room, around again, until we hear, "You girls, settle down up there." We muffle our giggles and tip-toe. We continue to parade, fully believing we are quiet, but soon the heels begin to clomp again from behind our small feet. We hear another, "Girls!"

We slip the shoes off, shuffle in bare feet. But our giggles grow louder. One of us—my idea, or my sister's?—suggests we look at ourselves in the mirror. To look in the mirror, however, we have to climb up on the bed. Now we sashay around in a bouncy circle on the bed, glancing over our shoulders to see ourselves in the dresser-top mirror. We mimic the angle models take on the covers of *McCalls* or *Ladies Home Journal*. At first, the bounce is just an inevitable rebound from our awkward stepping. Then one of us trips on a hemline, springs back. Soon the bounce is the thing. Then one of us realizes that we can get a higher bounce if we jump from the dresser to the bed. We take turns. We giggle. Louder. Louder still. We're on about the third round when there she stands, looming at the door, her jaw set in that no-nonsense look. "I told you girls to settle down!" Before any of us realizes it, the Lady Catherine hairbrush is in her hand, then coming down, fast and hard, on the one nearest her. Before she's through, both our backsides sting where red marks will soon bloom. "Now get off that bed and straighten up this room." She turns and leaves as abruptly as she had appeared.

We cannot be quiet now, though we try to choke back sobs. This has never happened before. There have been occasional swats on well-padded rumps, warning spanks. More common were clipped, angry words, later in adolescence, an actual slap or two. What lingered was the betrayal of the hairbrush, the fact of the beating, more than the actual sting. Yet my conscience stung even more. My sister was still too young, but I knew it was my job to bring this moment to the confessional: "Bless me Father, for I have sinned. I disobeyed my mother."

It's a miracle, in a way, that this was an isolated event, overwhelmed as she must have felt by a household bursting at the seams with children, eventually nine in all. In the early days, there was no running water; it had to be hauled in from the well house. Even after the house was remodeled and indoor plumbing had been installed, the work was still relentless. Though water no longer had to be heated on the stove to do the wash, the washing machine set up in the newly built-out basement still needed hands to feed clothes from the washing tub, through ringers, into the rinsing tub, and back through the ringers again. The laundry needed strong arms to carry the wet basketful outside, and hang it on the line, then pay attention and bring it in when it was dry—and before it rained. In winter, arms carried those baskets upstairs, hands hung the clothes over racks and clotheslines strung wall-to-wall in hallways and bedrooms. Hands took down the shirts, pillow cases, hankies, and underwear, rolled them up in a basket. Legs and back stood over the ironing board, hot and steamy in the summer, while arms sprinkled water from a cork-stopped bottle and moved the iron—electric, luckily, by this time—over every inch of moist or remoistened fabric.

That was just the laundry. There was also bread to be baked. Eggs, when we still had chickens, to be gathered and washed, then gingerly stacked in cardboard trays and set in boxes for the egg truck to pick up on Tuesdays. In the barn, the milkers and ten-gallon milk cans needed to be scrubbed and sterilized. All the while there were three meals a day to prepare and clean up after, a house impossible to keep clear of mud tracks and dust, and a garden to be planted, tended, harvested, and preserved. Work never ended. My sister and I helped as much as we could, of course, taking on more as we grew taller, stronger, more capable. Not without rebellion, certainly. But even after spells of foot-stomping and complaining, we settled in to the task at hand, just to get it done. Mostly, we worked without words.

That is not to say without communication. Communication with my mother was clearer sometimes in the absence of language. This was especially true after I graduated high school and left home. In the early 1980s, when I was living in Colorado, for example, I dreamed there had been an earthquake in Iowa. Aware how rare such a geological event would be, yet nervous nonetheless, I called home. Mom told me my grandfather—Dad's dad—had died from a heart attack. She had been just about to call me, she said, when the phone rang. A decade later, the dream was more literal; I dreamed Dad had a heart attack. This time I called home from St. Paul, Minnesota, to learn that, though his heart was fine, his lung cancer had come back. After being in remission for nearly five years, it now bounded through cells all over his body. More than once, as his condition worsened, when I reached for the phone to call Mom, there she would be on the line even before I had dialed her number. When her time came, I needed neither the language of dreams nor the telephone. I just knew—without knowing when or how I knew—that Mom wasn't going to be living for much longer.

That summer in 1990, we hadn't been speaking to each other at all on the physical plane. In those years, I was, in dizzying succession, recovering from childhood wounds and coming out as a lesbian. Mom had agreed to meet with me in the presence of a counselor, but she changed her mind. I'd written and asked how we could meet, what circumstances would make it comfortable for her to talk. She refused to answer my letters. Into this came first my knowing, then my brother's call: Mom was at Mayo Clinic with a probable diagnosis of cancer. The next day I drove to Rochester, praying all the while to those two ponies in James Wright's famous poem, "A Blessing." I needed their presence in a field along Highway 52 to steady me. I was on my way to reopen a conversation with my mother, one I knew could not last long.

On a Sunday just a couple of weeks later, I spoke to her for the last time. She was soon to be transferred home to Charles City, Iowa, to the hospice unit of the hospital. I was headed home to the Cities from a wedding in Charles City, one Mom was especially sad to miss since the bride was one of her favorite granddaughters. Annabel, our neighbor from the farm who had remained a good friend of Mom's, had spent the whole day with her. My siblings from out-of-state would be coming by to see her later in the evening. While I was driving, I imagined

Ruby and Annabel praying together, though Mom was Catholic and Annabel Lutheran. Perhaps they said "The Lord's Prayer." Perhaps they simply talked about death. Mom, of course, wouldn't say. When I asked, she only offered that it had been a good day. She did seem to me less anxious than on previous visits.

"I only have this much left," she said to me, gesturing with her right hand along a line beginning at her left shoulder and ending near her right ear. Though I dared not ask, I took this to mean that much of her soul was already making the crossing. I told her I hadn't meant my need to heal to hurt her. I said I was sorry, that I loved her. She said, with the old steel-blue snap back in her eyes, that I had hurt her. Then she added, "I guess, if you want to think you're a lesbian, that's okay." The rancor didn't leave her voice until she said as I was turning to leave, "Have a nice life."

In the end it was my brother Jim who rode shotgun at her bedside the moment she passed over. I didn't need words, or even dreams, to know the moment.

August 25, 1990, mid-afternoon. I am at a Take Back the Night rally in Loring Park, downtown Minneapolis. I'm involved in a conversation with my girlfriend and some friends when I suddenly feel lifted out of it by a question: "What would happen if Mom died right now?" I shift into another envelope of time, just for a moment. Then the answer comes: "It'll be all right."

I returned to my apartment soon after, to the message from Jim on my answering machine. His calm, tired voice simply says: "Give me a call as soon as you get back." When I reach him, he describes every detail of her passing. How there was no pain during her last hour. How, when she asked what we would do with her money, he replied that we would use it wisely. How she spoke random sentences, like, "Don't take the bus that way!" How, at the very end, she raised her right hand, as if to shield her eyes from a light, and said, "I'll go with you now."

Neither of us cries audibly over the phone, but I sense from his voice and pauses that tears are sliding over his cheek and down along his jaw line, as they were mine. He adds, "The hospice folks said it was the most peaceful passing they'd ever seen." We finish up with details about arrangements—most of which Mom had planned from her hospital bed—how quickly I could get home, whether he'd been able to reach our sister.

After our conversation, I take the suit—recently bought in case of an interview, I'd thought—out of the closet. I gather shoes, stockings, slip, earrings to go with it. Suddenly the whole upper half of the apartment is flooded with light—an odd light that brightens everything yet casts no shadow. As it passes through the three small rooms, I cross myself, though I haven't been going to Mass for years. I know she has just passed through, and that this is how we have always communicated best—in the fewest words possible. Finally, I know just the right thing to say: "Good-bye, Mom."

Acknowledgments

I am indebted to my mothers and mentors Cynthia Cone, Myrna
Kysar, and Marsha Velders. Thanks to the Anderson Center for Interdisciplinary Studies for solitude and to Anoka-Ramsey Community
College for time. I am grateful to all the women who made this book
possible: the staff at at the University of Minnesota Child Care Center
and Horace Mann Elementary; Katie Kreitzer and Gloria Santa Cruz;
Ann Regan, editor-in-chief at the Minnesota Historical Society Press,
mastermind and midwife; and, most of all, the authors who, with
honesty and clarity, share their mothers with us. Finally, my deepest
gratitude to my husband, Scott Velders, and to my children, Cole and
Ada, whose patience, love, and support makes this all worthwhile.

Contributors

JONIS AGEE is the author of five novels—*Sweet Eyes, Strange Angels, South of Resurrection, The Weight of Dreams,* and *The River Wife*—and five collections of short fiction—*Pretend We've Never Met, Bend This Heart, A .38 Special and a Broken Heart, Taking the Wall,* and *Acts of Love on Indigo Road.* She is Adele Hall Professor of English at the University of Nebraska–Lincoln.

ELIZABETH JARRETT ANDREW is the author of *Swinging on the Garden Gate, Writing the Sacred Journey: The Art and Practice of Spiritual Memoir,* and *On the Threshold: Home, Hardwood, and Holiness,* a collection of personal essays. She offers writing instruction and spiritual direction in Minneapolis.

SANDRA BENÍTEZ is the author of the novels *A Place Where the Sea Remembers, Bitter Grounds, The Weight of All Things,* and *Night of the Radishes.* She was a recipient of the National Hispanic Heritage Award in Literature. Her latest book is *bag lady: A Memoir. The Triumphant True Story of Loss, Illness and Recovery.*

BARRIE JEAN BORICH is the author of *My Lesbian Husband,* winner of a Stonewall Book Award from the American Library Association, and *Restoring the Color of Roses.* Her essay in this volume is from a work-in-progress entitled *Body Geographic.* Her awards include a Bush Artist Fellowship and Loft-McKnight Award of Distinction. She teaches in the MFA program at Hamline University.

TAIYON COLEMAN's work has appeared in *Ethos, Knotgrass, Sketch, Cave Canem Anthology IV, V,* and *VII, DrumVoices Revue, Sauti Mpya, Bum*

226 *Rush the Page: A Def Poetry Jam, A View from the Loft, Maverick Magazine #9, Gathering Ground,* and *The Ringing Ear.* A two-time Loft Mentor Series winner and a member of Cave Canem, she lives with her family in Washington, D.C.

. HEID E. ERDRICH's poetry collections are *National Monuments, The Mother's Tongue,* and *Fishing for Myth.* She co-edited *Sister Nations: Native American Women Writers on Community.* A member of the Turtle Mountain Band of Ojibway, she was raised in Wahpeton, North Dakota. She teaches writing and is curator at Ancient Traders Gallery in Minneapolis.

DIANE GLANCY is a professor at Macalester College. She is the author of nine novels, five short-story collections, and twelve collections of poetry. Her recent books include *Rooms: New and Selected Poems; In-Between Places,* a collection of essays; *The Dance Partner,* stories of the Ghost Dance; and a collection of poetry, *Asylum in the Grasslands.*

JAN ZITA GROVER is the author of two books of essays—*North Enough: AIDS and Other Clear-Cuts,* which won the Minnesota Book Award for creative nonfiction in 1998, and *Northern Waters* —and of *Dakota Goes Home,* a children's book. "Motherfood" is adapted from a chapter in the book she is writing about food and eating.

KATHRYN KYSAR is the author of *Dark Lake,* a book of poetry. A winner of the Lake Superior Writer's and SASE poetry contests, she has received fellowships from the National Endowment for the Humanities, the Minnesota State Arts Board, and the Anderson Center for Interdisciplinary Studies. She teaches writing and literature at Anoka-Ramsey Community College.

DENISE LOW, 2007–09 Kansas poet laureate, is Humanities & Arts Dean at Haskell Indian Nations University. Her recent books are *Words of a Prairie Alchemist,* a Kansas Notable Book; *Thailand Journal,* a Kansas City Star Notable Book; and *New & Selected Poems.* She is a fifth-generation Kansan of mixed German, British, Lenape (Delaware), and Cherokee heritage.

ALISON MCGHEE is the *New York Times* bestselling author of six novels, including *Rainlight*, *Shadow Baby*, *Was It Beautiful*, and *All Rivers Flow to the Sea*, as well as books for children of all ages. Her picture book *Someday* was inspired by her relationship with her mother.

SHEILA O'CONNOR is the author of two novels, *Tokens of Grace* and *Where No Gods Came*, winner of a Michigan Literary Fiction Award and a Minnesota Book Award. She has received Bush Foundation, Loft-McKnight, and Minnesota State Arts Board fellowships. An assistant professor at Hamline University, she also serves as the fiction editor for *Water~Stone Review*.

SHANNON OLSON is the author of the novels *Welcome to My Planet: Where English Is Sometimes Spoken* and *Children of God Go Bowling*. She has written for *The Guardian* (London), *InStyle*, *Good Housekeeping*, the *Star-Tribune*, *Minnesota Monthly*, and *The Rake*. She is an assistant professor of English at St. Cloud State University.

CARRIE POMEROY's writing has appeared in *The Laurel Review*, *Calyx*, *Slow Trains*, and *Literary Mama*. Recipient of a Minnesota State Arts Board grant, a Henfield Prize, and an honorable mention for a Pushcart Prize, she has taught writing at Metropolitan State University and the Loft Literary Center. She lives with her husband and two small children.

SUSAN POWER is an enrolled member of the Standing Rock Sioux Tribe. She is a recipient of a James Michener Fellowship, a Radcliff Bunting Institute Fellowship, and a Princeton Hodder Fellowship. Her first novel, *The Grass Dancer*, won the PEN/Hemingway Prize. Her second book, *Roofwalker*, was awarded the Milkweed National Fiction Prize.

SUN YUNG SHIN is the author of *Skirt Full of Black* (poems); co-editor of *Outsiders Within: Writings on Transracial Adoption*; and author of *Cooper's Lesson*, a bilingual Korean/English illustrated book for children. A 2007 Bush Artist Fellow for Literature, she is a community activist and is a frequent speaker on adoption issues.

228   SUSAN STEGER WELSH is the recipient of a Minnesota State Arts Board fellowship and a SASE/Jerome fellowship. Her first poetry collection, *Rafting on the Water Table*, was a finalist for a Minnesota Book Award. She mothers two mostly-grown children from St. Paul, where she lives with her husband and works as a writer.

ANNE URSU is the author of the novels *Spilling Clarence* and *The Disapparation of James*, as well as *The Cronus Chronicles*, a trilogy for young readers. She has won a Minnesota Book Award, was nominated for Barnes and Noble Discover Great New Writers Award, and was a finalist for Borders Original Voices Program.

KA VANG was born in Laos and grew up in Minnesota. Her plays, *Disconnect*, *Dead Calling*, and *From Shadows to Light*, have been performed at venues in Minnesota and New York City. Vang's short story, "Ms. Pac Man Ruined My Gang Life," was featured in two anthologies: *Bamboo Among the Oaks* and *Charlie Chan Is Dead II: At Home in the World*.

WANG PING, associate professor of English at Macalester College, was born in China and came to the United States in 1985. Her books include *American Visa*, *Foreign Devil*, *Of Flesh and Spirit*, *The Magic Whip*, *Aching for Beauty: Footbinding in China*, and *The Last Communist Virgin*. She is the recipient of National Endowment for the Arts and Lannan Foundation fellowships.

MORGAN GRAYCE WILLOW has received awards in both poetry and prose from the Minnesota State Arts Board, the McKnight Foundation, and others. Her most recent poetry chapbook is *Arpeggio of Appetite*. A former American Sign Language interpreter, she published *Crossing that Bridge*, a guide for making literary events accessible to deaf audiences, funded in part by The Witter Bynner Foundation. She teaches at Minneapolis College and the Loft Literary Center.